"You have life before you. Once only
you can live it. What is the noblest
object of desire, the supreme gift to covet?"
—Henry Drummond in his devotional classic,
The Greatest Thing in the World

"For now we see only a reflection as in a mirror;
then we shall see face to face. Now I know in part;
then I shall know fully, even as I am fully known.
And now these three remain: faith, hope and love.
But the greatest of these is love."
—1 Corinthians 13:12–13 (NIV)

Savannah Secrets

Savannah Secrets

The Greatest of These

MARLENE CHASE

Guideposts

Danbury, Connecticut

Cover and interior design by Müllerhaus
Cover illustration by Pierre Droal, represented by Deborah Wolfe, LTD.
Typeset by Aptara, Inc.

Printed and bound in the United States of America
10 9 8 7 6 5 4 3 2 1

Chapter One

"Do you ever feel like the world is going faster and faster?" Julia Foley asked. She tucked her hand inside Meredith Bellefontaine's elbow as they walked through the park on the way to the City Market. "You try to keep up, but any minute you think you're going to fall off the edge."

"Happens every time I get on the treadmill," Meredith answered, her blue eyes merry. "But I know what you mean. Seems like just yesterday we were hanging our Christmas stockings from the mantel, and here it is nearly Valentine's Day!"

"I know. Go figure!" Carmen Lopez chimed in, catching up to Julia and Meredith. Their indispensable "Girl Friday" pushed back her luminous dark hair.

"Still chilly, though," Julia said, feeling the wind through her sherpa-lined jacket. But it was exhilarating too. It was good to be with friends—Meredith, who had reopened her husband's detective agency and brought her in as partner, and Carmen Lopez, their young assistant, whose life zest was nothing short of inspiring.

"Folks in the Midwest would call this weather downright balmy," Meredith said, turning to Julia, whose shiver must have been perceptible. "They would say you were lucky to enjoy temps like these in February. It's sixty-one degrees already!"

"What can I say?" Julia laughed. "I'm dyed in the warm wool of the South!"

Meredith laughed, lifting her head toward the sun. She pushed back a lock of blond hair that was already frizzing with the morning's humidity. "Well, it's a glorious morning anyway, and I love this trek through Forsyth Park at any season of the year."

"Me too," Carmen said, breathing the fresh air in deeply. "Even if it is Saturday, and I could be sleeping in." She rolled her brown eyes expressively.

Passing Mercer Museum, they turned onto Liberty Street, a straight shot for City Market, the attraction that drew hundreds of Savannahians year round and a host of visitors from everywhere. Today they would join the crowds delighting in the many colorful shops and galleries clustered in the four-block area.

The developer of the project, which began in 1985, had emulated the design of the successful Torpedo Factory of Alexandria, Virginia. Savannah's group of working artists occupied approximately 19,000 square feet of space in the Market. The environment was enhanced by food, entertainment, and retail businesses.

Carmen paused to cradle a pink camellia from a resplendent bush bordering the walk. Her dark hair lifted in the breeze and floated around her shoulders. She murmured her appreciation of the flower's beauty in her native Spanish, to which she resorted on occasion, though her English was more than adequate. "*Hermosa*, no?"

Julia smiled. She was glad Carmen had joined them for a Saturday brunch at the café/bakery that was a favorite of locals. As a juvenile court judge, Julia had seen in Carmen what was now evident to everyone. Despite a somewhat checkered past, the young woman in her midtwenties was intelligent and resourceful and had become a valuable assistant. Though separated in age from the two partners by four decades, she had quickly become a friend.

Carmen held out the flower for their inspection. "So gorgeous!" she raved. "If I were a flower, I would be a camellia." She pressed her face into the pink bloom which, against park rules, she had nipped from the bush. At Julia's disapproving glance, Carmen shrugged good-naturedly, brown eyes innocent. "It's just one, no? It was hanging loose; it would have dropped off any minute."

Meredith leaned in to study the flower in Carmen's hand and gave Julia an indulgent glance. "Where else than our beloved South can you find evergreen shrubs that flower during the dull days of winter?"

Julia nodded, grinning. Meredith knew a lot about flowers and tended them carefully around her Italianate-style home that overlooked Troup Square. Her camellias burst into flower weeks before Julia's garden came to life. "Long live our beloved South!" Julia quipped as they hurried on toward the Market.

The café/bakery proved to be every bit as enjoyable as everyone said. They breakfasted on frittatas and sweet crepes with caramelized pears. Meredith ordered a double chocolate muffin and cut it in thirds to savor with their gourmet almond coffee. More than satisfied, Julia joined her friends afterwards as they headed into the stream of eager shoppers.

"I'm dying to see the new designs at Pottery Paradise," Carmen said. "Their ads claim to have some of the best Talavera pottery pieces."

"I hope it's at least a block or two away," Julia said, patting her stomach. "Breakfast was fantastic, but I'll need to hit the treadmill from dawn to dusk to compensate." She grinned. Beau used their treadmill on occasion, but left to her, it was doomed to live out its days as a clothes rack.

"Treadmills should be good for something," Meredith put in knowingly.

"Just because you never need one," Julia said teasingly. Meredith wore her stylish clothes well, but she had even more to offer in spirit and character. Any man would be lucky to win her affection. Meredith had lost her husband far too soon. She had loved Ron and grieved deeply for him, but Julia couldn't help hoping her friend would find someone to spend the rest of her life with. Someone as wonderful as her own Beauregard Eugene Foley.

Julia turned to Carmen, who had set a challenging pace. "I didn't know you were interested in pottery."

"Well, not just any pottery. It's the Talavera variety I like. I have a set of salad plates I bought at Crate and Barrell for forty-four dollars, but someday I may be rich enough to buy some authentic pieces."

Carmen could surprise you, Julia thought. After her Guatemalan parents were killed when she was only ten, she'd been shifted from one foster home to another. In a way, she'd practically raised herself, and she got into some early trouble with the law as a teenager. But she'd been amazingly resilient and had made giant steps to finish her education and advance herself. For Julia, Carmen's rise had been deeply satisfying to witness, and she'd been eager to help the young woman succeed.

"You know, creating Talavera pottery hasn't changed much since the early colonial period," Carmen continued in her animated fashion. "They start by mixing black sand from Amozoc and white sand from Tecali. They wash it and filter out the best particles and shape it on a potter's wheel. Then it must dry for days before it's fired. Then comes glazing, more firing, and hand painting. It takes about three months for most pieces, but some can take up to six months. *Es muy bonito.*"

Julia raised her eyebrows, impressed.

"I googled it," Carmen admitted. "You can learn anything on the internet."

Carmen was a whiz on the computer, it was true. She could navigate sites with speed and determination. Her skills had come in quite handy in the investigation business.

"You know," Carmen continued, still rosy with praise for her favorite artistry, "the process of making Talavera pottery is so complicated and the pieces so easily damaged that during colonial times, artists prayed special prayers over them, especially during the firing process."

"Very wise artisans," Julia said. "It might be what's missing in a lot of arenas today. Not just art." She smiled apologetically. Did she sound like she'd donned her old judge's robe and was about to pontificate? Or like her pastor on a Sunday morning? "Prayer is certainly underrated by a lot of people," she finished, drawing in the strap of her purse as they bustled through the crowd.

Prayer unquestionably had made a difference in her life over the years, Julia realized, not for the first time, and especially in guiding her and Meredith in their work at Magnolia Investigations. Their first case had been a daunting one, by anyone's measure. They might have abandoned the venture if God hadn't shown up.

Sometimes she marveled over the way He sent just what and who they needed at the right time—like Maggie Lu, who had made it possible for them to solve the mystery of the young girl who disappeared from the Besset mansion sixty-five years ago. Since that first case, the intrepid woman had assisted them in solving others as well.

Julia had hoped she could ask Maggie Lu to join her and her mother for supper later that day, but Mom had said she wasn't up to it. She had pleaded for a quiet meal at her house with just her daughter for company.

Julia felt her chest tighten. Lately her eighty-four-year-old mother had been distant and sometimes even morose. Julia was aware that elderly people could fall prey to depression. Was that what was going on with Bonnie Jean Waverly—B.J., as her family and most of her friends called her? Julia shook away a vague sense of regret and guilt. She wouldn't think about her mother now. She would simply enjoy this part of the day with friends who knew how to find joy in life.

"Well, that style definitely wasn't designed for me," Meredith said wryly, interrupting Julia's reverie. They were passing a boutique featuring a model in a trendy high-waisted skirt. "I'd look like a reject from a Holland tulip field."

"But look at that ruffled blouse!" Carmen said, pointing to an adjacent window. "It's to die for. I'd love it in red." She mimicked a cha-cha-cha, swiveling her hips.

"Let's check out that pottery place you're so crazy about," Julia said, grabbing Carmen's arm and propelling her forward.

The streets were busy, even in February. Most were wide enough for a dozen people to walk abreast and still afford space for a horse-drawn carriage. Outdoor patios, with huge wooden planters blooming with flowers and greenery, were set for alfresco diners. Every window was designed to draw attention. The eye simply wasn't quick enough to take in the myriad sights.

Meredith stopped at a tall iconic clock, a gift to the citizens of Savannah that commemorated the hundredth anniversary of the founding of Rotary International. "They dedicated that clock in 2005 when I was director of the historical society," she said. "It's a real landmark and quite a draw for tourists."

"I'm sure Beatrice points it out to visitors of Savannah now. In her over-the-top Southern speak, no doubt," Julia said, not unkindly. Beatrice Enterline, the current historical society director, often set them musing over her flamboyant and sometimes unnerving demeanor. "I reckon she'd say it was enough to make a possum roll over dead."

"Or a frog spit in a rabbit's eye!" Meredith added.

Carmen laughed, rolling her eyes. "Come on, you two. Pottery Paradise is in the upper-level section. It's always fun to meet the artists and watch them create."

Julia had enjoyed doing just that on more than one occasion. There was always something new and exciting to see. Even Beau was willing to endure a shopping trip to observe the eclectic items on display at the Market. Paintings, pottery, wood turning, sculptures, glass works, jewelry—the variety was amazing.

"Let's check out the downstairs galleries first," she said before Carmen could begin climbing the black wrought-iron staircase to the upper floor.

"Looks like the Winston Gallery has reopened," Meredith said, pointing across the wide street to an attractive smoke-colored brick building with high-set windows in glossy black casements. "It's been closed for a while, but someone must have taken it over—unless Eduardo is back."

"Didn't I hear he was in a rehab facility after his stroke?" Julia asked, zigzagging through the crowd.

"Since last November," Meredith answered. "The Winston was one of the classiest in the Market. Apparently, there was no one to keep the place going in those intervening months."

Julia entered the high-ceilinged gallery and gazed around at the works of art placed on three long walls. Paintings were carefully arranged and illuminated to draw the eye around the room. "Lucky Eduardo didn't lose his lease," she said. "New businesses are always clamoring for a spot here. How did you find out? Was it in the paper?"

"Quin had something to do with helping to retain the lease for him." Meredith spoke somewhat absently as she peered at the dazzling display of color and form.

Arthur "Quin" Crowley was an attractive lawyer who had recently come from Columbus to Savannah. He and Meredith had met in the process of securing information about the owner of the Besset mansion.

"I wonder what Eduardo would say about his gallery now," Julia said, drawing in her breath. "He definitely preferred beautiful landscapes and classic works from an earlier era."

"As I recall, he had some fine Winston Churchill paintings for sale," Meredith said, glancing around with a slight frown. "I always liked his *Lake Near Breccles in Autumn*."

The gallery was quite changed, filled with modern works from the first half of the twentieth century and contemporary offerings produced after 1950 and even later into the twenty-first century. Such art, Julia knew, was globally influenced and culturally diverse. Of course, it would naturally reflect the advancing world of technology.

Julia released a surprised breath. "I guess it's a good thing Maggie Lu didn't come along today." She'd been invited since she loved art but had begged off to visit a good friend who was ill. The wildly chaotic forms in the Winston today might not be to her taste. *Or to mine either,* Julia thought. But it was a new age and keeping up with it could be a challenge.

Meredith surveyed each work with a critical eye. "Art really helps us look more closely at people and emotions, doesn't it?" she said. "It helps us see what doesn't readily or easily appear to us."

Julia nodded, appreciating once again her partner's deep insights into things. Among her other fine qualities, she might make a first-rate philosopher.

Carmen had gone ahead and roved from one display to another without comment. Now as Julia caught up to her, they were a few feet from a large painting covering half the rear wall. It was a striking piece. Bold crimson and orange geometric shapes like stylized flames erupted from some black maw and penetrated an invisible sky. In the center of the squares and triangles, a small white oval pierced the brilliant oranges and crimsons.

Julia felt a quick shudder—like fear. Yet something compelled her, drew her eyes back, held them. The forms were beautiful, entrancing, but at the same time dark with mystery and dread. Something of hope shone through as well, and Julia was deeply touched. What was the artist saying? And why at this moment did she think of her sister, Cassie? Other visitors must have been affected too, for a small crowd lingered near the painting, whispering excitedly.

Carmen continued to peruse the art. Silence was uncharacteristic of the outspoken young woman peering now at the signature at the bottom, which read DESDEMONA.

Adjacent to the painting was a sign, which the three of them seemed to catch sight of at the same time. Meredith read in a hushed voice, "'Desdemona, known to some as the "runaway artist," has come to Savannah and is scheduled to appear on February 16 for a gala event to which everyone is invited. A collection of the artist's paintings titled *Spectrum of the Soul,* will be available for purchase from 7 until 9:30 p.m. This is her signature piece, appearing at the Winston for the first time. Fans of her exciting work will want to be on hand to greet her.'"

"Runaway artist?" Julia repeated.

"Curious," Meredith agreed, narrowing her eyes. "I'm afraid where modern art—or should I say contemporary art—is concerned, I'm somewhat of a runaway fan. Realism and impressionism are more my line, but I'm no connoisseur, that's for sure."

"I read something about a 'runaway' artist," Julia said. "There was a showing in Chicago at a prestigious grassroots gallery. Since then it seems this Desdemona has developed a cadre of enthusiasts." Julia tried unsuccessfully to draw her eyes away from the painting.

Meredith studied it closely. "Everyone loves a good mystery, I suppose."

"A lot of theories have grown up about her too," Julia said. "Someone suggested that she's a descendant of the great Marc Chagall, an early modernist. Or a wealthy dowager who funds her own exhibitions and caters to the rich and famous."

"Or brings new clothes to the emperor," Meredith said wryly. She touched Carmen's shoulder. "What do you think?"

Carmen, who was still studying the painting, appeared not to hear.

"Carmen?" Julia urged.

She turned to look up at Julia, wonder in the olive oval of her face. "Desdemona," she said under her breath.

"What do you think?" Julia asked.

Carmen straightened. She stepped back with a troubled expression. "It reminds me of something—from a long time ago," she said quietly. She pursed her full lips, dark eyes nostalgic, as though peering into some long-forgotten memory.

"We should move along," Julia said, nudging Carmen. A group of admirers was pressing in for a closer look. The galley was full. Besides, she was eager to get outside—away from whatever drew her to the strange painting. She felt edgy, uncomfortable. The gallery was so changed, so unexpected. She had been here before, often with Beau. Neither was a collector of art, but it was fun to peruse and to "listen" to what the various paintings had to say. This display had unnerved her. "Come on. I'm ready for coffee."

They turned into the nearby Cinnamon Bear Country Store and settled at a table outside. It was a favorite place that also had locations in Hilton Head, Amelia Island, and Midtown Savannah. Beau was partial to this store in City Market and was content to enjoy a Cheerwine while Julia finished her shopping. Now she sipped her Coco Mocha Nut Delight and waited while Carmen slowly stirred a cup of Jamaican Dark.

"So, what do you think?" Meredith asked, as she wrapped her hands around her cup of Amaretto Light and watched Carmen. "You seemed interested in that exhibit. What did it say to you?"

Julia was glad Meredith hadn't asked her, for her thoughts were disparate, troubled, far too personal, even bringing Cassie to mind.

Meredith continued thoughtfully. "Art should speak truth, some reality to enhance the human condition. At best, art should bring beauty and light to a dark world. Maybe, too, art says something about the human condition of the artist."

"I don't know," Carmen began thoughtfully, still stirring coffee that didn't need stirring. "Like I said, that painting reminds me of something from a long time ago. When I was—you know—on the streets." She fluttered her eyelashes in Julia's direction. "Well, one of the girls I knew then was a talented graffiti artist. We used to hold cans of spray paint for her and hand them to her when she needed them."

"A graffiti artist?" Meredith repeated. "I suppose that large, sweeping style could have roots in graffiti."

"She didn't write bad words or stuff like that. She just made pictures—and they were so good that no one painted over them right away. Like maybe they realized they were special." Carmen's eyes glowed. "She never signed a name, but somewhere in every painting she would put this swirling white thing sort of like an alien bird." She cocked her head to one side. "That's how she got the name. We called her 'The Dove.'"

Julia had seen the swirl of white in the center of the bold red and black forms, though it didn't resemble any dove she'd ever seen. It did look alien, though. A fanciful, almost alien birdlike flourish.

"I—I don't suppose you ever ran into her on the bench?" Carmen aimed her question at Julia but kept her eyes down. "I mean, she did get into some trouble like I did."

Kids defacing property was a perennial problem, but Julia hadn't dealt with many such cases in Chatham County during her tenure in juvenile court. While practicing in Atlanta, she had dealt with a few instances—all involving boys.

A nostalgic mist hovered in Carmen's eyes. "She was a little older than the rest of us, but in a lot of ways she was a child. All she ever wanted to do was paint. Brick alley walls, abandoned billboards, anything she could spray. It was like an obsession with her. And she could climb like a mountain goat! She was fifteen; I wasn't quite thirteen. I thought she was beautiful. I looked up to her. But she was *ingenuo*, you know?"

"Naive," Julia translated.

Carmen nodded. "You could tell her anything, and she'd believe it." She released a long breath. "She used to draw the white bird on everything she painted. We never knew why." She frowned. "It was a long time ago—twelve years or more since I saw something like that."

Carmen paused again to stir her drink, staring into it. "She said her name was Ophelia, but sometimes she called herself Virginia or some other name she thought was exotic. She was sort of mysterious." Carmen bit her lower lip. "There was a little boy too. He followed her around like a puppy. He was about seven or eight, and he could get in and out of any place quicker than you could blink." She clasped her arms around herself as though she were suddenly cold.

Her eyes flashed and filled. She was quiet for so long that Julia became alarmed. "What is it, Carmen?"

Carmen swallowed. Her whisper seemed to come from some deep, impenetrable distance. "He was climbing a scaffold of a building that was being renovated, and he—he fell." She gasped. "He was so small, so still."

Chapter Two

MOMENTS AFTER HER PRONOUNCEMENT ABOUT the little boy's death, Carmen sprang to life, and in her usual spirited optimism broke the shocked silence and announced that she had to run.

"Hair appointment," she said, lifting her voluminous locks off her neck. "I may get a whole inch cut off this time. Hot weather's coming!" It was something of a joke when Carmen talked about getting a haircut. It always looked the same after as before—lovely, glossy, and full, but not shorter.

Meredith too departed. She had plans to meet her son Chase downtown for lunch. The still unattached, extremely eligible history professor kept tabs on his mom, never letting too much time pass between visits. Today she would meet him at the agency, where she and Julia had left their cars so they could walk through Forsyth Park to City Market early that morning.

Julia waved them off, explaining that she had a few errands to run, including a trip to the nearby florist to pick up something for her mother. Red tulips—perfect for this February day that yearned toward spring. She would give them to Mom when she joined her for supper.

Red had always been her mom's favorite color. Dad had bought her red roses, the undisputed symbol of love and devotion. Julia released a long sigh, recalling the wonderful sense of being loved. Protected from all the dangers that might befall a child. She swallowed hard, imagining a little boy's fall in an abandoned alley. She couldn't remember a time when she hadn't been certain that her parents would keep her safe.

Many other children, like Carmen, had not been so blessed.

The second cup of coffee she'd ordered had grown cold. Julia pushed it back and tried to dispel the picture that Carmen's words had imprinted on her mind.

Whoever the creator of *Spectrum of the Soul* was, she must have confronted something dark and dangerous in her life. What had led to the painting? Julia wondered. It had affected her strongly. Why? Perhaps it was just the story Carmen had told or the reminder of Julia's sister, whose face came flooding into her mind again. She pushed it away. She would not think about Cassie now.

"Get on with your business," Julia told herself sternly. She had tulips to buy and life to live. She left the table to a couple eyeing her spot while trying not to appear impatient. The florist—her favorite place to buy flowers—was just ahead past the gallery they had perused. She loved the Flowerpot's blooms, which were always fresh and beautifully arranged with matching tissue and ribbon and placed carefully in long white boxes. Surely they would cheer her mother, who had grown increasingly solemn and withdrawn of late.

She walked with a quick step, determined to hurry past the elegant brick gallery without looking into the wide, gleaming window. Still, as she approached, she could feel her steps slowing, sensed a strange magnetism as her eye was drawn once more to the prominent exhibit inside. Perhaps because it was the lunch hour there were no patrons milling about—inside or out. She could clearly see the exhibit that had attracted so much attention. The paintings of Desdemona, the runaway artist.

As she neared, she saw a man standing close to the focus painting—the splendid wash of golden and crimson forms that had so enraptured Julia's thoughts. The visitor stood alone—tall, erudite in appearance, and wearing a gray suit. His silver head in profile inclined toward the exhibit as though he was studying it or communing with it. Adoring it? Strange, the feeling that gripped her—as though she had intruded on something not meant for her to see.

Julia watched, curious about the lone gallery visitor who seemed stopped in time, leaning in as though mesmerized. Presently, he raised his left hand and traced the edge of the glossy black frame before stepping back. Then he tapped the frame as though to bid it farewell and turned away. In a fleeting glance at his face in a quarter turn that was still profile, Julia thought she saw a look of satisfaction or knowing. Maybe even triumph? Or...

"Well, I declare! Is that you, Julia Foley?"

Julia spun around at the bright voice that broke into her odd reverie.

"It *is* you!" Beatrice Enterline, black pixie hair ruffled, smiled a beaming pink-lipped smile and grabbed Julia's arms. She held her back to look her full in the face. In her exuberance, her purse slipped off the shoulder of her lime-green suit set off by a green-and-white polka-dotted scarf.

"Beatrice!" Julia greeted her, recalling in an instant how her name had come up as they walked through Forsyth Park that morning. "How nice to see you," she said, enjoying the flamboyance Beatrice could bring to life.

"Why, it's been too long," the historical society director exclaimed in her practiced Southern drawl that she believed her patrons expected. Her carefully penciled brows arched high in her forehead. "And that marvelous partner of yours! How is Miz Meredith Bellefontaine?" She drew out the last name with scrupulous enunciation.

"You just missed her," Julia said. She struggled with Beatrice sometimes, but Meredith said she was harmless, even though Beatrice had taken over a job Meredith had enjoyed so thoroughly for years before leaving it to reopen her husband's agency. "We were enjoying City Market with Carmen this morning." Julia smiled, thinking that Beatrice had a hundred-watt bulb inside that she switched on at will.

"You two darling detectives," Beatrice intoned, hazel eyes shining. "I can't tell you how grateful I am—how utterly indebted our great city is—for the way you turned things around with the Besset estate."

"You're just too kind, Beatrice," Julia said, suppressing a sigh. It had been their first case, and one Beatrice had hired them for, and it had resulted in the restoration of a grand old mansion. "I trust things are going well with the society?"

"Fine as frog's hair split four ways," Beatrice said with a chuckle and then drew a breath, as though depleted by her enthusiastic rhetoric. She gestured to the gallery window. "And now that the Winston's reopened, we'll be able to share it once again with all our guests to Savannah."

Julia turned to stare into the gallery window again, noting immediately that the gentleman observing *Spectrum of the Soul* was no longer in sight. Curiously, she had not seen him leave the gallery, but she had been distracted by Beatrice. And now another group of junior high and high school age young people was pouring inside the Winston, their voices eager. "Yes, it is open again, and people have been coming. It was pretty crowded when we were inside a little while ago."

"That just makes me happier than a hound with a bone," Beatrice said, shaking her head. She looped an arm through Julia's and propelled her ahead of the gathering tourists. "And what did you think of it?" she asked.

"Well, it's—" Julia searched for words to describe it. "Quite changed, but bright and airy—very welcoming." It occurred to her that Beatrice should know something about the Winston's affairs. Even though she'd just had coffee, it would be an opportunity to ask. "Beatrice—" She patted the hand on her elbow. "Do you have a few minutes? We could have a cold drink or a sandwich over there." She pointed to a small bistro across the street beneath a red-striped awning.

"Why, honey, what a grand idea," Beatrice said, her eyes widening further. "Mind you, I have a meeting this afternoon. Chamber of Commerce, and you can't keep those folks waiting."

It was vintage Beatrice, pompous tone and all. The historical society director graciously added, "But I can spare a few minutes— especially for you, dear."

When they were seated with two raspberry lemonades and a sub sandwich they decided to split between them, Julia asked Beatrice if she had heard about the current exhibit.

"Why certainly, dear. We keep up on these things. We make sure our guests have a list of Savannah's current sights."

"Then you've heard about the featured artist?" Julia asked.

Beatrice cocked her head to one side and considered it. "One of our guides mentioned something about a mysterious artist who is supposed to exhibit here." She paused. "Some visitors from Chicago were talking about it. Of course, you hear a lot of things in my line of work. I just hope he's up to the standard we've come to expect from the Winston."

Apparently, Beatrice didn't know that the artist was female, and before Julia could correct her, Beatrice launched into a history lesson.

"The gallery is named after Winston Churchill," she said, warming to her subject. "And you did know, didn't you, that the famous statesman from the other side of the pond visited our beloved Southland?"

"Well, I—" Julia began.

"He fell a bit short of Savannah, of course, but he did review the troops in Jackson, South Carolina, shortly after Pearl Harbor. He witnessed our brave men parachuting. Said he'd never seen a thousand men leap into the air at the same time. He was mightily impressed."

"That's very interesting—"

"He called our troops a mighty army, an achievement that soldiers of every other country would study with admiration and envy. A great statesman was Churchill, and to think he was also a superb artist. Eduardo DeLuca was quite the collector of the great man's art." Beatrice smiled and raised an eyebrow at Julia apologetically.

"It's part of my speech, don't you know? Folks like to hear about famous people."

DeLuca, Julia thought. Yes, she'd heard her mother mention the name. Mom knew everyone—or used to—from the committees she had served on.

"I hope this new owner makes us as proud as Eduardo did. I was so sorry to learn about Mr. DeLuca's illness." Beatrice finished off her drink and seemed eager now to be on her way.

"Do you know the new owner?" Julia asked.

Beatrice exhaled sharply, gave a little shrug of her shoulders. "Well, no. He's not from around here, but I'm told he knows his stuff." She stood. "And now, I must get to my meeting. Madam Chair will be mad as a mule munching on bumblebees if I'm late."

She tripped off in her open-heeled pumps, turning to wave farewell with pink enameled fingernails. Julia felt the smile frozen on her lips. There was only one Beatrice Enterline. Julia glanced at her watch. The visit had lasted a mere twenty minutes. She hadn't learned anything about a so-called runaway artist, but she'd survived it and learned something about Winston Churchill in the bargain.

It had been quite a day so far, from the journey through Forsyth Park with Meredith and Carmen to the chat with one of Savannah's most colorful citizens. She gazed around at the people laughing and pointing as they viewed the Market's sites, munching on little sacks of candy or swirling ice cream cones with quick tongues. The sun beamed down like a benevolent courtier. Life was good. Only the strange painting in the gallery had punctuated the otherwise warm and enjoyable day, evoking a sense of sadness and anxiety.

What had the runaway artist been thinking—feeling—as her brush moved across the canvas? Julia felt a strong urge to know—to lift whatever dread seemed to pervade the beautiful lines, to let that tiny spark of light that teased at its center break through with joy. She bent her head to petition the God of all goodness and blessing on behalf of the runaway artist, whoever and wherever she was.

Chapter Three

IN HER BEDROOM JULIA DRESSED for the visit to her mother's. She chose a pair of black jeans and a red twin sweater set. She didn't need anything fancy to visit her mom.

Growing up she had been proud of her mother, who was hardworking, genuine, and attentive to her family. They were not wealthy and couldn't always compete with Savannah's more affluent society, but neither did they lack anything. Mom was who she was and had no patience for airs. Julia had never felt inferior in handmade blouses and skirts and knew her mother had sewn them with love and pride.

Bonnie Jean, blond and trim, with a quick smile and perceptive blue eyes, could hold her own in any arena. She enjoyed homey things—walks in the woods, ice cream sundaes on the porch in summer, good books. She preferred simple attire, but when she did dress up, she could be absolutely stunning. Julia glanced at the photo on her dresser where her mother posed in a black velvet dress. At her throat was a dazzling diamond necklace. Next to her, Julia's dad was fitted out for their twenty-fifth wedding anniversary.

"Isn't it the most beautiful thing you've ever seen?" Mom had exclaimed those long years ago when she had inherited the necklace from her great-aunt Faith. It had been a complete surprise, but she had loved it and worn it to every dress-up function, including church. Often she would touch the magnificent stones reverently when she thought no one was looking.

Julia paused as she affixed a pair of small gold earrings. How long had it been since she'd seen her mother wear that necklace? Too long. Mom didn't go out much anymore except to church. But even there she had not worn the diamonds in ages. Why? It was completely puzzling. Julia turned away from the photo at the sound of her husband's footsteps.

Beau threw his favorite fishing jacket on the bed and kissed her lightly on the cheek. "How was the Market today?"

"You're back early. Fish weren't biting?"

"Tolerable for February," he said. "But there's a Georgia Bulldogs game on I want to see. Alabama Crimson Tide doesn't have a prayer."

"And you may not have dinner. I'm at Mom's tonight, remember?"

"Sure, I remember." He gave her a wink, which was more compelling now that cataract surgery had ended his need for glasses. His blue gaze, infused with light and intelligence, lay gently on her. "Don't worry about me. I'll grab something before the game starts." He pulled on his favorite Savannah Tigers Basketball shirt.

Julia couldn't help feeling proud of her retired anesthesiologist husband who still had a full head of wavy gray hair and had retained a trim physique well into his late sixties. A heart healthy diet—a necessity for someone who'd experienced a triple bypass—had helped on that score. He could still get her pulse racing as he had the first time he had treated her in the ER when she was a summer camp counselor and he a young intern. She'd blessed the infected insect bite that took her to the hospital ever since.

"So, you and Meredith had a good time spending all our money?" Before she had a chance to answer, he wiggled his brows Groucho Marx style. "But if you brought back my ginger cookies, all will be forgiven."

"Not this time," she said ruefully. She heard herself sigh and realized she was still preoccupied with what she had seen and felt at the Winston. And with Carmen's nostalgia as she studied the artist's work. Before they'd parted, Julia had agreed to go with her to the exhibition the following Tuesday. But now, seeing in her mind's eye again the disturbing painting, she wished she had declined.

Beau gave her an appraising glance. He could be remarkably sensitive to moods and situations. It was just one of the traits she loved about Beau, who'd been the love of her life for nearly four decades.

"The Winston has reopened," she remarked, tucking her hairbrush inside a dresser drawer. "Don't think you'd recognize it, though. Not a Monet or a Dutch Master anywhere in sight. It's pretty upscale and very modern." She paused. "Not that there's anything wrong with that, but it will take some getting used to."

"Give me a James Whistler or Joseph Turner any day," Beau said. "It seems to me that Eduardo was partial to Winston Churchill's paintings. When the British prime minister wasn't making history, he was making art."

That, of course, was why Eduardo had named his gallery "the Winston." Julia recalled Beatrice's history lesson. After a pause, she said, "There's going to be an exhibition there by an artist who apparently shuns the limelight. She goes by the rather pretentious name of 'Desdemona.'"

Julia felt herself frowning as she remembered Carmen's account of a graffiti artist and the little boy. She grabbed a jacket and the box of red tulips. Her mother was a stickler for punctuality. "The story is she promises to appear but doesn't show up for her exhibitions. She's been dubbed the 'runaway artist.'"

"That can't be good PR," Beau said. "Eventually her audience will run away, won't they?"

"You'd think so," Julia said thoughtfully. "The talk is, though, that people are intrigued by the mystery. They want to know who she is and where she comes from. Kind of got me hooked too."

Beau slipped his arm through hers. "Come on, I'll walk you out," he said, hefting the box of red tulips for her.

They walked downstairs arm in arm and out onto the wrap-around porch. The ceiling fans were stilled, as were the rocking chairs, where in summer they liked to sit and read or talk or be silent. Julia loved this house, its soft moss-green siding and glossy black shutters, the spacious green lawns and ancient elms that surrounded it. The house made her feel protected and loved, and she hoped she'd never have to leave it.

Beau walked her to her car, placed the box in the back seat, and sent her off with a warm hug. "Greet your mother for me. I hope she's feeling better."

The two got along famously. He was a bit less understanding of Cassie, who was forever reinventing herself and wasn't above hinting about her need for money.

Julia rolled the window down a crack as she drove. Who could fathom how the mind of her younger sister worked—or when she really used that mind? Cassie had gone to the West Coast years ago to "find herself," leaving nine-year-old Wyatt behind for her parents to raise. And they had taken him in, strong, responsible people that they were.

Now Wyatt was a forensic auditor in Savannah and the father of two girls, Madison and Kennedy, who called Julia's mom "Grandma." Julia, though in fact their great-aunt, was "Nana." As for Cassie, she lived in upstate New York now, but it might as well be Mars or the moon.

"Life's messy sometimes." Cassie's philosophy, however true, was little comfort to the family. She'd been the "messy sister" when they were growing up, getting into mild scrapes, causing anxiety for the family, and in general making home life a challenge. But she was talented and bright, and Julia had adored her little sister. Now it was hard not to be angry with her and the choices she'd made.

Julia drove into the old neighborhood where she had grown up. Savannah had electrified its streetcar in 1888, extending two lines from the Victorian District south along Whitaker Street and creating the suburb. The district had been designated a National Historic Landmark in 1997, but time had left its mark on many of the old nineteenth-century houses that lined the streets. The air smelled different somehow, though Julia doubted it was any different here than in the rest of Savannah.

The sturdy Queen Anne home her mother still maintained brought a wave of nostalgia. How often she'd climbed those six steps to the broad front porch with its decorative white pillars and settled into one of the old sheltering rockers. Windows with black shutters glistened beneath overhanging eaves, and a polygonal slate roof gave the house a distinctive geometric shape. She looked up at the window of the room that had been hers. Cassie had occupied a rear bedroom, though as a child she'd frequently bartered for a trade, employing an assortment of incentives.

"Don't let her railroad you," her father had said on more than one occasion. "She's just as likely to want to switch back in a day or two." Not that Dad hadn't indulged his restless daughter at times. It was difficult to say no to the queen of charm.

Cassie had left home within days of high school graduation. Off to the College of Charleston with two best friends as restless as herself. She'd stayed nearly a year before eloping with a Cinematic Arts major bound for LA. The relationship hadn't lasted, as they had all feared, nor had the next. But she had rallied, gone east, and tried her hand at modeling, then enrolled in beauty school and set up shop— briefly. A boutique in Trenton, New Jersey, had followed, then a short stint in the real estate business. And now?

Now at almost fifty-five, Cassie was still searching for herself. Or running. From something? To something? Always there was a new interest—sculpting, interior decorating.... It was hard to keep up. She hadn't been home since their father's funeral, and then she'd just breezed in and out—at Mom's expense. She kept in touch from time to time with her mother and Wyatt, sent presents to the girls, but she lived on another plane, scarcely touching down to the reality of her estranged family.

Julia parked beneath a spreading oak and climbed the familiar steps. Her mother was always careful to keep the porch well swept and inviting—even including a wreath on the door. Some seasonal thing she put together herself that said welcome. She didn't fuss over such things, because she always had some community event to prepare for—the PTA, the local food bank, the arts committee, or some other cause that needed attention. She was known to be a hard worker and one who had the fortitude and ability to get things done.

"If it's worth doing, it's worth doing right," she always said. And she held her children to the same high standards. She had encouraged Julia every step of the way from dream to the judge's bench.

Mom had given up most of her community work and did little entertaining now. It was to be expected. She was eighty-four years old. But she had withdrawn more and more. Something had definitely changed internally, maybe more than age-related depression that some older women suffered. Julia rang the bell rather than rummage in her purse for a key. Besides, a woman needed privacy, even if she was your mother.

She heard no approaching footsteps, rang again, then turned the doorknob that had grown smooth and shiny over the years. The door yielded easily, and she stepped into the wide hallway and set the box of flowers on the hall table. "Mom?" Why wasn't she locking her door? A woman alone was vulnerable.

After a few seconds Julia heard the creak of an upstairs door, and her mother appeared on the landing. Julia did a double take.

Her mother was wearing a bathrobe, the tie hanging down to her bare feet. Her hair, usually carefully groomed, strayed carelessly around her face. Though she'd lost an inch or two, she was still tall and carried herself erect. Until recently she'd done the mall walk three times a week to keep fit.

She peered down at Julia, then at the watch on her slender wrist. "Why are you here so early?" Rebuke mixed with confusion hovered in her pale blue gaze.

"You said to come at six thirty," Julia said, consulting her own watch. "I'm not early. Are you all right?"

Her mom squinted at her watch once more. "Of course I'm all right. I just—well...I'm sure I said seven thirty, because I knew you were going to be busy all day."

"Why are you still in your robe?" Julia asked.

"I'm not *still* in my robe," came the quick response. "I was in the process of changing clothes to get ready for dinner." Then her lips softened into an apologetic smile. "Never mind. You're here now. Dinner's in the oven." She turned in to her bedroom, pulling the tie around her waist. "I'll be down in a jiffy."

Julia wandered through the living room, which had changed little since its remodel in the '80s. She could smell the lasagna—her mom's specialty—bubbling in the oven. She walked into the kitchen. Fifteen years ago, her father had surprised his wife on her birthday with brand-new appliances and real granite countertops.

Julia ran her fingertips over the uncluttered counter's smooth surface and recalled her mother's happiness that day. Two days later, Malcolm Lewis Waverly was killed, the victim of a car crash.

Julia had been devastated. She'd always been close to her father. Where her mother was ultradisciplined, Dad had enjoyed life with abandon. Julia had loved his big billowy embrace, his teddy-bear gentleness, which even now she imagined she could feel, warming her inexplicably.

"Well, there you are. Might as well make yourself useful."

Julia jumped. She hadn't heard her mother come quietly into the kitchen in her favorite beaded slippers. Malcolm had bought them for her at a Fair-Trade event that featured handcrafted wares from developing countries. She was wearing a green blouse with a black cardigan and slacks. Her hair had been ordered in a short bob that curved around her face. Her reading glasses hung around her neck on a silver chain. Bonnie Jean Waverly was still a stunning woman, but she looked tired and preoccupied. A small frown wrinkled her forehead.

"Since you're early you can set the table," she said, grabbing a pot holder and opening the oven door.

"I'm not early," Julia began. She let the protest dwindle and opened the lower cabinet where her mother stored the good dishes.

Her mother gave a slight shiver, though the kitchen was warm from baking. "Let's use the French Garden china. It will make us think of spring."

"Speaking of spring, I brought you something from City Market." Julia opened the box she'd brought into the kitchen and watched her mother's eyes light at the beauty inside it.

"Oh, lovely. Absolutely lovely." She gave Julia a warm smile, then said in an offhand voice, "Put them in some water, will you? There's a vase in the right-hand cupboard." She sat down at the table, seeming suddenly weary. "So, you went to City Market, where you bought my tulips. Since you're early you can tell me all about your day."

Julia sighed. She wanted to ask her mother about her health. Had she gone for the checkup she promised to get? Was she eating properly? She'd always been thin, but she seemed to have lost weight. It couldn't be easy, however determined she might be, to keep up this house and property. Had she considered some household help?

Mom frowned as she folded her hands in her lap. "Has the Winston reopened yet? Eduardo put so much of himself into that gallery." She stared into some space beyond Julia. "Working with him on the arts committee was a real privilege. He's done a lot for our city." She nodded her head slowly. "That stroke really laid him low, though. Poor Mr. DeLuca. He doesn't deserve this adversity."

Julia saw the flash of sorrow in her mother's eyes.

"Your father and I liked visiting the Winston back in the day." Mom's eyes misted. "He got to know Eduardo through the arts committee. Occasionally we met at his home—we got to know his wife too. Oneta sure has her hands full now taking care of him." She sighed heavily and looked down at her hands. "Your father would be sad to know what happened to him."

"The gallery has reopened," Julia hastened to say. "The facade has been refurbished and the stonework looks almost new. New sign too, but it's still 'The Winston.' Meredith, Carmen, and I stopped in after breakfast."

"I heard someone had stepped in to run the place," Mom said, sadness still etched on her face. "I just hope Eduardo will be able to come back."

"The gallery has changed a lot, but it seems to be going strong," Julia said gently. "Maggie Lu was going to come with us, but she had to visit her friend who is ill."

Mom's face suddenly clouded. She looked down at her lap, clasped and unclasped her fingers. After a pause she looked off into some space beyond Julia. "You mean the woman who inherited the Besset plantation."

Her mother knew exactly who Maggie Lu was. She had met her at a dinner at Julia's house. Had she forgotten? She and Meredith had talked about her often enough too—how she had helped them in their agency work. Maggie Lu would make a good friend for her mother. They were both proud women, strong women, who fought for good causes and cared about their communities—their world. Since their first meeting Julia had tried to get them together again, but her mother always had an excuse not to come.

Was it Maggie Lu in particular, or was it that Mom was simply disinclined to social interaction these days? She spent too much time alone. Julia swallowed. It wasn't good for anyone—let alone the elderly—to isolate themselves.

"You remember, Mom. Maggie Lu turned the plantation over to the historical society to benefit all of Savannah. She's a very civic-minded lady. And a generous one." She paused, wondering what it was that bothered her mother about Maggie Lu. "I think you'd really like her. And I know she'd like you."

Mom pushed back her chair in one quick motion and went to the oven. Over her shoulder she said, "Grab the salad from the fridge, and let's eat. It's time now. It's seven thirty."

Chapter Four

LIGHT RAIN FELL FROM AN overcast sky as Julia dressed for the exhibition at the Winston. Forecasters had predicted that it might become a full-on thunderstorm.

Savannahians could expect up to eight days of rain in February, leaving twenty-two of sunshine and moderate temps. Just her luck. This was one of eight!

She had whisked through supper after a busy day at the office with briefings related to recent cases and catching up with paperwork. At least there was a bit of downtime now with no immediate cases on their docket. As she added small rhinestone earrings to complement her favorite black sheath, she wondered what the gala evening would hold and how visitors would greet the new exhibit. She wrapped a scarf dotted with silver sequins loosely around her neck and went into the den.

"Is it a black-tie event?" Beau asked, appraising her appreciatively.

"People wear anything to art exhibits these days," she said, happy for the admiration in his eyes. "This dress is as old as the hills, but it will do."

"Well, you look marvelous, *dahling*," he parroted in his best Billy Crystal imitation.

"And you look infinitely more comfortable than I feel," she countered. "If I hadn't said yes to that special gallery showing, I could be lounging on the sofa with you...*dahling*."

She smiled as she got in the car, still feeling the glow of Beau's warm embrace. How fortunate she was to have found a man who took such good care of her and seldom missed a chance to compliment her.

When she arrived at the Winston, she spotted Carmen waiting for her under the broad awning. She was waving brightly as Julia made her way to the gallery.

"*¡Hola!*" Carmen called in greeting. She was wearing an attractive serape that hung below the hips of her skinny black pants. Her hair had been secured at the base of her neck under a perky red beret. She looked artsy and chic, striking just the right note for an art gala.

Julia felt a swelling of pride. Unlike some young women Julia had tried to help, Carmen had blossomed once assured that someone really did care about her after all.

"We'd better get in before the rain comes," Carmen said as a loud rumble of thunder echoed around them.

They ducked into the gallery. "Have you seen any sign of the 'runaway artist'?" Julia asked, dropping her umbrella into the stand by the door.

"No one I recognized," Carmen said, grinning and shrugging grandly.

Has she already forgotten about the memory the exhibit stirred? Julia thought. *If she has, I haven't.* She marveled at the mix of reluctance and anxiety she felt at the prospect of seeing it again.

Some two dozen guests wandered among the exhibits, most glancing toward the door as Julia and Carmen entered, then returning their attention to the paintings. Clearly, the promised guest artist had not arrived. A few patrons hovered near a refreshment table featuring a punch bowl glistening with an amber-colored beverage. Chocolate-covered pretzels and assorted nuts were arranged in cut-glass dishes.

The large painting signed by the elusive Desdemona remained on the prominent wall where they had seen it earlier in the week. A few smaller paintings in the same sweeping style had been carefully arranged next to it, left and right.

The collage drew a larger group of onlookers than other works clustered around the gallery, each representing modern, contemporary, or abstract genres. Julia decided to start on the left and work her way to the main exhibit after the crowd cleared a bit.

Julia paused at a painting that looked like a stained-glass window, the geometric panes outlined in heavy black strokes. The card indicated it was "A Tracery Abstract" by Timothy Norr and listed at six thousand dollars. Julia wondered how many people could spare that much money for a painting. Only the most ardent and wealthy collectors, she supposed.

Some paintings were considerably lower in price. A card adjacent one read: A GICLÉE IS THE FIRST AND ONLY FINE ART PRINT TO BE MADE WITH AN INK JET PRINTER AND IS SUPERIOR TO ALL OTHER FORMS OF PRINTING. PRONOUNCED ZHEE'CLAY, THE WORD COMES FROM THE FRENCH, MEANING "TO SPRAY." Julia studied it, amazed how startlingly good it was, rivaling the quality of original art.

She moved on, noting an abstract by Larry Poons that employed allover fields of pulsing color. She surveyed paintings attributed to

Cody Hooper, Phyllis Kapp, and Sigmar Polke, each unique but all unfamiliar to her. She sighed. *Sadly, my knowledge of fine art—original or giclée—is minimal.*

"Do you think he's the owner?" Carmen whispered, tilting her head toward a refined-looking gentleman in a suit that might have been Armani or Versace. Whatever the brand, it was not off-the-rack merchandise.

Julia stared. Something about the slender, slightly bent body, was familiar. He was forty, perhaps, with premature gray hair expertly cut and sleek as fox fur. The model of old-world grace. She could be mistaken of course, and she'd seen his face only in profile, but Julia was sure he was the man she'd seen all alone through the gallery window studying the Desdemona painting. He was speaking to a well-heeled, middle-aged couple standing close to the featured exhibit.

Julia squinted to make out the nametag affixed to his lapel and was surprised to read a familiar last name—DeLuca. Was he Eduardo's son? Grandson possibly? MARCO DELUCA. She scrutinized the dark features, the pencil mustache—à la Clark Gable—that barely moved as he spoke.

Almost imperceptibly, visitors merged as one toward the man and the Desdemona art, abandoning other exhibits in the gallery. DeLuca's mild baritone accents carried easily, as easily as the smile that didn't quite reach his eyes. They were brown, Julia noticed as he turned around to face his audience. Brown but with a glint of amber, and the left one closed and reopened in rapid-fire succession. A nervous tic perhaps, which he seemed to bring quickly under control. He stretched an arm toward the painting.

"We had hoped, of course, to present the artist herself to you this evening." His accent was cosmopolitan. Affected or genuine? It was anyone's guess. "But it appears that she has chosen to remain invisible." He bowed his head briefly as one might in deep regret, then raised it, chin jutting out as though in brave determination. "We shall have to content ourselves with the majesty of her work that graces our walls."

He gave one more ingratiating bow, and the silence in the room quickly descended into sighs and whispers. When he stepped aside, one was able to get a clear view of the painting with its carefully framed description. Julia moved closer to read it:

WHILE DESDEMONA'S ORIGIN AND PROVENANCE ARE LESS FACTUAL THAN THEORY, HER WORK HAS BEEN HAILED AS SOLIDLY SENSATIONAL, TYPIFYING THE TERM AVANT-GARDE. HER BOLD TRIANGLES, TRAPE-ZOIDS, AND SQUARES ARISE OUT OF DRAINED AND SOBER FIELDS OF COLOR. SHE HAS BEEN HERALDED AS AN ARTIST WHO SPEAKS TO THE DEPTHS OF HUMAN EXPERIENCE YET TO BE REALIZED. HER WORK APPEARING AT PRIVATE AND PUBLIC GALLERIES HAS QUICKLY BECOME A FAVORITE OF CONTEMPORARY ART FANS.

Julia's concentration was broken by a clap of thunder that rever-berated through the gallery. Almost instantly, rain clattered like stones pelting the roof.

"Here it comes," Carmen said, rolling her eyes ominously.

"I guess we'll have to stay and look around some more," Julia said. "I don't think our umbrellas would do much good out there. It's raining bullfrogs!" Some guests reacted to the sudden downpour by heading for the refreshment table, which sounded like a good idea to Julia. Something of a relief from the troubling featured painting.

"I'll join you in a minute," Carmen said. "There's Jenny Milford. Jenny!" And Carmen rushed toward a young woman with a blond ponytail and flashy gold earrings.

At the refreshment table, Julia lifted a cup of fruity punch to her lips and turned to look back at the display she had left. Everyone seemed to have drifted away except for one lone figure, a woman whose well-cut clothes were spotted with rain. She must have just arrived and without benefit of an umbrella, though a shiny green raincoat hung dripping over her arm.

A people watcher by habit, Julia sipped and watched. The woman was likely in her early seventies, average height and dressed primarily in black. A green shawl-like drape attached at one shoulder crisscrossed her full bodice. Her thick hair was braided and coiled on her head in a style of long-ago antiquity. She moved with surprising energy, causing a few white strands to escape despite the beaded combs caught in its depths.

As the woman leaned in closer, her snowy hair reflected the deep reds and golds of the painting. She took a few steps to the right, then paced back to the left, her low heels thudding softly on the hardwood floor. Eyes fixed on the painting, she suddenly faltered and bent over as though in pain. Was she ill? Was she going to faint?

Julia set her punch cup down on the table and started toward her. But suddenly the woman stood erect again, her feet planted firmly in well-made shoes. She began to pace some more, then, after spotting the gallery director, made a beeline for him.

When Julia saw her eyes for the first time, she caught her breath at the hostility in their dark depths.

"Where is she?" the woman demanded, grasping DeLuca's coat sleeve.

"Excuse me?" Stepping back, DeLuca brushed his coat sleeve, as though to remove the effects of her touch. "To whom are you referring, madam?"

"You play games," she returned hotly with a thick accent Julia couldn't place. The lips, without benefit of makeup, formed a grimace beneath a Romanesque nose. "You play games, but this is no game. I want to know where my granddaughter is."

"Your granddaughter!" He took another step back, then released an exasperated sigh. "Madam—"

"You must know. You have her work on these walls. It did not simply fly up there." She swept one arm wildly toward the large painting signed with the single name *Desdemona*. Then suddenly, she seemed to deflate like a spent balloon. Her arms dropped to her sides, her knees buckled, and her face paled to a white that rivaled her hair.

Heads turned at the raised voices as Julia stepped in beside the woman. DeLuca's color had likewise drained. He seemed completely at a loss and didn't move to get the lady a chair or to summon assistance. Julia took her arm gently but firmly.

"She needs to sit down," Julia told DeLuca. "Somewhere quiet," she urged, gesturing to a door off to one side, likely an office.

DeLuca seemed to regain his composure. "Of course." He gestured with a sweep of his arm to usher them inside. He gave surprised patrons a genteel smile as Julia helped the troubled guest out of the fray and into a chair near an expensive-looking cherrywood desk. "Please, continue to enjoy the exhibit," DeLuca told the milling crowd and stepped inside after Julia, closing the door. He frowned at the intruder then directed his gaze to Julia, the tic in his left eye working madly.

"Are you all right?" Julia asked the woman, supporting her in the chair.

"I am all right. I am all right," she said, breathing heavily. "Just let me sit a minute." Her eyes bored into DeLuca's, challenging him.

Julia angled her head toward DeLuca, who stood rigidly steps away from a watercooler. "I think she could use a drink."

DeLuca frowned but went obediently to place a paper cup under the spigot. Visibly displeased with the unwelcome disturbance, he handed the cup to Julia to pass to the woman. He released an impatient sigh. "You've no idea how many people claim Desdemona is their long-lost sister or aunt or—"

"Helena!" the woman spat, nearly choking on the water. "Helena Meyer! Whatever name you are calling her, she is my Helena, my granddaughter." The dark eyes snapped like hot coals.

"Madam," DeLuca began with strained impatience, "whether she is this Helena you speak of or not, I do not know. I acquired the artist's work through a colleague who recommended it as a good investment." The tic winked, then steadied. He drew a breath and let it out in a sigh. "These paintings are part of my private collection and have recently come into prominence. Desdemona—"

"Desdemona—runaway artist! Bah!" The incensed woman broke off into another language Julia couldn't identify. Latinate perhaps? Julia's mind raced. Whatever the outraged woman said was laced with scorn.

"She is Helena Meyer, the child of my only daughter, and I must find her. You know who she is. You know where she is!" She pointed her index finger at DeLuca's chest. "You must tell me." With each sentence, she grew more agitated.

"I have told you, madam. I have no knowledge of the author of these paintings." He shook his head, the thin mustache unmoving. "Many have claimed to know who she is, but they have been wrong, deluded. I am sorry for your trouble, but it would be best if you went home. I have guests waiting—"

"Something has happened to my granddaughter." She emphasized the second syllable of the word. "She does not run away. I come all the way from Athens." Her voice broke on the last few words. From an expensive-looking purse she drew a flowered handkerchief and held it to her mouth.

Had she come from Athens as in Greece? Julia caught her breath. Of course, there was an Athens, Georgia, which was four hours inland, but this woman wasn't American. Julia touched a hand to the woman's shoulder, felt its rigidity beneath the fabric of her dress. Clearly she was not well. "Is there something we can do for you, Mrs.—" Julia hesitated. "I'm sorry we don't know your name. I'm Julia. Julia Foley."

"Iris Floros," she said with a rolling accent that sounded like waves rushing in to shore. She lifted her head, seemed to gain control of herself, and tucked the handkerchief back into her purse. She stood and extended the paper cup toward DeLuca, who had remained a distant six or seven feet away. He stepped forward wordlessly to take the cup, in the process revealing a watch that couldn't be purchased at any local department store. *Marco DeLuca has expensive tastes. As does Iris Floros*, Julia thought.

Julia smiled. "Mrs. Floros. I'm pleased to meet you, and I'm so sorry that Mr. DeLuca and I have not been able to help you." She hesitated, taking note of the woman's hands. Her fingers looked strong and capable yet sensitive. Maybe she was a musician like her name sounded. A pianist or cellist. Or a painter like her granddaughter. *Alleged* granddaughter.

She must be staying with someone in Savannah. Someone she might call. Julia hesitated for only a moment. "I have a car. Could I take you home?"

Iris pursed her lips and released a weary breath. Challenge glittered in the dark eyes lifted to Julia's face. "I am not going home. Not yet." She glared again at DeLuca. "But in any case, you cannot drive all the way to Greece."

So it was true that she had come from Athens, the great city famed for the Byzantine Museum, the Agora Marketplace, and the Acropolis. Julia felt her pulse race.

Iris shrugged her shoulders. "Never mind," she said. "I have a taxi waiting to take me to the Andaz."

The Andaz Savannah by Hyatt was a popular hotel not far from City Market. Julia swallowed. Had Iris Floros traveled from Greece alone? Something in the determined jaw, the proud lift of the regal head said she might have done just that. But clearly, she was not a well woman. "I see," Julia said simply. How awful it would be to come this far and not learn the whereabouts of her granddaughter.

"You are very kind," Iris said, giving Julia a small, tired smile. She pivoted suddenly, her gaze boring through DeLuca. "But you— you I do not trust."

DeLuca spread his hands in a helpless gesture but said nothing. The tic in his left eye shivered like an icicle trembling from the eaves.

"We will speak again," she told him, and turned angrily toward the door.

"Let me walk you out," Julia said warmly. She picked up the green raincoat that Iris had apparently forgotten. "You may need this. Let me help you into it."

"You are kind. One does not always find kindness in this world." Her eyes flashed to DeLuca and back to Julia. "Actions speak louder than words. Is that not an American proverb?"

Julia said nothing but gently took her arm and steered her toward the door. Just outside, Carmen watched with a quizzical expression. Julia's assistant, who missed very little, had likely seen her disappear into DeLuca's office, though Julia hadn't been inside more than a few minutes. She glanced at Carmen with a look that said, "I'll tell you all about it later," and guided Iris Floros out of the gallery.

On the stone landing she paused beneath the awning. The rain had stopped, leaving sidewalks and streets glassy with the glare of market lights and passing cars. A taxi idled at the curb. The young driver got out and stood at relaxed attention against his vehicle.

"I will be fine now," Iris said with one more tired twist of her lips. "And I thank you."

Julia hoped there was someone waiting for Iris at the Andaz or some relative in Savannah to call on if she needed help. On impulse, she pulled a business card from her clutch bag and handed it to her. "My address and telephone, in case I can be of help."

Without looking at it, Iris Floros stashed the card into some hidden pocket in her dress and strode away.

"I hope you find her," Julia called after her.

Without another word, the lady stepped to the waiting taxi, her regal white head bent against the February chill.

"*¿Hay una problema aquí?*" Carmen quipped, eyes wide with curiosity.

Julia sighed. "She thinks Desdemona is her granddaughter. Came all the way from Athens to find her."

"A four-hour drive for nothing. I hope she didn't take a taxi all that way." Carmen laughed, pulling her serape closer around her.

Julia lifted her eyebrows meaningfully. "That would be Athens— as in Greece!"

Chapter Five

THE DAY AFTER THE ART exhibit at the Winston, Julia climbed the fifteen steps leading to the Carnegie Library. She had always admired the stately brick structure with its twin columns topped by round orbs that mimicked the globe-shaped lights on either side of the double green doors. Outside and in, the Carnegie was an architectural wonder.

The East Henry branch originally opened in 1914 as one of twelve segregated public libraries in the South funded by philanthropist Andrew Carnegie. After desegregation it reopened as a branch of the Savannah Public Library but continued to serve a predominantly African American clientele. It was temporarily closed in 2000 when it fell into disrepair, but funds were raised to restore it. It reopened in 2006.

Julia never failed to marvel at the remarkable march of history when she entered the doors of the library, which was an important landmark of Savannah's African American saga. Former users included Supreme Court Justice Clarence Thomas and Pulitzer Prize–winning author James Alan McPherson. And now here she was joining that elite company of patrons!

Julia had no research project that drew her to the library today, but she wanted to check on Maggie Lu. This was one of her days to volunteer at the East Henry Branch, which was a quick seven-minute walk from her house on Le Grand. She had been away visiting her good friend who, in addition to having Alzheimer's disease, was recovering from a bout of pneumonia. Magnolia Louvenia King was amazingly resilient and self-contained in the face of chaos or misfortune, but with the imminent threat of her friend's death, Maggie Lu might need some cheering up.

It was early with only a few patrons taking advantage of the handsome library. She spotted the tall African American woman surrounded by several boxes and folders spread out on a wide, polished table. At seventy-six years of age, Maggie Lu still sat erect, her salt-and-pepper hair drawn back from a forehead remarkably free of lines. She looked the professional woman she was in a dove-gray dress with long sleeves and a lacy Peter Pan collar. Much as she must have looked during her years of teaching at nearby Spencer Elementary, now renamed Williams Elementary.

It had been nearly a year since Julia and Meredith had met her in the process of unravelling the sixty-five-year-old mystery of Harriet Besset, who had gone missing. So pivotal had been Maggie Lu's role in that unravelling that they had renamed the agency in her honor—Magnolia Investigations—and continued to find her assistance important to their success.

"Julia honey," Maggie Lu said, glancing up over her wire-rimmed spectacles. "I didn't expect I'd see you today." Her quick smile made her look a good deal younger than her age. "You on a mission today?"

"Well, I wanted to ask how your visit went. How is Delyse?"

The smile faded. She leaned back in her chair and folded her arms over her waist. She drew a breath and let it out in a long stream.

"Oh, honey, I just hate to see her getting so small. She's nothing but a little lump in that big old bed. The pneumonia has left her very weak."

Delyse Watson, with whom Maggie Lu had volunteered for many years in this very library, had been a patient at the nursing home when Julia met her. Now, in deteriorating health, she might not recover. It would be a terrible blow to Maggie Lu.

Julia recalled vividly the Jamaican woman—her warm brown face and brilliant white hair, in which often a blue ribbon or a silky red rose would nestle. She could almost hear the toothy Patois greeting, "*Wah gwaan wid yuh todeh*?" Loosely translated, it meant "How are you today?" Perky, clever, and remarkably well read, she had been a teacher too in a school across town.

"I'm sorry," Julia said, sitting down on a chair next to Maggie Lu. "You've known each other for a long time. I think she must know how lucky she is to have you for a friend."

Maggie Lu sighed softly. "It's the smile of a loving Father shining down on us both," she said, nodding slowly. She closed a file folder on top of a stack of other papers. "But she's goin' home, and it won't be long. Oh, I'll miss that sweet Delyse."

"Well, you're keeping busy, and that's a good thing," Julia said gently. "But what's all this?" She gestured to the formidable piles of paperwork spread out on the table. Several piles, in fact.

"They belong to Delyse. She asked me to go through her memoirs and letters and things—to save what's important. You know she was always writing down something she didn't want to forget. There are boxes of papers and folders with bits and pieces. One page of a letter but missing the next. Then I find it in another box. She's a dear, but the messiest, most disorganized woman God ever put on this earth." Maggie Lu smiled in fond remembrance. "She doesn't have anything valuable here really—except to her."

"I'm surprised she didn't want Reggie to handle it," Julia said. She knew Delyse had a son—a record producer who was always looking into the next big deal that would take an audience by storm.

Maggie Lu released a puff of air. "That boy? He hasn't been to see her in months. Sure, he's paying for her care—and leaving it to them. The caring, that is." She tapped the folder with a pencil. "So, she asked me to go through her things. He'd likely toss the lot out— although he did take Sydney in. Sydney the Third, that is. Don't know what happened to the first, but sometimes she addresses these jottings to Sydney the Second." She smiled, tapping a finger on a handwritten page.

Julia wasn't fooled. Maggie Lu had doted on Sydney the Third. She'd grown fond of the cat while she was hiding from the mansion owner who had promised to track her down to pay for what happened to his daughter. She'd hidden out in Delyse's secluded cottage until the truth came out that the man was himself responsible for what happened. He'd come to his senses—or rather God came to his rescue. In the end he had repented and willed his entire estate to Maggie Lu, and she turned it over to the Savannah Historical Society.

"I'm glad somebody's seeing to that querulous kitty," Maggie Lu said. She pushed the papers aside, indicating the end of that discussion. "How was the gallery reopening?"

"Interesting," Julia responded. "Carmen and I went. In the pouring rain, I might add." She paused, recalling the surprising run-in with the woman who had claimed Desdemona was her long-lost granddaughter. She shrugged. "It's quite changed from the way it used to be. Or maybe it was just that this was a special exhibit. Contemporary art—some of it very striking, but unusual. Very modern."

"I've always wondered how that can of soup became so iconic—worth a king's ransom." Maggie Lu chuckled as she referenced the famous Andy Warhol painting. "Reckon there's no accounting for taste—or tomatoes."

"Maggie Lu, do you know a Marco DeLuca?"

She shook her head. "Wasn't it a DeLuca who ran the Winston before?"

"Yes. My folks knew him—Eduardo DeLuca—through the arts committee that my mom served on. He had a stroke and is still recuperating."

Maggie Lu said nothing for a long moment. "How is your mother?" she asked softly as she tapped the eraser end of her pencil over a manila folder on the table. "You said you've been worried about her."

"Oh, she's all right, I think. Just lately she seems really bothered and withdrawn. It may have something to do with my wayfaring sister." Julia looked away.

Quietness reigned between them briefly as Julia recalled the recent dinner conversation with her mother. She felt her face grow warm.

"Families can be hard," Maggie Lu said quietly. "'Lovin' be hardest with your own,' Granny Luv used to say, and I know that's right."

Maggie Lu might have been thinking about her nephew, Luke, whom she had loved with such passion as a child. But he had broken her heart with his anger and drinking.

"But she also said, 'Prayin' is a power stronger than a mountain of dynamite,' and I know that's right too."

Prayer had helped bring Luke to his senses. He'd turned his life around and now brought new joy into Maggie Lu's life. Julia smiled into the wise brown eyes that had seen so much—the good and the bad. "You're right of course. We all should remember that."

Julia had prayed for Cassie for a long time, but when nothing changed, it was sometimes hard to keep on believing. It wasn't Cassie so much troubling her these days; it was Mom. The family hadn't been close since her father died. She felt it a singular failure on her part that she had done so little to draw them all together.

Maggie Lu turned to answer a question for a young man. "I'll be right back," she said and got up to show the visitor the way to a research section.

The interim gave Julia time to reflect on their discussion. She wished anew that Mom could get to know Maggie Lu better. Her mother was eight years older, but she had always retained a youthful aspect—at least until recently.

Her mind flashed to the previous November when she and Meredith attended a Historical Society fundraiser. She had purchased a table and convinced her mother to attend as one of her guests. Knowing Maggie Lu was coming as well, she planned to seat them together so they could become acquainted. But it wasn't to be.

Julia and her mother had come early enough to participate in a silent auction and were enjoying the various items offered for sale.

She bid on a Roberts Brothers first edition of Louisa May Alcott's classic *Little Women*. Mom placed a bid on a Renaissance Gold Wedgewood salad bowl to replace one she'd broken.

Meredith joined them, and the three of them were giggling and exclaiming over various treasures when they spotted Maggie Lu and her daughter, Charlene, coming toward the silent auction area. Julia waved and went to greet them and show them their table.

"There's still time if you want to place a bid or two," Julia said, helping Maggie Lu with her coat and pointing out the place cards with their names printed on them. "The silent auction is around the corner there."

"Oh, I'd love to have a peek," Charlene said. In her midfifties, she was taller than Maggie Lu but favored her mother with her lean athletic build, high cheekbones, and intelligent eyes. She was an excellent businesswoman and had worked hard to acquire the Downhome Diner, a favorite haunt for Julia and Meredith and a good many more Savannahians.

"This old woman don't need to be buying more trinkets," Maggie Lu said, lapsing into Ebonics for emphasis. Then, grinning, she added, "But ain't nothin' wrong with looking!"

And so, Julia steered them back to the silent auction tables and found Meredith studying a poster-size photo of a 1940s Keystone Dollhouse available for bidding.

"Jules, look! It has two stories and six rooms and it's in excellent condition," Meredith said, blue eyes dancing. "Kinsley would absolutely love it."

"Of course she would, Mere, and you're just the one to spoil her," Julia said knowingly. Meredith doted on her two grandchildren, nine-year-old Kinsley and eleven-year-old Kaden. Kinsley was a girly-girl from the get-go and especially loved dollhouses. Kaden was extraordinarily bright but struggled with social situations as did most children on the Asperger's scale. "And have you found anything your budding little astronomer might like?"

"Guess I better!" Meredith said happily.

"You might even find something for *yourself*!" Julia quipped. She scanned the crowd, peering around other guests examining the treasures that would help to fund the society's endeavors. "Have you seen my mother?"

"I did," Meredith said, straightening and giving Julia her full attention. "She asked me to tell you she felt a migraine coming on and decided it would be best if she went home."

"What?" Julia was dumbstruck. "She was fine just a few minutes ago. Is she all right?" Mom did suffer from migraines, but she was generally able to detect them coming on before heading to an event and would take medication to mediate the symptoms. Julia felt a keen disappointment. She had hoped to share the evening with all her friends and family. Of course, her mother was the only family member near enough to attend.

"I asked if she needed a ride, but she said she had her own car." Meredith nodded reassuringly. "She said you shouldn't worry about her. She'll call you."

Now, as Julia watched Maggie Lu return to the library table, she felt again that odd sense of distance. Distance and loss—indefinable but edging into her heart like prickly heat.

"That young man is writing his thesis on the social politics of Frederick Douglass," Maggie Lu said when she resumed her seat.

"Whatever that means." She lifted her eyebrows and said, "I think Douglass's social politics might be summed up in something from a speech of his that I read." Without waiting to be asked what that might be, she explained. "'It is easier to build strong children than to repair broken men.'"

"How true," Julia said quietly, trying to shake free from her earlier thoughts. "And that's what you are doing. Volunteering here in this library helps to build strong children as well as adults."

"Well, that's almost too much compliment for me this early in the morning," Maggie Lu said, looking at her with so much warmth that Julia felt the sting of unexpected tears.

What is the matter with me? She pushed back a little from the table. From the look on Maggie Lu's face, it was likely she hadn't missed the flash of melancholy or whatever it was that had come over Julia. She really needed to get to the office.

"We were talking about that art exhibit, weren't we?" Maggie Lu asked. She peered over her glasses. "I'm sorry to interrupt our talk. I'm not due to start work for another half hour, but I guess a volunteer is on duty the minute she appears."

What they had been discussing was the thorny issue of family relationships and the efficacy of prayer, but art exhibits were a much safer topic. Julia gladly switched gears. "Something strange happened while we were there. A woman came in and went straight to the focus painting of the exhibit.

"It's hard to explain that painting—so much turmoil and darkness, all crimson and golden trapezoids—then that oval of light in the center. Well, the thing about it is that no one knows much about the artist. She calls herself 'Desdemona' and apparently doesn't show up to talk to people or sign an autograph."

Maggie Lu pursed her lips. "Some students from the Art and Design College were looking for information about someone known as the 'runaway artist.' I'm not sure they found anything."

"Well, I guess there have been a number of theories about her. Theories and stories, but this woman—she was probably in her seventies—went right up to the new director of the exhibit and claimed the artist was her granddaughter. Demanded to know where she was."

"And did he know?"

"Said he had no information. Apparently, there have been others claiming kinship or speculating on her provenance. He was quite irritated and embarrassed by the interruption." Julia frowned. "I'm not sure she's well, because it looked like she might faint. I stepped in to see if I could help. We took her into the director's office and got her some water."

"Poor woman," Maggie Lu said.

"It all happened so fast." Julia released a long breath. "Turns out she came all the way from Greece to find her granddaughter. I'm sure Marco DeLuca thought she was *loca*, as Carmen would put it. I felt sorry for her, asked if I could help. She had a taxi waiting at the curb, and she left. It was quite an evening, and it was raining bull-frogs besides. I was glad to get home to my snug, warm house."

"DeLuca," Maggie Lu said thoughtfully, repeating the name. "It seems to me I recall a rumor about an art deal that went wrong. DeLuca was a name connected with it. It was something of a scandal for a short time, then seemed to blow over."

"Really," Julia said, curiosity instantly piqued. "When was that?"

Maggie Lu shook her head contemplatively. "Must be nearly five or six years ago. I don't really recall any of the details."

"Was it in the paper?"

"If it was, I don't recall—it was just some talk. May have been nothing important at all." Maggie Lu sighed. "Apparently, it hasn't affected the reopening. I'll have to get over there one of these days."

Julia made a mental note to research news stories connected to the Winston. "Anyway, I just wanted to make sure you got back all right from your visit with Delyse."

Maggie Lu didn't drive. Public transport in Savannah was all right, but Julia always worried when Maggie Lu took the bus out of the city by herself. Come to think of it, this branch of the Live Oak Library System wasn't in the best of areas. They had urged her to volunteer only in daylight hours. She squeezed Maggie Lu's hand warmly. "You know we worry about you, Maggie Lu."

"You're a sweet thing, aren't you?" she said, peering over her spectacles. "But you don't have to worry about this old woman. The good Lord's been taking care of me for more years than a body can count. Besides, worry is like a rocking chair. Gives you something to do but doesn't get you anywhere."

Julia's cell phone buzzed. She slipped it out of her jacket pocket and checked the screen. She gave Maggie Lu an apologetic glance and answered the call.

"There's someone here to see you." Meredith's voice held mystery. "She says you met the other night. A lady with an accent. Carmen told her she should make an appointment, but she wasn't taking no for an answer. I told you were out; she said she'd wait."

"Did she tell you her name? Say what she wanted?" But Julia was already seeing dark, angry eyes, a Romanesque nose, and white hair coiled like a snake ready to strike.

"Just that she must see you. She says she'll wait."

"Coming," Julia said and clicked off. "The lady from Athens I told you about? She's waiting at the agency." She searched Maggie Lu's face as though the answer to what might become a big problem could be read there.

"Nothing you can't handle," Maggie Lu said with a thrust of her chin. "You and the best help there is."

Chapter Six

JULIA DROVE TO THE AGENCY, heartened by her quick visit with Maggie Lu at the library and curious about a second contact with Iris Floros. After the night at the gallery, she had googled the Greek surname and discovered it meant "green" and might also be a shortened form of "Phloropoulos." Coupled with the first name, Julia had a vision of a budding green flower, but the woman who had confronted Marco DeLuca had been seasoned and prickly as a field of thorns.

Carmen rolled her eyes and inclined her head as Julia ducked inside Magnolia Investigations. "She's in your office. Meredith is waiting for you there too." She glanced meaningfully toward the small waiting area to the left of the reception desk.

Julia had been so intent on Carmen's warning expression that she hadn't noticed the tall, angular woman sitting there, clutching a small purse in her lap. Fiftysomething, thin and all angles, she wore a deep mauve dress with a matching tunic and an odd hat that dipped over her forehead at yet another angle. Thin lips beneath a long nose were etched into a straight line.

"This is Miss Angelos. She accompanied Mrs. Floros. I told her she could wait for her here." Carmen had supplied her guest with a cup of coffee that sat untouched on the small table next to the faux leather couch reserved for visitors. The unsmiling woman bobbed her head briefly, making the odd little hat wobble above brown hair of no discernible style. For all that, Julia thought, her features were regular, the bones in her face good. She might be a handsome woman with a little touching up and without the drab mauve outfit.

"Good morning," Julia said, glancing from Carmen to Miss Angelos, who nodded and flashed glittery amber eyes in the direction of the closed inner office door. She looked back at Julia with an unreadable expression. Impatience? Worry? Suspicion?

When no verbal greeting was offered, Julia moved on to her office. Her guest, seated inside with Meredith, turned at the sound of her entrance.

"Ah, there you are!" Iris Floros scrutinized Julia, taking her measure from her smoothly styled silver hair to her low-heeled pumps. She pursed her lips in a thoughtful gesture. "I found your card this morning when I was getting dressed." She produced it from her handbag and set it on the desk with a flourish. "When I see that the kind woman who helped me is a private investigator, I know the gods may smile on me after all." One white eyebrow rose in a graceful arch as she continued to hold Julia's attention. "I want you to find my granddaughter."

Julia took a chair across from Meredith. She flashed a glance at her partner, who was clearly as nonplussed as she was. "Um—"

"I am a woman of means," Iris put in quickly. "I can pay for your services. That is what you do, is it not? Find people who are missing?"

"Well, it's not a matter of—that is—" Julia knew she sounded utterly unprofessional. But who was this demanding woman?

Meredith jumped to her partner's rescue. "Magnolia Investigations is a duly licensed private agency in the state of Georgia, Mrs. Floros. But before we accept a case, there are certain things that need to be discussed. Certain—"

"Things! Things! What things?" came the impatient interruption from a woman who clearly was used to being in charge. "My granddaughter is missing. She is in trouble. I know! A grandmother knows!" Her voice caught, and she bent forward, much as she had done in the gallery.

Julia and Meredith jumped up at the same time. "Are you all right?" Julia asked. "Please, Mrs. Floros—"

As quickly as the woman had folded inward, she righted herself again. "I'm fine. It is nothing. No, don't call Celia!" She took a deep breath as Julia sat back down again with a glance at the door. "That woman will fuss and fume that I'm too old to travel. In the end she will be no help at all!"

Celia Angelos, the unsmiling figure in the odd hat. A nurse? Or a companion? Perhaps Iris Floros needed an angel. Maybe more than one.

Mrs. Floros pulled a small box from her purse and extracted something. A pill certainly, and Julia grew more uncomfortable as the woman popped it into her mouth and swallowed.

"I'll get you some water," Julia said.

"No need. Please, don't bother." The proud head lifted. "It is true I have a heart condition, but these pills are all I need. Celia can do nothing more, and I must talk to you."

Digitalis? Some other heart medication? Unsettled by the woman's explanation, Julia went to the cooler to get a cup of water. They could at least listen, even if they had to decline taking the case. It would be terrible if this distraught Greek citizen should have a cardiac episode. The words "international incident" flashed through Julia's mind. Yikes!

Iris clasped her hands in her lap and twirled them in a kind of mesmerizing motion. "My granddaughter is the only family I have left."

"When did you last see her?" Meredith asked quietly.

"A few years ago," came the offhand reply, as though it was insignificant. "2006, I believe."

A few years? Iris Floros was talking about a grown woman whom she hadn't seen in fifteen years! Missing? It sounded ludicrous. The so-called "missing" person was an adult with her own plans, who may have simply chosen not to include her strong-minded Greek grandmother.

"She is missing. It is true that I haven't seen her in a long time, but we were in contact by post." Iris's commanding voice cut the air, and she sniffed as though personally insulted. "She started art college three years ago and was very excited about what she was learning." A shadow crossed her animated features. "She never said thank you—" Again the pregnant pause. "But I know she was happy there."

"You were living in Greece?" Julia asked. "And where was your granddaughter?"

"Right here in Savannah with her father. Before that, they lived in Atlanta. It is in the same state, yes?" Iris drew her eyebrows together in distaste. "They moved for her father's work, I believe."

"You speak very good English," Julia said.

"We learned English in school, and at home my father insisted we must learn." She hesitated briefly, as though she'd temporarily lost track of her purpose.

"So, you were in touch while she was at school," Meredith put in. "How long has it been since you heard from her?"

Iris sat up straighter and reached for the water that had been left near her chair. "Last year," she mumbled softly, "about this time." Perhaps realizing how cryptic this sounded, Iris continued. "She left school because she met someone who was going to help her become a big success as a painter.

"'I wish you could meet him, Grandmama,' she wrote to me. 'He is strong where I am weak, and he likes my painting.'" Ending her parody of the letter writer, she set the cup down with a sharp click. "I was happy for her. She was doing what she loved to do, but her letters... They came more slowly—and then, no more letters."

Julia felt the pain in the older woman's voice. "Young people can be very focused on their own affairs," she said gently. "They often forget about their mentors or family or—"

"You don't understand!" Iris said, clasping her hands over her chest. "Art is everything to Helena. She couldn't wait to share her success with her grandmama, whose blood flows in her veins. Something changed. Her letters became short little lines, sad lines, and then nothing."

"Are you all right?" Julia asked, unnerved, for Iris had paled, her hands still pressed against a place near her heart. Julia glanced toward the door, thinking Celia might be of some use after all.

The moment passed, and Iris was again in control. "Of course, you cannot really understand, but all this talk of a runaway artist.

Bah! Helena was proud of her work; she would not do this. Something is wrong. She is not like her mother—" She stopped. "I know something is wrong; she is unhappy. I must find her." She shook her head, dislodging one of the combs in her snowy hair.

"Are you sure you want to continue?" Meredith asked in a business-like manner, deflecting the emotionalism that charged the air.

"Yes. Let me explain better." After a sip of water, she folded her hands in her lap once more. "Helena's mother—my daughter—left Athens when she was only eighteen years. Rhea was an artist—she grew up among artists." She paused to give Julia a direct glance. "I am a member of an artisans' guild in my country; I am a sculptor." The hands swirled in her lap, as though she might be molding clay.

"Felipe and I made a good living." She moistened her lips and started again. "We shared a studio. We were always busy. There were commissions. Many commissions. My daughter—" She shook her head but went on. "Rhea was gifted but always a troubled child. When she began to develop as a woman, she became more and more restless—and disobedient. We—we—feared for her, but we were very busy."

Always busy. Very busy. The words said so much more. Had they been too busy to make sure their daughter didn't get lost in the shuffle? Maggie Lu's recent reminder of Frederick Douglass's words swept through Julia's mind: *"It is easier to build strong children than to repair broken men."* Greek children. American children. All were vulnerable. All could break.

"Always she wanted to go away," Iris lamented. "She wanted to go to America. I said she is too young. I will pay for university in our country, but she—she had no ears for Felipe and me. It was a time of great trouble. Much trouble. Much anger. And then—" She drew a breath and let it out slowly. "Then one day she took all the money we had and a diamond ring—high quality gold, very expensive—and left us."

That statement fell like a physical blow on Julia's heart; she could think of nothing to say.

"I hear nothing. Nothing for five years." Something hard glittered in the dark eyes, then turned to resignation. "I was not surprised when she wrote that she is married. 'He loves me,' she says. I should not worry. I should be happy for her."

"You weren't invited to the wedding?" Meredith asked.

As though she hadn't heard, Iris continued. "She never wanted to know, 'How are you, Mama?' or 'I'm sorry about taking the money and ring.' No. Just that I should be happy for her." Iris closed her eyes as though the light burned them.

She leaned forward in the chair. "When Rhea said a baby had come, I was happy but still angry. I came to Atlanta, where she and her husband lived. I saw my Helena for the first time. Beautiful—dark hair like sable and eyes the color of blueberries like Rhea. But her father did not welcome me. 'Duke,' Rhea called him, but his real name was Donald. He worked at the shipyard—all hard muscle and angry eyes—no patience for art." She released a slow breath. "He hid her paints and pastels, threw away her pictures! She must cook good food, keep his house. Bah!" she said again.

Julia pushed a strand of hair behind her ear. Iris's story was appallingly sad. It made her angry too. What right had a husband to destroy something his wife loved?

"She went out with friends—dancing, drinking. Duke—he drank too. Too much. They argue, fight. Then the accident happened." Iris said it matter-of-factly, but a little muscle in her jaw quivered. "After Rhea died, Helena's father refused my help. He said I should go home—he will take care of his little girl as he always did with no help from his artsy wife. That's the word he used—'artsy' like it is something bad."

"So, you left and went home to Athens?" Meredith asked, pausing in her note taking.

"There was nothing I could do. I wrote letters, I telephoned, but I hear only silence. Then I got sick. I spent almost two years in the sanitarium and much time after that to get better. But the year Helena was ten—I came to Savannah for her birthday. I knew she and her father moved away from Atlanta and settled here. An ugly little house in an ugly place." Her lips formed a straight, angry line. "I could have given her—but what is the use? He would not listen. Like talking to stone."

"Did you see Helena then?" Julia asked softly.

Iris nodded. "Even a man as hard as Duke could not stop me. I came across an ocean to see her. But he watched us every minute and froze me with his cold eyes. He wanted me to go."

"That had to be hard for you. I'm so sorry." Julia touched her arm, felt the anger that held her in its rigid grasp.

"She asked me, 'Are you really my grandmama?' Her blueberry eyes were so full of sadness. And I think that Rhea has told things about me. Bad things." She lowered her head and said nothing for several seconds.

"Rhea left in anger, and anger never left her—or Felipe. He would not hear her name in our house. I think the poison between us reached Helena. I only had a few days with her, but—" She grew wistful, her voice devoid of its usual testiness. "You know how you can love someone in one second? It is like falling into Poseidon's arms—you can do nothing to save yourself. You are swallowed up."

The silence deepened. Julia marveled at the woman, who spoke of an angry sea god and of other gods who might smile on her. Orthodox Christianity was still the largest religious denomination in Greece, but perhaps for Iris it had not penetrated the heart.

"We wrote letters. She sent me pictures she made, pictures she had to hide from her father, and I hide from Felipe. How she loved to make pictures!" Iris shook her head. "Duke was afraid she would run away like her mother. That she would leave him like my Rhea did. But art was everything to Helena. He tried to keep her with him, but he could not do so in death. After he died, she went to school, and it has been over a year since her last letter to me."

Julia's mind raced trying to keep up with the family saga. So, Helena had left home and somehow reconnected with Iris while she was in art school. But she had since gone silent again. Her grandmother believed she was in trouble and had traveled thousands of miles to find her.

"How was it that you traced her to Savannah and to the art gallery?"

"I knew her father died. I tried to find her, but I had nowhere to go for help. No relatives to contact. Colleagues in my art guild at home couldn't help me. I hired a nurse from my city, and we flew here."

She had come all this way with her nurse companion, hoping to find Helena. Julia studied the troubled face, the deep lines across the regal forehead, the anguish visible in the bold dark eyes. Given her health condition, she had taken a huge risk. How sad if she didn't find this elusive granddaughter—perhaps even sadder if she did.

"I saw ads for the show at this Winston gallery," Iris went on. "And when I saw the paintings, I knew my Helena was the artist. I know her touch on the canvas. I can feel her spirit inside me!"

Julia pressed her lips together and regarded the noble face, wreathed in anxiety. "But you can't be sure." Even if the artist was Helena Meyer, suppose she didn't want to be found? Suppose she didn't want anything to do with her grandmother?

"A grandmother knows," she said again, this time with a soft, introspective voice. She straightened then and became all business. "As I say, I can pay you. I imagine your retainer is not beyond my means." She opened her large leather bag and pulled out a checkbook.

Meredith cleared her throat. "Mrs. Floros, we haven't agreed to take your case. Your granddaughter may not wish to be found. In missing person cases—"

"I do not believe this. She is unhappy; she is troubled. I know this." Her voice rose in increasing decibels. "How can I explain it? What am I to do? If only the gods would speak!" She appeared to crumple, causing Julia and Meredith to start fearfully toward her again.

"Please, Mrs. Floros. You mustn't upset yourself like this." Julia put a stabilizing hand on the woman's shoulder and glanced across at Meredith. "Look," she continued, reading something like pained acquiescence from Meredith, "we will look into the matter. No, you don't need to pay anything now. If we think we can help you, we'll bill you for time spent. There may be additional fees, depending on what happens."

"May the gods reward you," Iris blurted.

"We are not agreeing to take your case," Julia warned, "just that we will look into it and decide if we can assist you." It sounded cold to her own ears, and Julia deliberately avoided the anxious woman's eyes. "Now, I think it best that you let Celia get you back to your hotel."

They rose as one and moved to the door, which at Julia's touch opened. Celia sprang back, her face a wreath of surprise and confusion. At the same instant, Carmen came around the corner from the copy room; they all converged awkwardly in the hallway.

Had Celia Angelos been listening at the door? Julia glanced at the waiting area, where the coffee Carmen had brought to the nurse remained untouched. Carmen appeared flustered, as though she had somehow failed in her duties.

It was Celia who spoke first, stepping close to Mrs. Floros. "Are you all right?" Her sympathetic voice held none of the Greek influence employed by Iris. She had no accent Julia could recognize. Her eyes that had glinted amber when Julia had first seen her had deepened to gray-brown or perhaps they were simply clouded with concern.

"The taxi is waiting, and it's time for your meds. We should get you back to the hotel." She turned a stern face to Julia. "She has angina, and she mustn't get excited."

"My condition is stable!" Iris snapped. "The doctor says so. I am fine." She pulled back from Celia's grasp. To Julia she said, "I will call you tomorrow to hear your decision."

"We know where you are," Julia said firmly. "Better if you wait for us to call you."

"And you must be patient," Meredith put in. "We will be in touch. I promise."

Iris opened her mouth to speak further but suddenly closed it. She slumped with apparent weariness and allowed herself to be guided out by the sharp-featured Celia.

When they were gone, Carmen held her hands out in a helpless gesture. "I just went to copy some forms. I was only gone a minute or two. Is—everything okay?"

Julia sighed, feeling suddenly as weary as Iris Floros looked. "The lady wants us to find her granddaughter, the elusive artist she insists is in trouble and needs her."

"Our next case?" Carmen asked with a lift of one groomed eyebrow. At Julia's eyeroll, she added, "*Es una problema*, I think."

A problem indeed. Julia pondered the odd circumstance that had brought Iris Floros to the agency. If she hadn't visited the Winston Gallery when Iris did and intervened between the troubled woman and Marco DeLuca, the problem would never have come to their notice.

Chapter Seven

"Wow!" Julia exclaimed as she and Beau entered the Olde Pink House Restaurant on Abercorn Street. "I'd forgotten how cool this place is!"

"I wanted to treat my best girl to something special," Beau said. "It's a bit late for Valentine's Day but a perfect night to enjoy the Olde Pink House. Besides, this place has great history." He grinned down at her, blue eyes twinkling. He wore a crimson bow tie for the occasion and looked every bit the erudite professor. His field had been medicine, but he had a natural aptitude for academia—particularly history. "This place is amazing. They say that if you listen carefully you can hear the chatter of ghosts amid the tinkling of china and silver."

Julia grasped her husband's arm as they followed the waiter to one of the glittering tables. She had worn red to match Beau's tie and to commemorate the February holiday. They were to meet Meredith and Quin for dinner and had agreed to splurge on a visit to the upscale restaurant. "This place has gone through a lot of changes since the 1700s," Beau said. "Attorney's office, bookstore, tearoom, to name a few. But despite decay and neglect, it was always impressive, standing alone with whispers of the past hidden in its crumbling walls. It wasn't until 1992 that it was restored it to its original brilliance and became the go-to spot for tourists."

"And for us Savannahians," Julia added. "Great choice for dinner, Beau." She peered around the white-coated waiter. "Doesn't look like they're here yet."

"They'll be along. Quin said they might be delayed. He had a last-minute caller."

Arthur "Quin" Crowley had moved his law practice from Columbus to Savannah after the death of his wife. He and Meredith had bumped into each other—literally—in a parking lot when both were involved with the Besset case. At first on opposite sides of the investigation, they ended up bringing the matter to a satisfying conclusion and in the process began a friendship.

Julia cast Beau a sly look. "I'm glad Quin agreed to join us. I'm sure he would rather have had Meredith all to himself." The truth was, the dinner foursome would make things easier for her partner, who insisted that she and Quin were merely friends. Julia felt a bubble of humor, recalling that Meredith had left the office shortly after noon for a hair appointment.

"Here they come now," Beau said with a nod toward the door as he held out Julia's chair, preempting the waiter's move.

Julia watched their approach. Meredith flashed a warm smile, looking perfectly at ease in a soft pink dress, simply tailored with a slight flair at the hem. Her blond curls had been tamed into a smooth Helen Mirren bob that appeared effortless and carefree but probably wasn't.

Beside her, Quin cut a suave figure in a silver-gray suit that matched his well-groomed hair. He appeared tall alongside Meredith, but he probably surpassed Julia's height only by an inch or two. Moving with purposeful step, he leaned slightly forward as though a wind drove him. Meredith had once remarked about a calmness in him that made you feel safe—storm or not. Compelling but compatible at the same time.

"I'm sorry we're late," Quin said, shaking hands with Beau across the table and acknowledging Julia with a smile that lit his eyes.

"You're not late; we've only just arrived," Julia said. She was about to tell Meredith that she loved her outfit, which in its petal-pink softness didn't clash at all with her own cherry-red dress, but she stopped herself. In Quin's presence the compliment would embarrass her. Instead she offered, "Isn't this place amazing?"

"They've outdone themselves," Meredith said, touching the gleaming china at her place. "I used to love telling tourists the history of this place and how it got its name. How the porous native brick began to bleed through the plastered walls, mysteriously changing the color of the Habersham house from white to Jamaican pink."

As the former historical society director, Meredith was a wealth of information on Savannah. Julia was amazed at her knowledge and recall. She had wondered if Meredith would miss it, but she had plunged into the investigation business with avid determination, despite a not-so-carefully-concealed trepidation at the start. It had been a complete change for her. She had become familiar with some of her husband's cases and helped him with research, but she had been busy with her own duties and children. Julia looked across the table at her friend with admiration. She was a natural with amazing intuitive skills and a genuine drive to help people.

"Beatrice tells everyone that they simply *must* order the 'Olde Pink House pink lady' when they dine here," Meredith said, effectively mimicking the new historical director's animated speech. "It'll fry your taters for sure." She laughed but not unkindly. Beatrice was over the top with more affectations than Scarlett O'Hara, but she poured all of herself into her job and no doubt increased the tourist revenues of Savannah in the bargain.

"A pink lady," Julia repeated. "Minus the vodka, of course."

"Absolutely. It would spoil the lemonade, which I affirm is first rate here." Meredith scanned the menu over her tortoiseshell readers. "The Crispy Scored Flounder served with apricot shallot sauce, Geechie Boy grits, and collard greens sounds delicious."

"Is the Geechie Boy Mill still grinding dried corn after all these years?" Julia asked.

"Yes, since Native Americans first settled on the Ogeechee river in Georgia," Meredith said. "The term *Geechee* is a colloquial word used to describe the Gullah people who developed the land and still live there. There's an awful lot of Southern history in those grits."

"I think I'll go for some real comfort food. I'm going to have the braised pork shank with pineapple glaze, mac and cheese, and collards." Julia grinned at Beau and Quin, who were discussing the merits of the steak offerings. "It's a ton of calories, but as Susan Hayward said back in the day, 'I'll cry tomorrow.'"

The four of them chatted through appetizers of corn bread fried oysters and artichoke fritters stuffed with goat cheese. Julia sighed. She was enjoying a time to relax and savor good food and the company of friends. Still, the case of the strange woman who had come all the way from Greece to look for a missing granddaughter clouded her consciousness.

They hadn't gotten far looking into the matter, but it had been easy to confirm that Iris Floros was a citizen of Marousi, Greece. Marousi represented one of ten subcities of Athens dating back to the era of the ancient Athenian Republic.

"I've never known anyone from Greece," Julia said thoughtfully over a sip of her pink lemonade. "Imagine a client from so far away. Well, maybe a client," she amended, because they hadn't agreed to take the case, only to look into it.

Quin had been discussing the new pediatric wing at the hospital which Beau had championed before he retired. Now he turned a curious eye on Julia. "Are you telling us your fame has extended across the ocean to the land of fifth century BC landmarks? I am impressed!" he said.

"They met this woman at City Market's Winston Gallery exhibition," Beau explained. "My wife interceded over a little skirmish about some paintings, which the lady from Greece thought she recognized. Guess she gave the owner a generous piece of her mind. Must be a very gutsy person. Apparently, she trusted Julia enough to hire Magnolia Investigations."

"She certainly stood up to Marco DeLuca and insisted that the exhibited paintings were done by her granddaughter. Iris Floros is also a bona fide member of the Visual Arts Guild of Athens," Julia said. "She owns a studio and still receives some commissions. The studio's in her and her husband's names jointly, but he died a few years ago. Her own health isn't the best either." She frowned, recalling the artist's pallor, her sudden show of weakness, and the pills in her purse.

"So did the gallery have any information to offer?" Quin asked. "Was that what the 'skirmish' was all about?"

"The thing is," Julia began, "no one seems to have any information about the creator of the paintings in question. She's called the 'runaway' artist because she doesn't show up at exhibits of her own work and no one seems to know much about her. According to Marco DeLuca, who's running the gallery, lots of people think they know who she is and come up with all kinds of explanations. Some are quite preposterous. Apparently that mystique is what has everyone intrigued."

"Even Carmen was reminded at first of a graffiti artist she knew when she was a teenager," Meredith put in.

Quin's eyebrows drew together. "Wow, that would be an incredible coincidence. On the other hand, maybe this 'runaway' artist doesn't even exist. Everyone knows the art world abounds with frauds. In 2014, Switzerland's Fine Art Expert Institute estimated that half of all work on the market is fake. The figure was quickly second-guessed, but it remains troubling."

Julia studied Quin's features. She was aware, as he surely was, that in every discipline of life—personal and corporate—there were sharks who lurked in the shadows waiting to dupe someone out of their daily bread. Both lawyers, they had often dealt with the greedy and the victimized. Over their short acquaintance, Julia had come to appreciate Quin's dedication to justice.

True to his nature, Quin offered an example of his thesis, and she listened, noting Meredith's expression of admiration as he spoke.

"There have been some pretty high-profile scams like the disillusioned painter who developed a complicated system of baking his Old Master-style work to age it. He sold sixty million dollars in fake Vermeers to world-class museums. That was in the forties, but as recently as five or six years ago Sotheby's had to issue a refund to the buyer who paid ten million dollars for a Frans Hals portrait."

"Whether there's anything fraudulent going on at the Winston or not, what we're concerned with is this so-called 'runaway' artist." Julia paused. "And if she really is the granddaughter of Iris Floros, how to find her."

"The trouble is," Meredith said, "Mrs. Floros didn't give us much to go on. And the only photo she had was taken when her grand–daughter was four years old." She looked away briefly and added more softly, "It's really sad to miss all those years with your own grandchild. I know how much it has meant to be part of Kaden's and Kinsley's lives." A frown creased her features when she looked across at Julia.

Meredith was probably regretting her comment, thinking it was insensitive since there were no grandchildren in Julia's life. It wasn't a subject they discussed very often, and Julia knew her tender-hearted friend wished things could have been different for her. But Julia had no complaints. In the blessings department she hadn't been overlooked. The waiter approached with coffee and four china cups. It was the perfect opportunity to derail the subject of grandchildren. "Smells wonderful," Julia said, leaning back to allow room for the coffee to be poured.

They had declined dessert, despite the delicious-sounding offerings on the menu. They would simply enjoy the coffee and linger in the rarified atmosphere of this historic place. "I'm going to make a quick trip to the ladies' room before enjoying my coffee," she announced.

She had only taken a few steps away from their table when she was surprised to notice a familiar face toward the back of the large dining room. Marco DeLuca from the Winston Gallery dressed in an expensive pin-striped suit and black tie. He sat rigidly next to an elegantly dressed woman with blond hair drawn back on one side. Her hair on the other side draped over her face, nearly obscuring one green eye. Her deeply tanned face was heavily made up with dark arched brows. Bright red lips twitched petulantly as she spoke to DeLuca, her voice loud enough to turn a few heads.

Julia slowed her steps, taking in the scene and DeLuca's stormy expression. Obviously uncomfortable, he seemed to be trying to appease his companion. He looked up as Julia approached. Two red blotches appeared on his cheeks; eyes like deep wells roved from Julia to his decidedly unhappy companion. Julia held his gaze, registered the active tic in his left eye.

The woman closed her mouth and wrapped red-tipped fingers around the stem of her glass. She was older than Julia had first thought—mid- to late forties and wearing a dress probably designed for a younger woman. She shook back the hair that hung over her right eye, briefly uncovering a small scar on her cheek like a slice of crescent moon.

The restaurant was packed, the tables close to each other. Julia would have to walk directly by DeLuca and the lady. It likely was not the best moment for either of them, as they seemed to be engaged in some disagreement. But when DeLuca's eyes met hers, Julia smiled. "Why, Mr. DeLuca, how nice to see you again." She extended her hand. "Julia Foley—from the other night at the gallery," she explained, thinking that he couldn't possibly have forgotten their interchange at the Winston.

DeLuca rose, dropping his napkin to the floor. "Of course," he said, bowing slightly and taking her hand in a brief, sweaty grasp.

He turned to the woman without looking at her and made a little sweep of his hand. "This is Deirdre Jaynes."

Deirdre nodded but said nothing. She lowered her head, returning her concentration to her glass.

So much for introduction, Julia thought. His wife? But the last name was different. Maybe an ex with a new husband? A colleague in the art world? If they were friends, they were to all appearances at odds with each other. *Awkward!* Julia thought, taking a quick breath.

"I thoroughly enjoyed the exhibit," she said brightly. "The Winston was always a favorite place." She softened her tone. "By the way, I was sorry to learn about Eduardo. Is he doing any better?"

DeLuca cleared his throat and stood a little straighter. "He had rather a severe stroke, but we're hopeful he'll make a recovery in time." After pausing briefly, he added, "Have you known my uncle long?"

Uncle, Julia registered with surprise. "Not really," she said after a pause. "My mother served on the arts committee some years ago. I believe she and my father were regular visitors to the Winston."

"I see," he responded stiffly, looking her over with what might be mild interest or intense curiosity. A frown teased at his finely etched mouth. "By the way, I appreciated your assistance the other night with that unpleasant woman. I trust she got to her destination all right."

Unpleasant woman? Julia stiffened. The exhibitor had brushed off a distraught grandmother as just another tiresome critic who claimed knowledge she didn't have. He hadn't offered her a seat or a glass of water until Julia had intervened. "The lady came a long way to see your exhibit, Mr. DeLuca," she said quietly but firmly. "If she was unpleasant perhaps it is because she's very concerned about her granddaughter, whose work she apparently recognized in your gallery."

"Of course," he said, dipping his smooth gray head in a subtle bow. He cleared his throat once more. "In any case, it was good of you to help. I trust it didn't inconvenience you too much."

Julia recalled what she had seen when she had stared through the gallery window—the intense studying of the runaway artist's painting, the odd expression on his face. She smiled deferentially. "Well, it was nice seeing you. And nice to meet you, Miss Jaynes."

Deirdre Jaynes acknowledged Julia's words with a brief nod of her coiffed head, and Julia continued her trek to the ladies' room.

She took her time, refreshing her lipstick and finger combing her hair. She replayed the scene. It wasn't right to dislike a person before knowing him, was it? Still, first impressions had their effect, and it was hard to change them. But to be fair, DeLuca had been embarrassed by Iris Floros's outburst at the gallery. And it wasn't surprising that he didn't believe her story since many others had proposed affinity to the mysterious "runaway" artist.

Deirdre Jaynes hadn't been the soul of warmth either, but who knew what was going on in her life? Or what had passed between her and DeLuca moments before they'd been interrupted. Julia sighed, giving her reflection in the mirror a quick once-over.

She reentered the dining area to discover DeLuca sitting alone at his table. In front of him a stemmed glass lay on its side, spilling pink liquid onto the white tablecloth. A nervous-looking waiter was proffering a towel, but DeLuca had snatched up his napkin and was wiping his glistening face. The evening had not gone well for Marco DeLuca.

She was surprised to see Beau standing as she returned to their table, concern etched in his features that stilled all thought of the feuding couple.

He started toward her, his cell phone in his hand. She had silenced her own before entering the restaurant. "It's Wyatt," he said, blue eyes solemn. "When he couldn't reach you, he called me. Your mother has had a fall. She's at Candler."

Chapter Eight

THE SPRAWLING REYNOLDS STREET FACILITY came into view, its flags flying from three tall poles. The oldest hospital in America in continuous operation, the Candler was founded in 1804 as a seamen's hospital and poorhouse. Now it was home to the impressive 62,000 square foot Cancer & Research Pavilion, a renowned neonatal center, and a women's hospital.

Julia and Beau had driven the short distance in silence, Julia wondering about the extent of her mother's injuries. On the phone Wyatt had assured Beau that it probably wasn't serious. He had dropped in to see his grandmother and found her propped up against the wall near her closet where she had fallen.

"Wyatt got her in right away, and they've been treating her," Beau told Julia reassuringly as he maneuvered the car into a parking space. "But she's fussing big-time about going to the hospital. You know how she can be."

Julia felt terrible about having silenced her cell phone when they went into the restaurant. With the crowds and noise around her, she hadn't heard it buzz inside her purse. Then she had run into DeLuca and his companion on her way to the ladies' room and been completely distracted. Guilt washed over her. She should have been available to her mother. Mom might appear younger with her graceful movements and careful dress, but a fall at her age could be devastating.

Julia matched Beau's long strides to the emergency room entrance and hurried to the desk to inquire about Bonnie Jean Waverly. They were shown into an exam room and found her sitting upright in a chair, her left arm in a sling. Her complexion was pale against the green blouse she wore over dark slacks. A fawn-colored sweater draped her good shoulder, making her look small and vulnerable and very un-Bonnie-Jean-like.

A nurse in a lab coat sprinkled with Dalmatian puppies adjusted an ice pack against her patient's shoulder. Wyatt stood anxiously over his grandmother. As Julia entered, the nurse smiled.

"She has a mild radial sprain of the left wrist, and she's bruised her shoulder, but there are no breaks. She's very lucky. Doctor has ordered something for pain, but she should be fine. She'll need rest and regular icing to keep the swelling down. She'll need someone with her," she added, giving Julia an inquiring glance.

Mom's head snapped up. She glared at Julia and Beau and her fidgety grandson. "I just lost my balance for a minute," she said gloomily. "That's all. I was looking for something in my closet and just missed a step."

"Oh, Mom, I'm so sorry—" Julia began, reaching a hand toward her.

"I'm all right," she said. "It's nothing to get in a tizzy over." She smiled a tight smile that was more like a grimace. "It hardly hurts at all." She brushed at the wisps of hair that had strayed from their careful restraint. The proud independent lift of her head was exactly what Julia would have expected.

Whether her mother liked it or not, she would need help to get her meals, to bathe, and to dress. "We're here for you, Mom. I'm here. It's going to be all right."

"Sorry to cause all this fuss," she said, looking down. "I'm sorry."

"We're just glad nothing's broken," Julia reassured her.

"What were you doing up on that ladder anyway?" Wyatt broke in, as though the thought had just occurred to him.

Wyatt, in his midthirties, a successful businessman, still had that scrubbed little-boy look with full cheeks and well-defined lips. His hair was thick and curly like Cassie's. The gel he used for control gave it a high sheen as though the sun shone perpetually on it. His light blue eyes seemed to scrutinize life with thirsty intensity. He'd been left with his grandmother at nine years of age, flourished under Bonnie Jean's careful tutelage, and gone on to make his mark in finance. He had accidentally fallen into the role of forensic auditing when he discovered a hidden deficit in a major corporation's books. Now he was called upon frequently to translate complex financial transactions and numerical data into terms that ordinary laypersons could understand.

He matched his grandmother's stern gaze. "The last thing you should be doing is climbing ladders at your age." When she said nothing, he softened his tone. "Surely you could have called someone to get what you needed."

"Beau and I will take her home," Julia put in quickly, hoping to lighten the tension. Mom wouldn't take kindly to being reminded of her age by Wyatt or anyone else. Julia smiled at her nephew. "I'm so thankful you happened to go by, Wyatt."

"Me too," Wyatt said, buttoning the jacket of his suit coat. "I have a deposition first thing in the morning." He glanced at his grandmother and back at Julia. "You sure you can—"

"Of course. We'll be fine."

He moved to the door and Julia followed, leaving the nurse to finish placing Mom's things in a plastic bag. Once out in the hall together, Wyatt paused and pushed out his full lips briefly, as though analyzing something. He jingled his keys in his pants pocket. "Actually, you won't have to miss work. I called Mother. She's coming to Savannah."

Julia stared at Wyatt. Cassie was coming to Savannah? She hadn't been home in years and seldom bothered to call, even to ask about Mom's health. Her contacts had almost always revolved around some need of her own, usually involving money.

"She wants to take care of her while she's laid up," he said, averting his gaze from Julia. After a little silence, he added. "Probably be good for them both."

As a child, Wyatt had been morose after his mother left him. For weeks he waited for Cassie to come back. She would talk with him on the phone frequently, promising it wouldn't be long before they would be together again. But weeks turned to months and then years. Gradually, Wyatt had settled into life with his grandparents and developed his own friendships and interests. To all appearances he had overcome his hurt of being virtually abandoned by his mother. But, despite the tender care his grandparents provided, how much had he really been affected by Cassie's choice?

"And it's about time too," Wyatt said, jingling his keys again. Obviously, he was in a hurry to be on his way. He was attentive to his business but also to his soft-spoken wife, Gracie, and their young daughters, Madison and Kennedy. He nodded, giving Julia a quick smile. "She says she'll take an early flight tomorrow. She'll get a taxi or something from the airport."

Julia was too stunned to ask any more questions. Cassie hadn't come home even for her mother's eightieth birthday, which to Julia's mind was a signal milestone in a woman's life. Now a minor fall and a sprained wrist was bringing her sister home?

Had Wyatt exaggerated Mom's injuries? Or was Cassie at yet another junction in her journey and needed a place to rest and regroup?

After Beau dropped her off at her mother's house, Julia helped Mom into a pair of soft pajamas. Given her injury, pajamas would be easier to put on than a gown. She got her settled into bed and kept up a rapid string of commentary while she worked. The assault on Mom's fierce independence would likely be hard to bear. "Do you want the blanket or is the sheet enough?" she asked brightly as she stooped to right a tissue box that had fallen off the night table.

"The sheet will be fine," Mom said. She closed her eyes as though pretending instant sleep.

Julia sighed and looked around. Near the closet floor was a jumble of items that had probably fallen from the wire shelves above the clothes rack when Mom fell. They included a box of old photos, a round hat carrier with assorted figurines and keepsakes, and a plaid bedroll left over from camping days, complete with flattened plaid pillow.

Julia cringed, imagining her mother trying to steady herself on the stepladder as she began to lose control, knocking things down in the process. What had she been looking for on those shelves? Julia began to scoop up the strewn items.

"Don't bother with all that now," the definitely-not-sleeping Mom said. "You must be tired. You should go on to bed."

"It won't take but a minute, and I know how you hate things out of place." Julia tucked the bedroll back into the closet. She replaced a banded pack of letters and some empty perfume vials into the circular carrier that probably hadn't held hats in two decades. Inside the carrier, a narrow box lay beneath a small stack of lacy handkerchiefs. The dislodged lid revealed a necklace that sparkled in the light from the bedside lamp. It was beautiful—and instantly recognizable.

She turned to look at her mother, whose eyes were once again closed, and gingerly touched the diamonds in the filigreed silver coil. The treasured inheritance she had worn with such pride for so many years. The necklace she had worn for her and Dad's twenty-fifth anniversary. Why had it been relegated to the closet?

She gave a small gasp of wonder as she looked at the lovely necklace. Her mother had a hidden safe in the living room where she kept a few valuables—a first edition Holmes, a collection of late issue Buffalo nickels, a Lladro' Water Girl figurine worth about four hundred dollars. The safe was the obvious place for an expensive diamond necklace. Instead, it had been left on a bedroom shelf—not even in a drawer or jewelry box.

Julia held it up. "You haven't worn this in ages," she half whispered. The stillness that followed made her wonder if her mother had dozed off.

"Just put it on the dresser," came an abrupt retort, surprising Julia. "You don't need to bother—" The flow of words stopped, as though she regretted her dramatic protest. She shifted on the bed, rustling the sheet. "You should go to bed now," she said more softly. A few seconds passed before she added, "And thank you...." She rolled onto her side, facing the wall.

Despite the hectic nature of the day, Julia fell asleep quickly in her old room, which hadn't changed all that much in the forty-some years since she'd left for college. The walls had been repainted a pale gray, and her orange plaid '70s bedspread had been replaced by a white quilt and matching shams. But her mahogany carved bedposts and matching dressers remained, along with the scarred bookcase that had housed her favorite reads. An old set of Encyclopedia Britannica's Year Books (1969–1976) moldered on the bottom shelf like faithful ghosts.

She woke suddenly to sounds emanating from the kitchen. She scrambled into the jeans and sweatshirt Beau had brought last night along with her toothbrush. She'd slept too long, leaving her mother on her own to dress and prepare breakfast with one arm. *Fine daughter I am!*

She raced down the stairs in her bare feet, armed with an apology.

But the intruder with face obscured and peering into the refrigerator was not Mom. Julia froze. Some stranger had broken in and was shamelessly raiding the premises for food! Her voice echoed unnaturally in the hallway. "Who are you? And what are you doing in this house?"

The figure jerked up. A slim woman in faded designer jeans and an outrageous striped peasant blouse à la Woodstock turned slowly, lips pursed in her roundish face. Frizzy hair glinted red in the sun that streaked through the window. A voice, alien and familiar at the same time, broke through Julia's fog. "Is that any way to greet your only sister?"

Cassie! Julia steadied herself on the back of a chair and stared into the face of the sister she hadn't seen in fifteen years. In the flesh, that is. She appeared less glamorous than the image in photos she sent to the family from time to time. And she was older, but so was everyone else, Julia thought. Cassie's eyes were the same cerulean blue, and the familiar dimple winked in her left cheek above the forward thrust of her small chin.

Wyatt had said she would arrive that day, but Julia hadn't expected her to be standing in the kitchen of the house where they'd grown up as if it were the most natural thing in the world. "When did you... How did you...?" Julia stammered, unable to look away from her sister's half-smiling, half-apologetic face.

"I still have a key," she said, lifting her hands palms out like a defense attorney. "I took the red-eye in from Kennedy and got here early." She shrugged. "I didn't want to wake you." She frowned, revealing significant crow's feet at the corners of her eyes. Her voice softened as her eyes rolled toward the upper rooms. "How is she?"

Julia took a deep breath, willing herself to suppress her rapidly rising irritation. She faced her irresponsible sister, who'd left her nine-year-old in the care of their parents and now casually inquired about the state of her mother's health. "She suffered a bad sprain, but nothing's broken."

"That's what Wyatt said." Cassie pushed her lower lip out as though in deep thought. "He said she fell from a ladder in her bedroom. She's eightysomething now, isn't she?"

"Eighty-four," Julia said. "Last October, if you recall." It sounded bitter in her own ears. Her sister kept in touch from time to time with their mom and with Wyatt and the girls, but birthday cards, when they came, were usually late and accompanied by some out-landish apology. Family events took second place to whatever life challenge she was at that moment facing. Julia took a quick breath and tamped down her irritation. "It's good of you to come, though. Mom will be glad to see you."

Cassie stepped away from the refrigerator and pulled out a chair at the table. She sat down wearily. Her face, Julia realized, was the only thing round about her. Judging by the photos she'd sent at the beginning of the year, Julia saw that she'd lost weight. Her pale complexion made the freckles she hated as a teenager stand out like a spray of auburn stars. She had tried to scrub them away with a mix of bleach and Noxzema. Julia felt something crack inside like thaw-ing ice. At the same time, she recoiled, pushed back the melting. She let the silence press in.

After a long moment, Cassie looked up. She tilted her head toward the counter. "I started the coffee. Want some?"

Julia shrugged and rolled her eyes toward the cabinet over the sink. "Cups are in there." She studied her sister, who reached to retrieve the cups, revealing a thin tanned arm. Despite her redhead's complexion, Cassie had always loved the sun. As a child she had begged Julia nonstop to take her to the beach.

Cup in hand, Cassie paused at the coffeepot but didn't pick it up. She turned to Julia, her forehead wrinkling. "I know I haven't been a very good sister or daughter."

Or mother. Or grandmother. Julia added mentally.

Cassie ringed her lips with her tongue. "But I want to do this. I'll take good care of Mom for as long as she needs me."

Or you need her.

"Maybe I won't be as good at it as you." She stopped and bit her lip.

The straight-A student. The sister with a successful career and a husband who stayed. Perfect daughter for the perfect mother. Cassie had frequently thrown those epithets Julia's way—by inference if not in outright assault. A person grew weary of taking the blame for success. *No one's perfect, but everyone can take responsibility for their own lives and those affected by their actions.*

"Cassie?"

Julia turned to see Mom at the kitchen door, barefoot in her pink pajamas and hospital-issue sling. She folded her good arm over her chest. "It's been a long time since I had both my girls right here in my kitchen." She didn't rush to embrace Cassie, but her eyes lit like twin blue fires.

Cassie bolted toward her, hesitated a foot or so away, and cocked her curly head. "You okay, Ma?" she asked softly.

Cassie had always called their mother "Ma," but there was tenderness in the word. "I heard about your fall. I—I wanted to make sure you're all right."

"Of course I'm all right," Mom said, huffily, but her eyes gave away her gladness. "I'm not an invalid yet." Her glance roved between her two daughters, registering a host of unnamed emotions. "But now that you're here, it will give us all a chance to catch up."

"There's coffee," Julia said. "Sit down. I'll get your slippers." She hurried out of the kitchen and up the stairs, ashamed at her enormous relief to be away. Cassie would watch out for Mom and see that their mother had everything she needed. But how soon would she back out and leave the care of their mother to someone else?

Was she still letting herself be led around by the nose by the latest man to look her way? Perhaps that wasn't fair. She'd stayed with the same do-nothing man for a while now—a guy for whom no job offered was good enough. Therefore, he didn't do any. Was another letdown in the cards for their mom? One more disappointment?

Julia's cell phone sounded, bringing a welcome respite to her dark thoughts. Another world calling. The one she was comfortable in. The one she could control. Well, sort of.

"Jules? You okay? How's your mom?" Meredith, ever the voice of sanity.

"She's okay." She cleared her throat. "Cassie's arrived. Says she's staying as long as she's needed." After a pause, when Meredith said nothing, Julia added, "I'll be there in about twenty minutes now that the cavalry's here."

"Speaking of the cavalry, there's something of a skirmish going on here. Maybe you can calm Miss Angelos down."

"What's she upset about?"

"Seems she can't locate Iris Floros. Our client. Or potential client. Miss 'Angel' is beside herself."

Why was nothing ever easy? Julia retrieved Mom's slippers and her own overnight bag. She'd leave her mother in Cassie's hands and see what trials awaited at Magnolia Investigations.

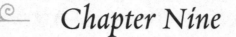

Chapter Nine

"OUR 'ANGEL' HAS LOST HER charge. She'll never get her wings this way. Iris absconded from the hotel before her keeper was awake." Meredith pushed back in her office chair and crossed her arms over her black Evan Picone dress with its contrast trim jacket. Unlike last evening's soft pink ensemble, this morning she was all business along with a fair amount of frustration. "Ms. Floros has a mind of her own apparently."

"She did the same thing the night of the exhibit," Julia said. "She's one determined lady, but her weak heart might just betray her."

"Yes." Meredith frowned. "I'm worried about her." She tapped her fingers absently on the desk and presently looked up. "She could be in trouble. But tell me, how's your mom this morning?"

Julia sat down across from her, feeling shabby after a night spent away from home and Beau's comforting presence. Not to mention, there had been no time for a shower, and the outfit Beau had brought should have been retired years earlier. "She's a little sore but feisty as always. She'll need her customary gumption to deal with Cassie."

"So, she's actually come back to look after your mother?" Meredith raised a blond eyebrow. "How did she seem? Your sister."

"Older—but then, aren't we all?" Cassie's pallor had taken Julia aback. Also, the lines of tension in her face and the way those blue eyes people found so charming didn't quite make contact. She was still Cassie—the same wild auburn curls, the flirty manner, the bell-like voice. But something had changed. Her twinkle had tarnished. She looked, to put it flatly, old. Julia shrugged away her disconcerting thoughts. "She says she'll stay as long as Mom needs her. Well, we'll see."

Meredith's fingers continued their rhythmic clicking. She said nothing for a long moment, the steam from her coffee mug blossoming upward.

"Maggie Lu was right," Julia said, releasing a long breath. "Families can be hard. Just the other day she quoted her famous granny again—'Lovin' be hardest with your own.'"

"Guess she knows that pretty well. Think of that nephew of hers. After all those years, he's turned his life around. Which, as I recall, Maggie Lu attributed largely to prayer."

"'A power stronger than a mountain of dynamite.' That's what she said when we were talking in the library." Julia swallowed. After their conversation she had felt bad for neglecting to pray for Cassie, and she'd vowed silently to be more attentive. Now her sister was back, something she should be glad about, but wasn't.

But why wasn't she? Julia felt a shudder. How many times had they hoped Cassie would break out of her cycle of irresponsibility? Stop lighting on every flower that beckoned like a crazed butterfly. What was she looking for anyway? Julia shook her head to clear the cobwebs. "I hope there's another cup of that coffee around. It's been a bear of a night."

Magically, Carmen appeared at Meredith's office door, holding one of Julia's old mugs filled with coffee. The mug read, I'M A LAWYER. TO SAVE TIME, LET'S JUST ASSUME I'M RIGHT.

How did the young woman do it? She was becoming indispensable to the effective running of the office, and she always knew when Julia or Meredith needed her ministrations. "Speaking of angels," Julia said, reaching for the mug like a thirsty prospector in the desert.

Carmen's eyes widened. She pursed her coral-tinged lips that highlighted the color of her blouse above the fashionable charcoal skirt. "Angel? *Moi?*"

Carmen liked to throw in a Spanish phrase from time to time. But the French word alluding to herself and spoken with such innocence made Julia smile. "Celia Angelos," she explained. "I understand she's lost track of Iris Floros."

"Ah," Carmen said, handing Julia the coffee. "She *was* pretty hinky on the phone a little while ago. Said she hadn't left her good job in Athens to chase after a crazy woman!"

Julia made a face at Carmen. "Hinky? What kind of word is that?" She smiled. Carmen employed a colorful and inventive vocabulary at times—English and likely Spanish too.

Carmen shrugged and sank down in the one remaining chair and gave her hair a toss over her shoulder. "Anyway, when Celia went in to check on Iris this morning around eight o'clock the lady was gone. No note, nothing. *Nada*. Celia was pretty upset. I thought she was going to bite my head off."

"And no wonder," Julia said. "Bet Celia wishes she'd never taken on responsibility for a woman as stubborn and driven as Iris Floros—even if it meant a free trip to America."

"I wonder why she did," Meredith mused. "Maybe the two have a special relationship—or the job pays well. Iris is a wealthy woman."

Julia sighed. She was beginning to wish she hadn't intervened at the art exhibit. That she hadn't witnessed Iris's tirade after she saw the paintings and lit into Marco DeLuca. That she hadn't tried to calm the woman down and offered her business card. Iris Floros was a loose cannon, and yet something about her and her story of a troubled granddaughter had touched Julia.

"Company!" Carmen announced at the sound of the agency door opening. She tripped out to the foyer in her stylish heels, which were higher than Julia thought should ever be introduced to feet.

"I must see the detectives!" came a thickly accented voice loud enough to be heard down the block. The voice grew even louder as heavy footsteps approached. Upon hearing the shuffling, Julia envisioned the visitor pushing past Carmen and heading toward the offices. "They are here, yes?"

Iris Floros pushed into Meredith's office, a red and gold paisley shawl flowing over a black calf-length dress. In her arms was a large flat package tied with plasticized twine. Her hair was swept into a white twist and held in place by ornate combs. Her cheeks bloomed an unnatural pink, and her eyes gleamed like wet coals. "The gods be praised. You are both here!" she intoned. "You must see!" Her breath came in ragged gasps.

"Ms. Floros!" Julia said, rushing to take the package before it fell from the woman's grasp. "You must calm down. Please."

"Are you all right?" Meredith asked, rushing to ease Iris into the chair Carmen had vacated a moment ago. "We've been wondering where you were. Celia is very worried."

"Ah, Celia!" the agitated woman said, flapping her hands in the air as though warding off a pesky insect. "I couldn't wait. I went to that gallery first thing this morning. I bought this." She pointed at the package Meredith had set on her desk. "Open! I will show you this is my Helena's work!"

"All right, Mrs. Floros," Julia said, "but first you need to slow down, catch your breath. Carmen will bring you something to drink. Water? Coffee? Perhaps some tea?"

"I am all right. I—" Iris coughed and pressed her hands over her chest. "Maybe some coffee." The rasping continued, and she shook her head as if to will it to stop. "No, no coffee. Water, please." She leaned back in the chair and clasped her hands in her lap, as though to tame them into submission. Briefly she closed her eyes. Carmen scurried away for the water. Her expression said *loca*.

"I had to go back," Iris began when her coughing had subsided. "I needed another look. The exhibit is the same, only that man— that Mr. DeLuca—he was not there." She made a face like something smelled bad, then she sniffed and jutted out her chin as though to summon more ladylike behavior.

"A young woman sold it to me." She nodded to the package. "For a king's ransom! But it is worth it. It is my Helena's. I don't know why she did not sign her own name instead of that Desdemona. But I will show you—" She nodded her head, urging them to open the package. She fumbled for her purse, which she had let drop to the floor by her chair.

Julia cringed. The pills were about to appear. Maybe she should call for medical help. Or for Celia. She silently willed Carmen to telephone Miss Angelos with the news that her charge had been located and was, for the moment, alive and well. *Wings on the way!*

But no pill box appeared. Instead, Iris pulled a small sheet of paper from her purse, unfolded it, and held it out toward Julia. "It is the last letter I have from my Helena."

Julia took it from the proffered hand and scanned the handwritten contents. Handwriting could be traced, analyzed.

"It is the only letter I still have. After Felipe died, there was a fire in my studio. My desk, where I keep mail...everything was ruined!" Iris continued. "This one I have in my bedroom. But you must look at the writing. You will see. It is the same writing as on this painting."

While Meredith began to unwrap the package carefully, Julia silently read the brief letter in her hand. It was dated a year ago September. Nearly eighteen months ago.

Grandmama,

You have not written in so long. I miss your letters. I am still painting—when Apollo's muses smile on me. They say my work is very good, but I must try harder and do as I am told.

The writing turned down slightly and righted again. Helena—or Desdemona or whoever—was having success with her work, but the part about doing as she was told raised a red flag. Told by whom? Apollo's muses? Her agent? Her teachers? Someone else? Julia knew that downward sloping letters often signaled depression. She read on.

I wait for your letters; I want to make you proud, to make Mama proud, but you say nothing. Perhaps you do not wish to write to me anymore. Grandmama, you were kind to me—and better than any muse. I pray that you are well. I pray for Mama....

The words trailed down again.

My friend said he will mail this letter to you because sometimes I think Dilly forgets. I must go. I must paint. I work; I pray, but the whispers of Melpomene grow stronger in my ear. Do not forget me, Grandmama.

    Your Helena

Whispers of Melpomene. One of those muses she spoke of earlier in the letter, Julia supposed.

"It is not true that I did not write," Iris said. "I sent many letters, but no answer comes."

"Who is Dilly?" Julia asked, peering up from the odd letter.

Iris clamped her jaw tight. "I do not know this Dilly—a friend perhaps." She grew more agitated. "But I wrote letters. So many letters. No answer!"

"Perhaps she has moved. Were your letters returned?" Julia asked gently.

"My letters do not come back. You see, she thinks I do not love her." A sob tore from her throat. "I told her I would come here to the United States if she would tell me how to find her. She doesn't answer, but I come. I—"

"What was the address on this letter?" Julia prompted, since there was no accompanying envelope.

"A post office box—only a post office box number. 264."

Julia returned her gaze to the brief letter. The round, flowing script sloped downward, then up, urgent, as though she'd written in a hurry or in furtive secrecy. Julia set the letter down, feeling an acute sadness. Iris had already lost her husband and her child. Would her only granddaughter be one more irreparable loss?

"The painting!" Iris urged. "Open. I show you."

Meredith untied the string on the package, and the wrapping fell away. The watercolor was as stunning as Julia remembered it from the exhibit dubbed *Spectrum of the Soul*. It was a series of overlapping circles with deep color in the centers that grew lighter as the multicolored circles expanded, filling the paper edge to edge. The colors bled into each other, producing a riot of color. In its center was a tiny teardrop of glistening white. The work was contained in a shiny ebony wood frame with a pale gray mat and nonglare glass. It was perhaps the smallest of the exhibit's paintings—11 × 14—and priced, if Julia remembered correctly, at $1,200.

"You see how she works her color with such splendid shading," Iris said excitedly. "She is a gifted artist."

Julia found herself mesmerized by the explosion of color that appeared to push relentlessly to its borders. The painting was beautiful, not nearly as dark and foreboding as the featured work at the gallery. But the style was clearly Desdemona's. Julia was aware of Carmen looking over Iris's shoulder, her face a mixture of awe and confusion.

The paintings in the exhibit had stirred an old memory from Carmen's troubled past—the mysterious graffiti artist who changed her name on a whim. Who was never seen again after the little boy died. Was Carmen remembering all that—recalling those days filled with angst and pain? Since the night of the exhibit, she hadn't spoken of the memory or the paintings again.

"Now, see!" Iris said, getting up from her chair and touching a blunt fingertip on the glass at the bottom of the frame. "It is signed 'Desdemona,' but it is my Helena. Look. Compare!" She bobbed her white head at the letter on Julia's desk. "See, the round letters are the same, and the *a* has little scroll at the end."

Julia studied the two signatures. They looked nothing alike, with possibly a slight similarity in the ending curl of the final letter. Of course, she was no expert in handwriting analysis. She released a dubious breath. Iris Floros was grasping at straws.

Perhaps guilt was part of it too. She and Felipe had allowed their pain to shut them off from their only daughter and from much of their granddaughter's growing-up years. She hadn't been around Helena in years and before that only briefly. Could she really recognize the artist's style? Or her signature? Did Iris want to believe so strongly that she saw what didn't exist?

Iris stared at Julia, then at Meredith, waiting for affirmation, which as the moment wore on she must have realized wouldn't be forthcoming. Carmen stepped back, holding Iris's glass, from which only a few sips had been taken.

Iris also took a step back and dropped into her chair, dejection on her features. She folded her arms over her chest and swayed slowly, shaking her head. Tears swam in her eyes. "Helena is here—or she has been here. I must find her. I know she needs me. Something is not right—" She seemed unable to go on.

"Why do you think she is in trouble, Iris?" Julia asked. The letter did have a melancholy note as well as an urgent ring, but nothing had been spelled out really.

"A grandmother knows," Iris repeated.

"Iris, what is—who is—Melpomene?" Julia asked.

The woman stopped swaying and swiped angrily at the threatening tears. She took a breath, seeming to struggle for calm. "Melpomene is one of the nine muses—the muse of tragedy." Her eyes widened as though a frightening omen threatened. "Melpomene is whispering in her ear. Helena is trying to tell her Grandmama she is unhappy. That maybe there is danger."

Iris believed that the mention of a Greek muse connected with tragedy equated a call for help. Was she right? Or was she deluded? After all, there hadn't been much contact between them until recent days. How well could she know her own granddaughter? No doubt feeling the pressure of eyes focused on her, she looked up.

Iris had been unsuccessful in stemming the gathering tears. Two fell down her cheeks and dropped onto her dress. "Have you—as you said—looked into it?"

Since first meeting Iris, life had encroached with hard-hitting intensity. The endless paperwork, other cases to finalize, Mom's fall and Cassie's sudden arrival on the scene. There had been little time to devote to the case of a missing artist who to all appearances didn't want to be found. Seeing Iris's tear-filled eyes and sensing her passion, Julia felt terrible for neglecting her. She glanced at Meredith.

"It's been a very busy week for us here at Magnolia," Meredith began, apparently finding Julia at a loss. "And some events of a personal nature have intervened."

Julia shot Meredith a frown at the uncharacteristic comment. They made it a practice to separate personal concerns from business ones. She quickly returned the conversation to business matters. "We will do everything we can to find the young woman you're seeking."

Iris pressed forward, covering her eyes with her hands, and more tears spilled over. "The gods be praised! I have found someone to help."

"But you must allow us to do the job, Mrs. Floros," Julia interrupted. "You mustn't run off from your hotel, endangering your health. We will give our earnest attention to finding Helena for you." She paused, reaching for the box of tissues to halt the flow of their client's tears. "You should know too," she added gently, "we put our trust in our heavenly Father, the Creator and Sustainer of all things, in every endeavor we undertake. We will seek His help for you and Helena."

There was no opportunity to assess the affect this pronouncement might have on Iris, for the strident voice of Celia Angelos came from the foyer. "Miz Floros! Miz Floros! Miz Bellefontaine! Miz Foley!"

Carmen nipped out of the office. Julia could hear her calmly but succinctly informing Celia that all was well. Her charge was indeed here at this very moment, conferring with the two best private investigators in the city of Savannah. In a voice that brooked no challenge to her authority, she told Celia, "Please wait here. I will see if Mrs. Floros has completed her business." Julia could hear the metallic tap of Carmen's stilettos and then the brief pause and urbane comment. "Charming hat. Did you find it at the Red Clover?"

Iris stood, extending both hands to Julia. "Thank you! Thank you from my heart."

"We'll call you tomorrow," Julia said. "But you had better tend to Celia now."

"Ah yes, Celia. *Mitéra kóta*. A mama hen! But at least I won't have to call a taxi."

Chapter Ten

"WHAT WAS I THINKING?" JULIA groaned, pulling her pinwale corduroy jacket closer over her knit blouse. Temperatures would climb into the sixties by afternoon, but February mornings gave a girl a very cold shoulder. "If ever we were hunting a needle in the haystack, it's now, and I sort of dragged you into it."

Meredith tucked an arm into Julia's as they rounded the corner into the Downhome Diner for a cup of coffee before heading to the office. She said nothing until they were pressed into one of the retro-style booths inside the busy diner. She pushed the stylish plaid shawl back from her shoulders and peered over her menu at Julia. "Well, we've seen a few haystacks before." She shrugged. "Besides, I trust your instincts for needles."

"To quote Louisa May Alcott, 'I'd rather take coffee than compliments just now,'" Julia said.

Meredith grinned. "She did say that in *Little Women*, didn't she? Trust you to glean that little gem, since it's your favorite book for as long as I've known you."

Julia sighed. "I'm not so sure I trust my own instincts for the particular needle pricking us just now." She frowned over her menu. She'd tossed and turned, keeping Beau up half the night, thinking over the events that had led to accepting Iris Floros's case. She glowed her thanks when Justine filled her coffee cup and gave her an all-knowing wink. "You're a life saver," she breathed to the young waitress.

"Just the coffee?" As Justine began to move away, Meredith added, "And two of those crullers with drizzly icing. You know the ones."

As usual, Meredith had read Julia's mind even before Julia knew she was craving one of the diner's morning specialties. "Ah, my hero," she intoned dramatically, clasping her hands over her heart. She swallowed another gulp of coffee, her mind quickly recalling how Iris had burst into the agency sporting a painting she'd paid $1,200 for. Escaping the watchful eye of her nurse/companion, she'd trekked on her own to the gallery in the early morning and then to their office. "She's determined, that's for sure. Not to mention aggressive. But there's something about her, something terribly tragic," Julia mused aloud, remembering Melpomene. "I mean old-world Greek tragic."

"Losing touch with a family member certainly ranks in the genre of tragedy," Meredith said. "She's genuinely frantic to find her granddaughter, whether she's this 'runaway artist' or not. And she did come halfway around the world to search for her."

"Despite her heart condition," Julia murmured. She paused, letting her gaze roam over the antique prints of Old Savannah that covered the lemony walls of the Downhome Diner. Her eyes roved over Fort Jackson, the old Cotton Exchange, and the vintage 1734 map of the city in bleeding sepia tones. She refocused to consult Meredith's blue gaze. "Where do you think we should start?"

"Well, we've made a start already, haven't we?" Meredith tapped an index finger on the table. "We know that Helena wrote at least one letter to her grandmother, who says there were others. Burned in a fire, sadly."

Julia took a bite of her cruller and dropped it back on her plate with finality. "A letter with no envelope and sent from a post office box."

"Which isn't hopeless, of course," Meredith said. "Typically, you can't rent a PO box without showing photo ID and having an alternate mailing address associated with it." She leaned back while Justine refilled her coffee cup. "Didn't you ask Carmen to do a reverse PO box search?"

"She's on it, but so far hitting a blank wall. And we don't know if the box is still rented out to the granddaughter." Julia toyed absently with her pastry. "Of course, we could slink around the post office in sunglasses and Sherlock Holmes capes to see who comes to number 264."

"Why didn't I think of that?" Meredith asked with an ironic grin.

Julia shrugged. "Just kidding."

They sipped in silence until Meredith said, "Maybe we should assume for the time being that Helena might actually be this 'Desdemona' and center our attention on the Winston Gallery, where we first met our client."

"Beats hanging around the post office, even if we knew which one of the nine locations might be the right one." She laughed, sensing a small relief from the tension of the moment. "And we should have some word from Curt Constantine regarding the two signatures. Curt's the best when it comes to signature analysis. He's busier than a one-armed paper hanger, but I have some pull from my old court days."

"If the signatures don't match, it will be a terrible blow to Mrs. Floros, I'm afraid," Meredith said thoughtfully. "But we need to know more about that suave fellow at the Winston."

"Mm," Julia mumbled.

"As you learned from Marco himself, we know he's a nephew of Eduardo's," Meredith said. "I've done some checking, and I found that Marco had an import/export business. It's probably where he made his money. A longtime collector of art too, and a critic. Some minor success as a painter."

Julia remembered Maggie Lu's comment about a rumored art scandal. She briefly relayed it to Meredith. "I've been scanning news stories but haven't found anything."

"Interesting," Meredith said. "We'll have to keep checking. Rumors start somewhere."

"Maggie Lu didn't know which DeLuca the story referenced. I wish we could talk to Eduardo, but in his current condition…" Julia broke off, reminded of her mother's connection to the former owner. She hadn't mentioned anything about a scandal involving him. "Marco stepped in rather conveniently after his uncle's stroke, but he maintains a strictly business profile. No personal details have cropped up, not even a social media appearance."

"He's young to have made his fortune," Meredith said.

"Yes. Sometimes, though, a person only appears successful on paper." Julia sighed. "In recent years, he seems to have convinced the art world that this mysterious Desdemona is worth investing in."

Meredith leaned forward suddenly and craned her neck toward the door. Julia followed her gaze to a tall woman with beautiful chocolate skin and iron-gray hair curled tightly to her head. Tasteful hoops hung from her ears. Charlene King Jackson, owner of the Downhome Diner. She had an efficient staff to keep things running, but she was a regular at the diner most days. At fifty-four, she was a commanding presence at nearly 5'11".

"There's Charlene," Julia said, delighted to see her friend who had played an important part in helping them solve their first case. A case that led them to Maggie Lu, who stepped inside the diner now at Charlene's side. A few inches shorter but tall by most standards, Maggie Lu looked a great deal like her daughter. Her carriage still erect, her skin clear and remarkably unwrinkled, she didn't look seventy-six.

Julia waved as the two women headed their way smiling. As they advanced, Charlene paused to have a quick word with one of the waitstaff. Julia was learning that Charlene was quite a remarkable woman.

Her mother, Maggie Lu, had lived through troubled times and had helped her daughter rise to become a successful businesswoman. She'd also passed on her strong faith in God and instilled in Charlene a passion to help others.

The now respected owner of the Downhome Diner often hired those who needed a second chance. She'd come a long way, first doing domestic work for wealthy families. Later came marriage and a daughter. But after being widowed in her forties, she kept alive a dream of opening her own restaurant one day.

It had been a hard-won dream for her, involving a time of estrangement from her family, particularly her mother, Maggie Lu. It made Julia warm all over to know she and Meredith had helped to bring the two together and at the same time solve a decades-old mystery that had plagued the city of Savannah. That original case involving the Besset mansion owner had given birth to Magnolia Investigations and to an abiding friendship. Maggie Lu had mentioned she might join them at the diner before heading to the library today, and Julia was eager to bring her up to speed on their latest case.

"I'm glad you take time to come see us now and then," Charlene said, extending a graceful hand to Julia, who grasped it in both her own.

"Now and then!" Meredith objected. "I think this booth has our permanent impressions on it. You have the best food in town. And these crullers!" She pointed at her plate, empty but for three stray crumbs. "They're the absolute best."

"I could say I taught her everything she knows," Maggie Lu said, sliding into the booth next to Julia. "But you can't believe everything an old woman tells you."

"Believe her," Charlene said, smiling a greeting to a patron across the room. She put an arm on her mother's shoulder. "But I need to leave you with these two amazing sleuths. I have a ton of receipts to go over from last week." She rolled her eyes heavenward.

"Oh, have a cup of coffee first, Charlene," Julia said. "We hardly get to see you, now that business is booming."

"The girl never stops," Maggie Lu lamented. She laid her hand over the one that rested on her shoulder. "Now, Charlene, you just slide in there next to Meredith. The receipts can wait a few more minutes. Mother's orders!"

Charlene sighed. "Maybe just for a minute, but no coffee. If I have any more this morning, I'll probably self-destruct!"

"How's Clarissa and that grandbaby of yours?" Julia asked. A scent of rosewater fell delicately on the air as Charlene eased into the booth.

"Well, the little man's perfect in every way," Charlene beamed. "Clarissa says he's a strong one—holds his little head up just as steady as you please. And he can kick the daylights out of the NFL mobile I got for his crib."

Maggie Lu took up the rave about her great-grandson's accomplishments. Meredith added her boasts about Kinsley and Kaden, Carter's children, who were the apples of their grandma's eyes.

Julia listened as the conversation bubbled over, delighting in the thought of a toddler's first steps or a party for a baby boy, complete with premature footballs and racing cars. "Jacob Philip sounds like a natural athlete," she said. She knew it must be gratifying to Maggie Lu that the little boy had been named after her deceased son, who died during Operation Desert Storm in 1991. Philip was Clarissa's husband's name.

"Is your mother doing all right after her accident?" It was Maggie Lu who suddenly switched the conversation. "I think one of my hand-grown violets might be just the thing to cheer her along."

African violets were Maggie Lu's love—well, one of them. She tended a slew of plants, began them with one leaf placed strategically in the soil. Then she would speak or sing it into a flourishing plant. Few people engaged in life with the wholeheartedness of a childlike faith as Maggie Lu did.

"Oh, you always come up with just the right thing," Julia said warmly. "Mom will heal nicely, I think. You can't keep Bonnie Jean

Waverly down. And now that Cassie's home, she'll perk up, I'm sure."

Of course, Julia wasn't sure. Wasn't sure at all. Violets or no violets. But she wasn't about to put a damper on their pleasant conversation. "There's nothing like flowers to brighten a woman's day. Don't you agree, Charlene?"

When Charlene said nothing, Julia glanced to her right. The woman who had raved on and on about her grandchild had become oddly silent. Her brows were drawn together, a look of shock in her eyes. Seconds ago, she had been expounding on Jake's glowing report from his well-baby checkup.

Now the proud grandmother was eerily silent. Charlene fiddled with a napkin next to her empty coffee cup. She stared down, divorced from the moment and from the conversation in which she'd been such an integral part. Something had happened. "How much did you say he weighs now?" Julia asked, disturbed by Charlene's silence. She looked around to see what might have distracted her friend but saw no one looking their way.

"I'm sorry," Charlene said. She glanced up, her expression like a deer in the headlights.

"He was a little under eight pounds when he was born, right?" Julia asked.

"Um—yes," came the halting response. "He's twelve and a half pounds now." Charlene balled up her napkin and gave Julia a tight smile.

"You must bring him around to see us," Julia said gently, wondering what had come over Charlene.

"I'll do that. Soon." Charlene stood to her feet. "I—I think my minute's up. I simply must get at those receipts. And I need to check on that new assistant cook we just hired."

The conversation across the table stopped. "You'll wear yourself out, girl," Maggie Lu remonstrated, looking up at her daughter. "My Granny Luv always said, 'A woman's got to stop long enough to smell the roses she's a'growin.'"

Charlene seemed to recover from her former distraction. "Granny Luv never met my assistant cook," she said, turning and sweeping a hand that took them all in. "But I have to go. Let's get together for lunch soon. My treat! At the best diner in town, of course."

"That girl!" Maggie Lu said, shaking her head as Charlene disappeared into the kitchen. "Ya gotta love her." Presently, she turned back to Julia. "Right now that violet is drinking in the sunshine in my window at the library, but I'll bring it by this afternoon, when I get off work. That suit the two of you?"

"Good," Julia said. "I'm sure Mom will be pleased at your thoughtfulness." But she wasn't sure about that, recalling her mother's reticence where Maggie Lu was concerned.

Perhaps it wasn't just Maggie Lu. Recently, her mother hadn't wanted to go out. Now with concerns about falling, she might be even less open to social interaction. Julia drew in her breath. Her father's birthday was approaching. Mom never spoke of it, but she was always pensive when that time of year rolled around. Maybe Cassie's presence would lift her spirits this year.

"So, tell me, how is our lady from Athens?" Maggie Lu shot Julia a perceptive glance.

"Difficult. Impatient. Determined."

"You've taken the case," Maggie Lu said.

"It really is the strangest thing we've ever gotten involved with," Meredith put in quickly. "She is convinced that her granddaughter needs to be rescued. She's come flying across an ocean to find her."

"Still convinced she's this runaway artist from the Winston showing?" Maggie Lu put her cup to her lips and sipped slowly.

"She brought us a painting from the show and wants us to compare the signature with one on a handwritten letter. We've called in an expert who will confirm it—or not." Julia sighed. "Probably not. Doesn't look anything like the writing in the one letter she showed us."

"One letter?" Maggie Lu asked with a lift of her graying eyebrows.

"One. She had others that were lost in a fire. This one was postmarked Savannah with a post office box number on the return. We'll try to find out whose name is attached to it, but that may not help us find her." Julia tried to keep the pessimism out of her voice.

"You'll find a way," Maggie Lu said. "There's always hope. You know, like the poet said: 'Hope and fear cannot occupy the same space at the same time. Invite one to stay.'"

It was vintage Maggie Lu—not just the launch into Maya Angelou's poetry—Maggie Lu was a teacher and a librarian, after all—but her focus on the positive. She didn't overcome the obstacles that had littered her landscape without keeping her hope high. "Oh, we're not giving up," Julia said, laughing. "We've just gotten started."

"It all began at the Winslow," Meredith said thoughtfully. "We need to find out if Mr. DeLuca can tell us anything more about this so-called runaway artist."

Julia thought about the incident at the restaurant and the embarrassing interchange. No, DeLuca wouldn't be anxious to see her again. She wondered what he thought of the most recent art sale, the Desdemona painting for which Iris had paid $1,200. "I don't think we can expect much of a welcome, but we'll favor him with another visit today."

Maggie Lu seemed to be thinking and didn't say anything for a long moment. Then she leaned back, folding her arms across her chest. "Odd that your current case involves an artist. I was wading through some of Delyse's stuff, and I found something about a student of hers, a girl who loved art. Was always sketching something when she was supposed to be reading or learning her multiplication tables."

"That could have been me, only I was always doodling—and daydreaming," Julia said with a grin. "Reading and spelling were my thing. And nothing could compare with the stories of Alcott or Grahame. I nearly flunked out of algebra once upon a time."

"What I read of Delyse's memoir was quite interesting," Maggie Lu said thoughtfully. "Mind you, it's only a few pages from her teaching days in Atlanta. Who knows where the rest is. For a smart woman, Delyse was such a scatterbrain." She smiled, a mist gathering in her dark eyes.

It might not be long until Maggie Lu could no longer trek to the memory care section of the nursing home where her long-time friend was struggling to recover. Perhaps she had been silently bidding Delyse goodbye for weeks, biding her time between visiting Delyse and volunteering at the Carnegie Library. Julia hoped her wordless expression of sympathy showed in her eyes.

Maggie Lu cleared her throat. "Well, I can't sit here all day. Carnegie is calling. Maybe I'll leave those snippets from Delyse's journal when I bring your mother's violet. In case you need a diversion." She got up and turned toward the door, smiling a warm farewell.

The buzzing of Julia's cell phone erupted, drawing her attention away from the departing Maggie Lu. "Cassie? What? Is Mom okay?" Julia held her breath.

"Fine. She's fine," came the quick assurance. "Sorry, I didn't mean to scare you. I just wanted—"

Julia drew in her breath. It was so strange that Cassie would call. She didn't even know that she had her phone number. Well, of course she would have it. Mom would have made sure she did.

"Just wanted to touch base and let you know Ma had a really good night."

"Oh. Well, that's good." Julia paused, painfully tongue-tied. "Really good."

"You okay?" Cassie's voice was hesitant. Apparently she was having difficulty conversing too.

"Fine. Fine," Julia said. "Thanks. I'll—I'll call you tonight."

Meredith raised an inquiring eyebrow. "All well on the western front?"

Julia nodded. "Seems so." She gathered her purse and zipped up her jacket. It would be a relief to work on a missing person case, to throw her concentration into the day's sleuthing.

Chapter Eleven

"THIS MAY BE A GOOD time for another visit to the gallery," Julia said as they left the diner. "I told Carmen we might have an errand or two to accomplish before we get to the office." She drew in her breath, still puzzled about Charlene's odd behavior and quick getaway.

Meredith raised an eyebrow. "You don't think DeLuca was telling everything he knows about his featured artist?"

Julia shrugged. "I've learned to be wary of men who look as good as he does. I mean, 'Mr. Suave' is like a cross between Brad Pitt and Cary Grant."

"Cary who?"

Julia gave Meredith a quick jab with her elbow.

"All right. I do have a faint memory of the clefted wonder. But is it fair not to trust a man just because he looks good? You don't seem to have a problem with Quin."

"Because I trust your instincts," Julia said, parroting her friend's earlier comment—and meaning it. "But as for Marco DeLuca's instincts—" She pursed her lips. "That may be another thing altogether."

They stepped into the spacious gallery where the Desdemona exhibit loomed in the center of the high-ceilinged room. A few patrons lingered near it, silently perusing the art. Two fortyish women in high-fashion dress exchanged whispers behind beringed fingers. Both looked prosperous enough to purchase even the most outrageously priced painting in the *Spectrum of the Soul* display. The geometric shapes in various red and orange hues flaming against a black background still gave Julia pause. She wondered what it said about the soul of the artist. What had she been thinking or feeling as she transformed a blank canvas into this dazzling conflagration?

"Spectacular, isn't it? It's getting rave reviews."

Julia whirled around to see a willowy young woman, her long hair an astonishing shade of blue. It hung like convex drapery at each side of her face. Almond-shaped eyes the color of mocha boasted pupils that shone like ebony buttons. High cheekbones bore perfectly round pink circles that, had they not been expertly applied, would be clown-like. She was young, likely in her twenties, and appeared to bounce on the small soles of her strappy shoes. She wore a coral mandarin dress with frog enclosures on the bodice. Her nametag read TWYLA ITO. Part of a lotus flower tattoo was visible along the side of her swanlike neck.

"Makes you feel all shivery inside, doesn't it?" Twyla smiled, revealing small, perfect teeth. "Have you seen the other paintings in this most spectacular exhibit?" She clasped small hands together and bent slightly forward in the formal manner of Asian humility that didn't jive with modern westernized expressions like "shivery."

Julia watched her with curiosity. Definitely Americanized. In Japan you could be banned from a lot of public places if you sported an unconcealed tattoo.

"We were here for the opening," Julia said, swallowing her surprise. If Twyla had attended, Julia was sure she would remember her.

"No, I had a class that night," she said, straightening. "Bummer." Her ruby lips protruded in disappointment. "I heard it was very good."

"Do you work here?" Julia asked.

"I'm a first-year student at the art college here. I'm studying animation. But I help here when I don't have classes and when Mr. DeLuca needs me. Doesn't pay much, but I like being surrounded by artists like Desdemona." The little bow again, then a shrug, the ubiquitous expression of modern youth. "Whoever she is, she's really cool."

"Ah," Meredith said, edging in front of Julia to engage the animated Twyla. "As wild and colorful as Yayoi Kusama, maybe?"

The young woman's almond eyes widened, and her red lips opened in an ear-to-ear smile. "You know her work?" She turned away from Julia, hands stretching toward Meredith. "I love Kusama's stuff!"

As Twyla began to rave about the artist, Julia held back as though perusing the walls. Who knew Meredith was so well informed? Whoever Yayoi Kusama was, Twyla was absolutely absorbed, exclaiming about the artist's forms that emanated from childhood hallucinations. She drew Meredith off toward an alcove containing elongated polka-dotted paintings, obviously intent on showing something to her newfound Kusama enthusiast.

Over her shoulder, Meredith gave Julia a conspiratorial wink and a nod in the direction of a partly open office door with the small gold plaque above it. M. DeLuca.

Julia meandered toward the office, aware that no one seemed to notice her. The high-fashioned patrons had gone off to other pursuits, and the gallery lay silent but for the muted conversation between Twyla and Meredith.

As her partner and the young woman disappeared from her line of vision, Julia stepped inside DeLuca's open office door.

Order reigned. The modest-size room was tastefully decorated in soft gray tones. A tightly closed Levolor blind covered a narrow window. An L-shaped executive desk stood out in front of an unusual maroon drape that might cover a larger window behind it. The desk was an elegant piece of furniture in steel and natural cherrywood and contained only a computer, a telephone, and a writing blotter. No stray files, coffee cups, pens, or pencils. Several canvases leaned against the wall, facing it so she could see only the backs of the paintings. In an alcove off the wall were many more rear-facing paintings. Is this what Marco had done with his uncle's paintings— stored them out of sight to make room for his own choices?

It might be quite revealing to talk to Eduardo DeLuca. She wanted to know what he thought about this nephew of his whose tastes were far afield from his own. She could hear Twyla's animated voice now; she and Meredith must be heading back toward the main part of the gallery. Julia sighed. Even though the door had been left ajar, it wouldn't do to appear to be caught "snooping" in the proprietor's office. Time to exit but not before having a peek at an attractive shopping bag leaning against one of the canvases.

The gold seal on the bag identified it as an item from a local upscale boutique. A beautifully wrapped package was quite visible amid the pink tissue paper stuffed around it. Julia detected a definite feminine fragrance. A gift for a lady friend, no doubt. The enigmatic blond who'd doused him at the Pink House?

For his wife? An ex? A girlfriend? She had discovered that he was divorced from one Katherine Ann Hughes, a model from New Orleans. Perhaps he'd met her while engaged in his import/export business travels, which to all appearances had been lucrative. Julia's research had revealed that he owned several homes—likely rented out—and even a villa. Managing his uncle's art gallery now was probably a hobby or a diversion. Who knew? For the most part, Marco DeLuca seemed to have escaped the twenty-first-century radar that allowed little secrecy for most people.

So, the man was a romantic. Not necessarily a philanderer. *Give him credit for that.* Maybe. She stood, allowing the invisible vibes to pulsate. Could you really discern a person's character that way? Probably not, and yet Julia felt a niggling discomfort.

She froze when the odd maroon drape suddenly parted behind the cherrywood desk. Like a magician suddenly materializing, Marco DeLuca emerged. He stared, his hand still clutching the fabric of the curtain he'd pulled aside. Julia could see that it obscured a door. She could make out a small portico and a bit of wrought iron railing that led down to the busy City Market street. He had a back entrance that opened directly into his private office!

DeLuca's eyes registered immediate surprise and, as quickly, anger. He was impeccably dressed in dark slacks and an open-necked shirt of some fabric that shone with silken newness. An unbuttoned tweed blazer hung perfectly on his trim physique.

Johnny Depp with prematurely gray hair. An attaché case held in one hand seemed suspended in midair.

"Something you wanted?" he asked, barely concealing the steel in his voice.

"I was—I was looking for you," Julia stuttered, willing her heart to stop hammering. "I noticed your door open and thought I'd wait."

Carefully he released the drape, bent to set his briefcase down, and rose slowly, perhaps composing himself. When he looked at her again, the dark eyes had lightened; he smiled, the left side of his trim mustache arching up. "And so, you have found me. Miss Foley, isn't it?"

"Mrs. Foley, actually. But Julia's fine." She cleared her throat. At least she hadn't had her nose in the shopping bag when he'd magically appeared.

"Care to sit down?" He extended his hand to a chair next to his desk. When she did as he invited, he pulled out his own chair and eased into it. Folding his hands on the immaculate desk, he looked at her inquiringly.

"Actually, I'm here on behalf of a client," Julia began. She waited briefly and resumed. "The Greek sculptor you met the other night at the opening? Mrs. Floros?"

An almost imperceptible quiver of his left eye and then recognition. "The irate lady who insisted she knows the identity of one of our artists." His lips drew together slightly as though trying to get a clearer picture. "A sculptor? From Greece, you say?"

"Yes. She has a studio in a small community near Athens. She's asked us to locate her granddaughter, and we've agreed to undertake a search for her. That is, my partner, Meredith Bellefontaine, and I." She paused, unable to read his expression.

"Bellefontaine," he repeated, musingly. "I've heard of a Bellefontaine Agency."

"Mrs. Bellefontaine's husband owned it previously. We are Magnolia Investigations now."

DeLuca's musing tone gave way to impatience. "Well, I wish you luck with your investigations, Mrs. Foley, but I really don't know how I can help you. I thought I'd made that clear in our previous meeting." His mouth twisted on the final word, no doubt referring to the covert nature of this most recent "meeting."

"I hope you understand that this is very important to our client. I'm asking if there is anything you might be able to tell us that could clarify who the artist Desdemona is." She recalled his seemingly rapt attention to the Desdemona painting when he had been unaware anyone was watching. Did he give that kind of studied admiration—almost intimacy—to all his possessions? She engaged him with a level gaze. "You say you've been a collector for several years; surely you can tell us how you came to purchase the paintings displayed in the exhibit and who your contacts are in order to facilitate our search."

"Mrs. Foley." Exasperated impatience. "Surely you understand that contacts—especially in the art world—are treated with special care. Our financial and professional interests are at risk. We simply can't be hounded and cross-examined by people looking in from the outside. However well-meaning those people might be."

Julia said nothing, though she felt her blood pressure leap. *Hounding? Cross-examining?*

He hurried on, perhaps seeing the smoke rising from Julia's ears.

"At any rate, as I said, I have no information for you. The paintings came into my possession a few years ago from a third-party private source. For whatever reason, the artist who calls herself Desdemona has chosen anonymity and gone to great lengths to preserve it."

"But surely if she knew that her grandmother had come all the way from Greece to see her…"

"Even if she came from Mars and was actually related to your client—which is highly doubtful—there is nothing I can tell you." He stood abruptly. "Now, I'll have to ask you to excuse me. I have a gallery to run."

"And we have a job to do, Mr. DeLuca." She rose, securing her shoulder bag. "You'll be hearing from us."

"I warn you I will not be harassed on this matter," he said in a level but menacing voice. "I'm sure you're aware that there are laws against invasion of privacy."

"Oh, I'm familiar with the law," Julia said, effecting a smile. She turned on her heel and left, nearly colliding with Meredith—sans Twyla Ito.

"You all right?" Meredith whispered as she hurried after Julia. "What happened in there?"

Julia pushed through the door onto the landing and hurried down the stairs to the street level. Meredith followed, asking nothing more until they reached Julia's car.

Julia started the motor but left the gear in PARK. She turned to face her friend. "Well, partner, the oh-so-delightful Marco has no intention of helping us. He all but threatened me with the law if we didn't stop 'harassing' him."

"But where did he come from? He wasn't around when we got to the gallery."

"Back stairs exit opens directly into that office. He caught me standing there, inches from his desk. I had no idea that drape covered a door." She frowned. "He wasn't pleased."

"Anything?"

"No." Julia groaned. "He's a very neat sort of guy—nothing lying around—except a shopping bag with a very expensive gift-wrapped bottle of perfume."

"Ah," Meredith said, releasing a quick puff of air. "He didn't give you any information about Desdemona?"

"No. He insists he knows nothing."

"Iris was so sure, so determined." Meredith crossed her arms over her jacket with a little shiver and grew quiet. "I haven't heard from her today. Have you?"

Julia shook her head. "Maybe she's taking the hint and letting us do our job. One can only hope!"

After a long moment, Julia murmured. "DeLuca. You know, there's something about that man that really gets under my skin. And what did Shakespeare say about someone who goes overboard to deny an accusation?"

"Hmm," Meredith said thoughtfully. "Hamlet referring to the queen: 'The lady doth protest too much, methinks.'"

"Yes. And methinks DeLuca must know something. How can he handle an artist's work without at least some communication or background? You'd think it would be a feather in his cap to introduce her to the world. And if he really doesn't know who Desdemona is, he should be glad for any leads from two experienced investigators who could help."

Meredith nodded.

"So," Julia went on, twirling a strand of hair around her ear, "maybe he knows something and for some reason isn't willing to talk. We could speculate about those reasons: Money or a scam of some kind. Who knows? Remember Quin's warnings about fraud in the art world. By the way, who is that Yayoi Somebody you captured Twyla with?"

"Never heard of her." Meredith grinned. "But I saw a giclée of one of her paintings in the gallery when we came in. Bingo! Got the girl's immediate attention. Apparently Yayoi Kusama is acknowledged as one of the most important living artists to come out of Japan. Twyla's a big fan."

Julia headed out of the parking lot. "She was kind of quirky, but I liked her, blue hair and all. The young these days can be uniquely creative, but I still have a hard time with tattoos."

"You and me both. Like my mother used to say, 'I was born too soon.'"

Julia maneuvered through traffic toward the agency, wondering what she could say to Iris. The intrepid grandmother would not be surprised, though, having had her own run-in with Marco DeLuca. Perhaps they were looking in the wrong direction anyway. Maybe DeLuca really didn't know anything. Maybe Desdemona simply was not Helena Meyer.

Meredith's cell phone rang with the jaunty "La Cucaracha," signaling a call from Carmen. Their clever assistant had fun coming up with that special ringtone just for them. It still made Julia smile. A song about a cockroach without his two back legs was hardly a grand theme for the jolly tune.

Meredith turned to Julia, excitement in her eyes. "Curt Constantine's analysis is in." She directed her voice into the phone once more. "We've been waiting for it. Go ahead and read it."

Julia tightened her fingers on the steering wheel. *At last, something definitive.* But when the pause seemed to last a good deal too long, she glanced to her right. Meredith's expression was grim as Carmen's voice came over the speaker.

"No match. Not even close."

"He's sure?" Julia knew that Curt was the best in his field; he wouldn't say so if he wasn't sure. She felt her heart drop. Helena Meyer was not Desdemona. Their one lead had dead-ended. Iris Floros had risked so much to find her granddaughter, and she was so sure she was the mysterious Desdemona. How would she take this news?

Chapter Twelve

JULIA PARKED THE CAR BENEATH the ancient oaks that fronted the Queen Anne home where she'd grown up. After supper, she had left Beau to work on a proposal to add a reading room to the hospital children's wing he had championed. Mom and the sister who hadn't been home in nearly two decades were expecting her.

She felt bone weary as she went up the walk toward the familiar structure with its polygonal roof and carved black shutters. Budding branches spread their shadows against the house, stroking it with groping fingers as though calling back something they'd forgotten.

It had been a less than satisfying workday in which she might have alienated a gallery owner and learned little to further their case. The signature on the artist's painting didn't match the one on the letter referring to "Melpomene," the muse of tragedy. Right or wrong, Iris had interpreted that reference as a plea for help.

They hadn't given her the news yet, and their client hadn't called. Tomorrow was soon enough to shatter a dream.

She climbed the steps to the porch and paused at the top, cradling the green ceramic pot with the violet Maggie Lu had sent for Mom. Its perfect purple blooms held no fragrance, but neither had the spring dandelions she had picked as a child to present with bursting pride to her mother.

She never approached that broad front porch with its round white pillars and natural wood rockers without a sense of timelessness. So many years had passed like stones skipping on a pond. Yet at that moment, she felt every ripple with sweet expanding pain.

For the most part, the years had been good, and she was grateful for so much that had been given her. Friends who had journeyed with her, Beau who loved her deeply. And God, who despite her failures, had never given up on her.

She dropped down onto one of the rockers, steadying the pot of violets on her lap. She would go in presently, enter that small cloud of unknowing that was Mom and Cassie—her enigmatic little family. A spray of stars shone in the darkening sky. It had been a warm day for February, and the sun's heat hadn't yet departed. It was twilight, the time of two lights, one descending and another ascending to meet somewhere in the middle.

This time of day always brought the Wordsworth poem to her mind:

Between the dark and the daylight, when the night is beginning to lower, comes a pause in the day's occupations that is known as the children's hour.

Twilight was one of God's recurring mysteries, His "children's hour" too seldom heralded, too little appreciated by His own. *Today I see,* her heart whispered.

"I thought I heard someone."

Startled, Julia turned to see Cassie in the open doorway, her hand on the screen latch. The double light gave a soft aura to the copper hair drawn back in a bushy ponytail.

She stepped out onto the porch. "I think Ma's asleep on the couch," she said in a hushed voice. "We were watching television." She closed the screen door quietly and looked from Julia to the violet. "For Ma?"

Julia started to rise. "Yes, a gift from a friend."

"Don't get up," Cassie said, her step light as she approached. "I'll just set it on the hall table, and I'll come out and join you."

Julia watched her go inside with the plant and return in a few seconds with a nylon jacket from the rack in the hall. "Everything okay?" she asked quietly.

Cassie secured the jacket over her shoulders and sat down in the adjacent rocker. "She's fine. She had a good day, I think. At least I didn't poison her with my cooking." She smiled at her little joke and looked up at the stars, then into some space beyond the oaks and pitch pine. "It's not too chilly yet," she said. "It's warm for February."

"Makes you believe spring won't be far behind," Julia murmured, aware of her sister's wide blue gaze that had somehow not changed since she was a little girl. Seeing Cassie yesterday for the first time had been something of a shock. Photos had shown the passing years, of course, and face-to-face she had appeared old and tired. Now, in bare feet, skinny jeans, and a yellow shirt under her jacket she seemed younger, more vulnerable.

Their rockers creaked in the stillness as each seemed to search for words to breach the distance. A few cars passed on the street, motors whooshing softly by. It was quiet enough for Julia to hear Cassie's cell phone vibrate in the pocket of her jeans. She watched her sister glance at the screen, silence the phone, and return it to her pocket without a word. Quietness reigned again.

It seemed odd to be sitting there. Odd and yet familiar in a way that intrigued Julia. She leaned back onto the floral pad that cushioned the slatted back. Mom bought new chair pads every year, always in some floral or leafy pattern.

After several moments, rockers creaking, Cassie made a sound halfway between a giggle and a sigh. Julia turned to see her clutching the arms of the rocker, much as she used to do as a child when she wanted to go fast, make her head bob like a woodpecker's until it seemed the chair would upend. Only now she made no attempt to propel herself forward. Her bare feet remained anchored to the porch floor; her fingers gripped the ancient wooden arms.

"Remember how we used to sit out here?" Cassie asked softly. "You'd be doing your homework, intent on getting the very best grades. And I would be bouncing around or playing with my Barbies, thinking school just wasn't any fun at all." She chuckled lightly, her voice rising. "I found two of them in an old trunk upstairs today. Malibu Barbie and Italian Barbie."

Julia smiled. "And I found some old tests and an essay on De Tocqueville stacked on a shelf. I don't even want to think how long it's been since I was in junior high. Imagine Mom hanging on to all that stuff."

Cassie sighed. "I guess mothers are like that."

"At least ours is," Julia said. Had Cassie saved any baby things that belonged to Wyatt? How she could leave a child and go off to a faraway place was beyond Julia to understand.

They fell silent again until Cassie spoke. "I wish—" She stopped, changed course, interrupting her wish. "She is going to be all right, isn't she? I mean, she's so thin now, and Dad's not here to take care of her."

A bit late for regret. He hasn't been here for more than fifteen years. Julia was glad for the anonymity of thought, though surely Cassie could read into the silence. She nodded. "The doctor says she'll be fine. And Mom has always been on the thin side. But she does forget that she shouldn't climb ladders and scrub floors on her hands and knees anymore."

"Daddy's gone, but you've been here," Cassie said, almost too softly to be heard. "Ma could always count on you."

An awkward silence followed. Julia heard what Cassie didn't say—that she, the younger sister, had been a disappointment. Their father's death in 2005 was the reason Julia had left her practice in Atlanta and returned to Savannah. Wyatt had his own family and business to tend to, and Cassie was—well, still trying to find herself. There had been no one else. Julia hadn't regretted it. Mom could be difficult sometimes, but she held a place in her heart that no one else could fill or ever would. She wondered if her mother knew that.

The shock of her father's hit-and-run accident had come close to unhinging her, Julia recalled now. How could someone be so alive in one moment, whistling to the music of Glenn Miller in this very house, and then silence? How could that magnanimous, fun-loving light be extinguished in one terrible second? Steeped in memory, she didn't realize right away that Cassie was speaking again.

"Remember how Daddy would come bounding up those steps like seeing us was the greatest thing in the world after a hard day's work? He'd have that green twinkle in his eye and say, 'Now there they are, my two best girls in the whole wide world!'" Cassie leaned forward in the rocker, as though she might bolt into his arms.

Julia felt the ache that never quite went away. His birthday was next week. Mom wasn't the only one who got misty-eyed when the day rolled around each year.

"You'd put down your books," Cassie went on, her voice high with enthusiasm. "And I'd drop my Barbies into the bushes." Her blue gaze drifted to the forsythia hedge that hugged the porch floor. Come spring the branches would explode in a yellow riot of color, but now they were a mash of empty brown stems.

Julia shut her eyes, feeling as dry and brittle as those branches. Sixteen years were but a hiccup as the reality of her father's death came thudding back. She could barely look at Cassie. Cassie, who'd come flying in for the funeral—at their mother's expense, of course—and flown abruptly out, like her father's death was an inconvenience too much to bear. Accusations trembled on Julia's lips, but a muffled sob stopped the words.

She turned to see that Cassie's shoulders were shaking. Displays of emotion—that is, real ones—were not like her little sister. At least not her grown-up little sister, who wrote that she was living life free as the breeze and rolling with any punches that threatened. As a child she could employ a pout or a giggle or a flood of little girl tears to achieve her ends. The sounds Julia heard now were nothing like that.

She waited, not knowing what to say. Only moments ago, she had been doing a slow boil, wanting to shake her sister and demand an explanation for her cavalier behavior. Now an urge to give comfort pressed in on her. She sat rigid, conflicted, and breathless.

Cassie hunched in her chair, all movement stilled. After a long moment she said in a trancelike voice, "I couldn't stand it, you know. All the flowers, the words, that wooden box trapping him inside. The look on Ma's face. I had to get away. Even now, going into the house I used to love..."

Julia drew in her breath as a dove's haunting call echoed in her ears. Had she gotten Cassie all wrong?

Cassie had been her daddy's darling, but had she clung so tightly to him that even after all these years she hadn't yet come to terms with the reality that he was gone? But she'd been running long before her father's passing. Running to something? Running away? *Dear God, life can be so complicated sometimes!* Another small sob jolted her.

"It's still your home, Cassie," Julia heard herself say just above a whisper. "It will always welcome you." She swallowed a lump in her throat. "And you've come because Mom needs you now. That means a lot."

Cassie began to rock slowly, rhythmically, saying nothing, even when her cell phone buzzed again like a petulant bee.

Wyatt had needed her all those years ago when she'd left him with Mom and Dad to raise. Madison and Kennedy had needed their grandmother too, hadn't they? But they were to receive only scraps of attention now and then through letters, short visits, promises. What good were Cassie's wishes now, her seeming regret?

But there was no more time to consider these troubling thoughts. There was a scraping behind them, and the screen door opened. Mom stood on the threshold in an oversized white blouse and loose slacks. Her blue eyes were watery and pale as a winter sky, her hair flat on one side where her head had lain against the couch pillow. Her feet were bare.

"I thought I heard voices," Mom said. She glanced at the two of them, a frown creasing her forehead.

"We didn't want to wake you," Julia said. "Are you feeling okay?"

"Just resting my eyes," Mom said, drawing herself up. She cocked her head. "Are you coming in or what?"

"Where are your slippers, Ma?" Cassie asked in a mock severe voice as she stepped inside, revealing her own bare feet.

"Same place as yours, I imagine," Mom said drolly. "Now do I have to get my own tea? Or will one of you put the kettle on?"

Mom had been partial to an evening cup of tea after supper for as long as Julia could remember. Lemongrass herbal was her favorite. She would occasionally switch to other varieties and could wax eloquent on the health properties of each.

"I'll get it," Cassie said, then looked from her mother to her sister with sudden confusion. She'd only been home a day; likely she hadn't yet learned where everything was.

"Julia can show you," Mom said. "Let's have tea in the kitchen, if that's all right with you."

"Sure. Won't take but a minute," Cassie said.

"I'll get your slippers," Julia said. She picked up her mother's sheepskin mules from the living room floor and retrieved the plant from the hall table.

In the kitchen, Cassie fumbled through cupboards. House-keeping wasn't her forte, but Julia had hoped that age or necessity might have sharpened her little sister's skills to some degree.

"I'll get these dishes later," Cassie said, banging a cupboard door shut and balancing a small stack of china on one hip. "I was going to do them, but when Julia came, we sat out on the porch a while like we used to do." Cassie's thin face blushed pink, heightening the blue of her eyes. Embarrassed, she added, "Look what Julia brought you, Ma." She nodded to the plant on the table.

"It's a gift from Maggie Lu," Julia said, sliding it gently toward her mother. "She works wonders with violets. She starts them from a single leaf, and the green shoot just pops up like magic. She's grown them in every color and type. She wanted you to have this one."

Mom scooted herself in closer to the table. She drew her brows together as though she was studying the plant for a science project. She gave a small sigh and leaned back in her chair, closing her eyes. She put a thin hand to her bruised left shoulder in a rare display of weakness.

"It's lovely, isn't it?" Julia pressed.

Mom opened her eyes and nodded toward the window. "Best put it over there where it will get the morning sun."

"Isn't that the African American lady Wyatt told me about?" Cassie asked, setting a cup in front of her mother. "The one who volunteers at the library and works with you sometimes?"

"Yes, she's been an excellent resource for the agency and a good friend too."

"Your sister has made quite a name for herself," Mom broke in, drawing the subject away from Maggie Lu. "She and Meredith have cracked some important cases here in Savannah."

"I'm sure," Cassie said, leaning against the sink and effectively hiding the stack of unwashed dishes. "She was a really good judge too. Wyatt says she was one of the best."

She said it without rancor, but Julia felt the old tension rise. Cassie was always comparing herself unfavorably to her successful sister.

Cassie's cell phone buzzed again. She pulled it out with an apologetic smile. She silenced it but this time put the phone to her ear and walked away into the dining room, mumbling something in a fractious voice. Julia heard only, "I asked you not to call me here."

When she was out of earshot, Julia poured her mother's tea and asked how her day was, what Cassie had fixed for lunch, and if the doctor's office had phoned. How was the pain in her arm? But her mind was on Cassie. No doubt the caller was Calvin. Calvin Harlow, whom Cassie had joined up with some dozen years ago and threatened to leave as many times, according to Wyatt.

"She needs to get rid of that do-nothing leech." Wyatt didn't speak of his mother often, but when he did, he minced no words. *"He gets her into one lousy deal after another and leaves her to pick up the pieces."* Wyatt didn't think Calvin abused Cassie physically, but he seemed to have the power to cripple her psychologically to the extent that she had no will of her own.

Cassie had been so excited when she and Calvin had landed a franchise for a fashionable boutique. What glowing reports she wrote to Wyatt and Mom. The next thing they heard, it had all come unraveled, and they were on to something else. They just needed a little money to tide them over.

"Sorry," Cassie said, returning a few minutes later with the haggard pallor Julia had seen yesterday. A look that had vanished while they sat together on the porch talking about Dad and Barbie dolls. "Nothing important." She turned to the sink of waiting dishes.

Mom took up her tea with studied interest, avoiding eye contact with either of her daughters. Julia bit her lip. How soon before Cassie announced that she had to go? When would she once again give in to Calvin's wheedling and leave Mom's care to someone else?

Chapter Thirteen

AS HE OFTEN DID, BEAU met Julia at the back door, having heard her car in the driveway. "Hey there," he said, draping an arm across her shoulder. He was dressed in his faded Bulldogs shirt and sweatpants. Close at his heels Bunny rasped a welcome, her striped tail weaving around his legs.

Nothing could take the prickly out of the world like coming home. "Hey to you too." She let him take her windbreaker and stooped to pet the rescue tabby Beau called Jack—for Jackrabbit because of her long legs. Having accomplished her welcoming duty, the cat loped off to more interesting pursuits.

"Everything all right at your mother's?" Beau asked, following Julia to the kitchen, where she dropped down in a chair.

"Mom's okay. She was asleep when I got there, so Cassie and I had a chance to catch up."

"How'd that go?" Beau's left eyebrow lifted in tentative curiosity.

Julia shrugged. "It was okay. I may be too tired to tell you now, though. This has been some day. I spun my wheels on the missing artist case to begin with, then at Mom's, Cassie was... Well, let's just say it wasn't exactly a successful end to a perfect day."

"Poor baby," Beau wrapped his arms around her neck from behind her chair. "Want anything? A cup of tea?"

She loved the warm feel of his sinewy arms around her, the spicy scent of his aftershave, which some strange alchemy rendered completely different from the fragrance in the bottle. "Nope. Had some with Mom and Cassie just a little while ago. Lemongrass herbal."

"Sounds like something you clean windows with," he said.

"It's supposed to be full of antioxidants, lower blood pressure, and burn fat." She smiled wearily. "But it does taste a little like Windex."

He laughed, kissing the top of her head. "And when was the last time you had a sip of Windex? Are you coming up?"

"It's still early," she said, stifling a sigh. "I think I'll stay up a little while and read. I need to unwind a bit. Maggie Lu left something for me from a journal belonging to Delyse Watson." *"In case you need a diversion,"* she had said. And she did need one. If she went to bed now, she'd lie there hashing out sticky family issues and keep Beau from his rest.

In the living room with Bunny already claiming a section of the couch, Julia took up the pages of rambling script she'd tucked into her shoulder bag. She wedged herself into the cushions. The last time she had visited at the care home, Delyse Watson had been a mere shadow of herself, lost in some dream, a smile lingering gently on her lips. Alzheimer's was a dreadful scourge that struck fear into the heart. But in the terrible thrall of it, did God send some special message or memory to calm His beloved ones? Some unique and unmistakable sense of His presence?

Let it be so, Julia thought. *Let it be so for this vibrant, dedicated woman who had risen from poverty to lift others to a higher plane.* A minister who visited her native Jamaica had seen something special in the small, wiry Delyse and taken her home to America.

Delyse's hard work and God's grace had resulted in literacy for some of the poorest children in Georgia.

The Delyse of twenty plus years ago wrote in small, quick strokes, the letters crowded on each line to make the most of the space. She'd learned to be frugal in all things—except perhaps generosity. Maggie Lu had told her how Delyse would scrounge supplies to provide for children who came empty-handed to school, much as Maggie Lu had done.

Delyse hadn't dated this entry, but at the top of the first page, Maggie Lu had placed a sticky note that read, D.W. CIRCA 2006? Julia settled herself among the couch pillows, prepared for the mini escape that would push the day's worries into the background. She imagined Delyse's husky voice writing her memoir and addressing it to her cat. Her mock scold of Sydney the Second would likely be accompanied by a sweep of her hand over the silken fur.

Dear Sydney,

Your furry ears can't hear what I say, and your crafty yellow eyes can't cipher what I write on this paper. You sweet little bag of bones, you're good for nothing but chasing those poor mice round this old house! DaVinci says the smallest feline is a masterpiece. Just don't you go taking on airs like you some prince or something. But, speaking of a masterpiece, I may have seen one today, and that brings me to this tale I'm about to recall.

It's the last day of the semester; summer vacation looms. I should be glad for the respite, but I'm feeling all blue and moody today. Teaching is what I love, what the good Lord set me on this earth for, but I suppose they'll be wanting me to retire soon.

Seems like yesterday I started teaching in that one-room schoolhouse a world away from here. Wasn't but a log cabin with an old cookstove for heat, but those were halcyon days for sure. That bunch of children had next to nothing and got only the dregs of what some other schools couldn't use, but they were in school! At the start, I had all I could do to hold them to their rickety seats so they could listen for five minutes.

It takes a while to get to know the children you're supposed to teach, so in the beginning it's just kind of aim and shoot and hope you hit something that will stick in their heads. I had to be tough, to small up myself and make no room for shenanigans or too much sentimentalism.

Gracious! You ain't never chased a mouse as full of tricks as they were. Reminds me of the proverb old Granny Brown used to say: "Mischiff kum by de poun' and go by de ownse." The boys made the most ruckus, but some of those sweet little girls were no angels. You can bet your kibble on that! They were my first students, and I loved every one of them, watched them rise like butterflies from a cocoon.

C.S. Lewis understood how even the smallest souls want more. They want to be more. "We do not want merely to see beauty," he says, "though, God knows, even that is bounty enough. We want something else which can hardly be put into words—to be united with the beauty we see, to pass into it, to receive it into ourselves, to bathe in it, to become part of it."

The world changes and keeps on changing. A lot of years have passed since that one-room segregated school. Now blacks and whites can learn together, and a poor Jamaican orphan can be considered good enough to teach them. But poverty and blight don't end, no matter how much higher learning people get.

I'm not likely to see any of my sixth-grade students after today. They flew out the doors when the last bell rang. They went to homes anyone can see have fallen victim to urban blight. Their parents, most factory workers or dock hands, struggle to keep their jobs and put clothes on their children's backs. Makes the heart of this ole woman shudder, and I pray that my students have not only seen beauty but by some miracle will become part of it. They'll go to the middle school when the new term starts, but this old school will be shut down before it tumbles down around our ears.

Many inner-city public schools like this one are challenged by declining enrollments and surplus spaces. Neighborhoods riddled with vacant and abandoned properties—indicators of area deterioration. City officials explore urban renewal or revitalization strategies but focus much of their energies and resources on downtown or financial districts. Neighborhood structures like public school facilities receive little consideration or are ignored totally.

My heart is heavier than stone when I think of all that needs to be done and what will happen to the students I'm leaving, or rather who are leaving me. Enough of this. You ain't listening, Sydney. You an idle jubie *(lazy one), that's what you be. Sleep on; don't worry; be happy.*

I'm the one to worry, Sydney! I am going to miss all my students, but there is one who lies especially heavy on my mind. I keep seeing her face and wondering what will become of her. She has a gift. She sees beauty, and she creates beauty, but I don't think it has become part of her, like Mr. Lewis says. I remember the first day she walked inside my classroom. The semester had started a week before, and I had noted that a student on the roster was absent.

She was a skinny, whiter-than-white child. Mind you, we had all colors, every shade from white to black, and some who didn't speak English. Most had little in the way of worldly goods, and some faced frightening trouble at home. I thought this girl with big ocean-blue eyes and black hair all tangled up like Medusa might be an immigrant. Because when I asked her very sternly why she was late, she just looked at me like I had two heads. Maybe she couldn't speak English.

Wouldn't do any good to keep on asking so I told her to sit. She looked at me with those eyes deep as an ocean and sat down at her scarred desk in a chair that didn't look like it could hold much weight at all. Which didn't matter because you could spit through her. Gracious, I never saw such a bony thing, like a good stiff wind might blow her down. She was wearing an oversized blue shirt with long sleeves over capri pants that might once have been white. "What is your name?" I asked, keeping my voice firm.

When she made no answer, I asked again, more insistently.

She bit her lower lip, looked away, and after a long pause said, "Elise."

"That's all? Just Elise?" I asked, gentling my tone.

What I got was a shrug. It was impertinent for a student to refuse to answer a teacher's question, but I couldn't know anything about this girl or what she might be going through. And who really knew what went on in the mind of a girl on the cusp of junior high school?

I let it pass and went on with the day's lessons. Curriculum for the day included math and geography, a short lesson on post–Civil War American History, and English. Books were scarce in inner-city schools—at least the updated versions— so I usually made up assignment sheets to work on in class as well as for students to take home. Elise hadn't raised her hand or responded to any questions but had dutifully stared ahead in my general direction.

The English assignment toward the end of our day was to write an essay about a topic I thought my students might enjoy. And it would help me get to know them. "Imagine that you could go anywhere in the world and do anything you wanted. In 150 words—no less—where would you go, and what would you do?"

Elise continued to stare ahead. It dawned on me that she hadn't brought anything with her to class—no notebook or pen or pencil. I produced a sheet of paper and a pencil and placed them before her. "Please be prepared when you come to class tomorrow," I said, and went to my desk as the children bent to work.

I don't walk around and hover over the children when they're writing. I feel that given their freedom within bounds they do better work. So, I left them free to write until it was time to end the day. I told them to bring their papers to me. Eager to flee the stifling classroom, they rushed to bring their work forward.

Only Elise remained at her seat. She appeared startled, as if she had been sleeping, but I had seen her pencil moving steadily. I watched her turn her paper over and stare at the blank white side. As she set the pencil down, it rolled suddenly onto the floor. She bent to pick it up, and that's when I saw the ring suspended on a long chain around her neck. It was a sparkly thing, almost gaudy in its brilliance and far too large for a young girl. She quickly pushed it back inside her shirt, glancing at me nervously as though she hadn't wanted anyone to see.

She secured the pencil in a groove in her desk and sat with hands folded in her lap. Her long hair draped her shoulders, half hiding the downturned face.

"Have you finished?" I asked, coming close and waiting for her to look up. When she didn't respond or move, I waited a few seconds and then turned over her paper. I peered into a drawing that covered the paper—top to bottom, side to side. Beautifully shaded lines, angles and circles coruscated in stunning detail to form an intricate design that left me speechless. Ten, maybe eleven years old, and she had completed this beautiful drawing in thirty minutes.

In the silence the wall clock's tick-tock was like a jackhammer. Regaining my composure, and still surveying the artwork, I said, "The instructions were to write an essay on where you would like to go and what you would do if you could do anything you liked."

I waited, but Elise remained still, unmoving. I looked at her, saw something like peace or satisfaction on the small white face. Those dark blue eyes seemed to look beyond me, beyond her drawing, to some place only she knew. I had expected perhaps belligerence or, should a miracle occur, penitence.

"Why did you not complete the assignment?" I felt the pull of the design, drawing my attention like a magnet, but I kept my eyes on hers. "Well?"

Her voice when it came was soft, steady, but she did not look at me. "This is where I want go. This is what I want to do." She paused. "More than anything."

Now I was the one without words. I knew I should reprimand her, insist that she stay behind and write the essay as instructed. But I was overwhelmed not only by the obvious talent she demonstrated but by the quiet yearning in her manner and words. And the cleverness of her response. "I see," I managed. Though I couldn't see at all. Would she bolt at any minute, flee the empty classroom and the teacher standing so close she must hear me breathe?

"Elise," I began, "this is beautiful—really very good indeed, and I can see how much you must love to draw, but—" I stopped, felt a wave of tenderness. I put her small masterpiece down on her desk and lost the rest of my sentence. "You may go," I said gently.

Abruptly, she stood and walked briskly away, making no move to take the drawing.

"Wait! You forgot this. Surely you want to take it to show your mother."

She stopped and turned around. "No!" She said it as though I'd suggested she burn it. After a few seconds, she said, "My mother is gone."

Gone? Gone to the store? Gone as in dead? "I'm—sorry," I managed. "But this is the end of the week and students need to take their things home."

He eyes fluttered to mine briefly, and she turned away, her small shoulders rigid. And she was gone, leaving her penciled masterpiece behind.

Julia shuffled through the pages, hoping there might be another page, something she might have missed. But here was the end of Delyse's tale. Delyse Watson could write such scholarly prose and then lapse into charming patois phrases like "idle *jubie*" or "small up myself." What a character—strong and passionate. It hurt to know her voice might soon be silenced—except for scraps of notes addressed to Sydney the Second. Her words deserved a far richer destiny.

Would Maggie Lu find other entries to pass on? The girl named Elise had been ten or eleven, a sixth grader in 2006. That would make her roughly twenty-six now. But Maggie Lu had written "circa" meaning "around." She couldn't be sure of the exact year. Still, Elise was near to the same age as Helena would be now. Hair and eye color could be the same, possible age too, but the name was wrong. Crazy to draw parallels. There were likely many talented ten-year-old girls in Atlanta in 2006.

It was as much of a stretch too, to imagine Elise as Carmen's supposedly naive graffiti painter, "The Dove." Julia sighed, remembering that Carmen didn't even know the painter's real name. *"She said her name was Ophelia, but sometimes she called herself Virginia or some other name she thought was exotic."* Was Elise one more name the girl had made up?

Julia sighed again. Diversion ended. But since Carmen had been so intrigued by Desdemona's art, she might be interested in reading Delyse's two-decade-old memoir about a talented sixth grader. She put the pages back in her briefcase to take to the office.

"So much for unwinding," she said to Bunny, patting her soft fur. "I'm going to bed." But she doubted that she would be able to sleep anytime soon.

Chapter Fourteen

ON MONDAY MORNING JULIA ENTERED the antebellum house that had become Magnolia Investigations and made her way to her office. It had once been the dining room with floor-to-ceiling windows through which the morning light now flooded. It shone with gilded splendor on the white fireplace that dominated the room. If one had occasion to conjure the past, one might hear the tinkling of china and the muted tones of nineteenth-century table talk.

It was quite a different scene now with modern office furniture and equipment, but Savannah was still the enchanting jewel of the South and the only place she wanted to be.

Her office, decorated in soft gray tones, was a good place to think and work, and she blessed the day Meredith had suggested they join forces and reopen her husband's business. It was suited to her high energy and need to do something productive, something valuable in the world. Not that jurisprudence hadn't been satisfying, but when retirement came, she'd had no wish to sit back and let the world move on without her.

She glanced at her reflection in the mirror above the fireplace, saw the shadows beneath her eyes. Ugh! Today could prove difficult, especially for Iris Floros, who would be waiting for the verdict on the signature that she was sure belonged to her granddaughter. But the lead had come to a dead end. Or so it seemed. Who was Helena Meyer and where was she? Julia had a feeling Iris wouldn't be willing to fold her hands and return to her studio in Marousi, despite the news she would hear today.

Then there was Cassie and Mom and their delicate family relationships. Julia had spent some time on Saturday and then again after church on Sunday with them, but Mom was withdrawing into herself. Cassie continued to flounder after a half century of living. How had time gotten away from them and taken so many opportunities for warmth and understanding in its relentless march? Nobody said life was easy. But one should not give up on a knotty problem without looking under every bush and scouring every potential route to its solution.

Carmen's cheery lilt and Meredith's mellow accents filtered through to her office. The day had begun, and already the phone was ringing. Whatever transpired in this day, she would give it her best. There was still time. And so long as there was life, there was hope.

She waved to Carmen, who shouldered the phone and scribbled something on a pad. Moving on to Meredith's office, she found her partner studying the day's calendar, a lock of blond hair falling over one eye.

"That could be Iris Carmen's talking to," Julia said as she sat down across from her partner. "Or maybe she won't call; maybe she'll just come storming in any minute."

"Good morning to you too," Meredith said dryly, tipping her head to one side. "Rough night?"

"Do I look that bad?"

"Like a mile or two of bad road." Meredith grinned and leaned back to survey Julia. "You heard from Iris?"

"No. You?"

Meredith shook her head. "The lady is respecting business hours, but I'm sure she's anxious to know about the signatures."

"I'm not looking forward to telling her. She was so certain about it." Julia sighed.

"Yes. Well, I think we should talk to her in person rather than give her the scoop over the phone." Meredith narrowed her perceptive eyes. "Truth to tell, I'm surprised we haven't heard from her yet. Let's see if that was Iris on the line a minute ago."

"Nope. Wasn't her." Carmen stood in the doorway, hands on her hips. "It was Clemmons, Inc., saying our supplies are in and ready for pickup." She winked one brown eye.

Julia was always amazed at Carmen's ability to intuit what was on your mind without verbal clues.

"I'll pick them up when I go to lunch," Carmen continued. "I'm meeting Harper."

"That sounds like fun. How are things going at the *Savannah Morning News*?"

"Harper wants to pick my brain. She's been trying to get the scoop on Desdemona ever since the showing in Florida. Jacksonville, I believe. But don't worry. I won't let her worm anything out of me. And I'll pick up the supplies after we leave Big Bob's."

Julia rolled her eyes.

"I know, Big Bob's is cheap, but they make a great fish taco."

"Better your stomach than mine," Julia said as Carmen left Meredith's office with a chuckle. She shook her head, feeling better about the day despite what loomed. Carmen had a way of lightening the mood. Julia wondered if Carmen was still interested in Chase, Meredith's younger son, the sandy-haired, blue-eyed dreamboat who was still single. A history professor at Atlanta's Emory University, he was admired by many a searching debutante but interested in few, though Carmen seemed an exception. His true love was history, and he was obviously in no hurry to replace it.

Meredith leaned forward and put both hands on her desk, fingers splayed. It was a gesture that usually signaled she was coming to a decision. She looked up. "Well, you want to call the Andaz or shall I?"

"Go for it," Julia said, making no move to leave the room. "She may want to come here, but we could go to her. Save her the trouble."

Meredith punched in the digits and put the phone on speaker. "This is Meredith Bellefontaine. I'm calling for Iris Floros."

"This is Celia," came the familiar stilted voice. "Iris is still resting. I have arranged for calls to come to my suite so she will not be disturbed. It is important that she has her rest."

"I see," Meredith said with a dubious glance at Julia. "But it's important that we see her. When do you think she will be available?"

Julia glanced at the clock on the wall. It was 9:15. Perhaps for someone with a heart condition that was early, but Iris had gone off by herself to the gallery even earlier than that.

"Please tell her that Julia Foley and I have urgent matters to share with her." She paused. "We'd like to come to your hotel in about an hour." Meredith's voice was businesslike, straightforward, but her expression showed her consternation as she hung up.

Julia frowned. "Maybe she had a bad night. Seems funny to me for strong-willed Iris to be asleep at this hour."

"I agree." Meredith tapped her desk with an index finger. "Well, an hour it is."

Forty-five minutes later, Julia and Meredith approached the imposing Andaz Hotel that looked out on Ellis Square, one of Savannah's most exciting spaces. With its fountain for kids to run through, shaded tables, and a life-size chess set, it was a popular spot. A steady stream of tourists took advantage of its unique grandeur only steps away from City Market with its great shopping and dining.

They made their way leisurely to the suite number that had been provided. An hour exactly had passed. Julia knocked on the door.

Celia's amber eyes narrowed as she cautiously opened the door. "Good morning," she said, thin lips curving in the slightest semblance of a smile. Her brown hair drawn back from her thin face made her seem older. "Mrs. Floros is expecting you," she said formally.

She was dressed in a tan mid-length skirt that buttoned down the front with a white blouse secured high at her long neck. It gave the impression of a schoolmarm rather than a nurse. Upon first meeting her, Julia had noted her strong bones and attractive features obscured by her rigid bearing and gaunt angularity. Celia Angelos might have once been pretty. Julia was vaguely reminded of someone, though she couldn't put her finger on who.

"Bring them inside, Celia!" Iris scolded, pressing forward and elbowing Celia to one side. She appeared to have dressed hastily in a blue and white printed caftan over wide-leg lounge pants. Her abundant white hair was piled atop her head, secured with clear plastic combs.

"We're sorry to call so early," Julia began, noting their client's pale complexion in contrast to her dark, flashing eyes. She looked haggard, despite her bluster.

"It is no problem. Please, come in!" She splayed her arms in a wide arc, indicating a striped couch and two overstuffed green chairs surrounding a low glass coffee table.

"Calm yourself; you mustn't get all worked up," Celia said, placating her. She took Iris's arm and attempted to shepherd her to one of the chairs.

"Don't fuss over me. I am perfectly fine." Iris glared at Celia. "I never sleep so late. Why didn't you wake me up before?" She put her hands to her temples as if to clear her mind.

Celia looked from her charge to Julia and Meredith. "She needed her rest." She made a palms-up gesture. "All of this has been hard on her. The traveling, the worry and all." Then in a burst of impertinence that surprised Julia, she added, "I told her she needs to stop all this gadding about and go home."

Iris gave her companion a look of fury. To diffuse the storm Julia feared was coming, she said brightly, "Celia, you traveled with Iris from Athens, so I assume you are also Greek, but you speak excellent English, and you have no accent at all."

The veins in Celia's temple appeared to pulse. She looked down at her hands briefly, then shrugged her narrow shoulders. "That's because I am American. Raised in Baltimore, but I married a man from Greece who died five years ago. When his mother became ill, I went to Athens to take care of her." She paused, jutted her chin out briefly. "I felt it was my duty.

"After she died, I decided to stay in Athens." She looked down at her hands again. "There was nothing for me in Baltimore anymore. So, I entered the home health care system. When I heard Mrs. Floros needed a nurse and travel companion, I responded." She gave her charge an indulgent smile that quickly dissipated. "It's a good fit. I understand artists. Studied myself once upon a time. I still dabble with pastels. And I know this country, whereas Iris—"

"Now that we have heard your life story," Iris interjected in a quick flare of temper. She waved a dismissive hand at Celia and turned to Julia and Meredith. "Can we get on with our business?" She put her hands to her temples and shook her head, as though groggy from sleep.

"Certainly," Julia answered.

Iris sank more deeply into the couch cushion. "I am sorry we don't have any refreshment to offer."

"No need," Julia assured her. She paused. Not only had Iris slept late, she appeared to have wakened unrested. Had she had breakfast? "But are you sure you're all right? You look very pale."

"Please. I am fine, only anxious. You have some news. Your expert—did he compare signatures?"

Julia nodded. "He examined them very closely, and the truth is—" She hesitated, wishing the news were different. "We're sorry to say that the two signatures don't share any characteristics. We don't think the same person signed both the letter and the painting."

Iris's hand went to her mouth, and her eyes widened like inkwells.

Meredith put a hand on her shoulder. "We're sorry. We know you…"

"That cannot be," Iris said sharply. Her eyes roved back and forth, seeking each face in the small semicircle. "Your expert—he has to be wrong."

There was only a slight possibility of a faulty analysis, and that was if some catastrophe had altered the personality. It was extremely rare. Julia wasn't about to mention it, lest Iris be further drawn into her own self-deception—if that was the case. "Iris, how can you be so sure? You've had so little contact with your granddaughter. So many years have passed since you've seen her."

"I know. A grandmother knows!" she said, repeating what she had said before. "I had a painting she made for me. It was destroyed in the fire, but the style is the same. The way she mixes colors and circles within circles, angles inside angles—so beautiful. So like my Helena!"

Julia exchanged glances with Meredith. She cleared her throat and folded her hands in her lap. "Mrs. Floros—Iris, we can't trace your granddaughter through the painting, but there are other avenues, if you want Magnolia Investigations to continue looking for Helena."

Iris kept her focus on the painting lying aslant against the cabinet. She shook her head slowly from side to side, her lips working. Celia was silent, arms folded across her thin chest, sharp features inscrutable.

Julia waited, wondering how long Mrs. Floros planned to stay in Savannah. Could she afford the significant cost of living at the Andaz along with the other expenses involved? Could she afford a private investigator?

"I must find her." It was just a whisper, but it contained a world of pain. "You see, it's all my fault. I let Rhea go, allowed anger and hurt to make a big distance—like an ocean—to come between us." She flung her arms wide, the caftan's sleeves sweeping the air. "I lost Helena too for a long time. Then we came together." She intertwined her expressive fingers. "We made a little bridge, and now…" A sob caught at her throat, and her eyes spilled over with tears.

Meredith's voice broke into the silence. "I think Mrs. Floros needs some water. Better yet," she added, addressing Celia, "would you mind bringing us all some coffee from the coffee shop downstairs? Perhaps some pastries too. We will need a little time to discuss what Mrs. Floros wants to do next."

Maybe Iris and Celia always interacted this way, but it seemed to Julia that Celia injected herself too personally into her charge's affairs. Celia glanced at Iris, who was dabbing at her eyes with a tissue. She was obviously reluctant to leave. Julia smiled encouragingly. "Iris will be fine."

When the door closed on Celia, Julia turned to Iris. "Do you intend to remain in Savannah and look for Helena?"

"It is something I must do," she said. "And I want you to help me. These other ways you talked about…" She bit her lip. "Maybe they will help to find her?"

"We'll need to compare notes, Iris. Go over everything from the beginning and see what other information you can give to aid in our search," Meredith said. "For instance, did Helena say anything about friends at the art college? Did she give any names?"

Iris let her breath out in a resigned sigh. "No. None that I can remember."

"Did she mention a roommate? Anyone she spent time with? A boyfriend?" Julia pressed.

The shaking continued. "My Helena, she wasn't so good at making friends, you know. It was always that she wanted to paint—only to paint."

Julia reached for her purse and pulled out the letter Iris had given them for signature comparison. She read it again silently as Iris watched. When she came to the troubling line, she read it aloud: "'I am still painting—when Apollo's muses smile on me. They say my work is very good, but I must try harder and do as I am told.'" She looked up. Did it have something to do with the man she had met—the reason she had left school? "What do you think she meant by that?"

Iris gave a little shudder. "I wish I knew," she said. "I know she met someone there. She said that I would love him." She paused. "I think when she was a little girl, she was afraid of her father. He was a hard man. He was afraid that Helena would go away like Rhea did."

Once her father was gone, she had freedom, but would she know how to handle that freedom? Julia wondered. It would not be surprising for Helena to fall under the influence of someone. A mentor, a teacher, or a boyfriend.

"It is this letter that makes me afraid," Iris broke in, her voice a whisper. Her eyes darkened. "My Helena is sad, and she speaks about Melpomene." She shuddered at the mention of the muse of tragedy. "I have to find her."

"Try not to worry," Meredith said. "We will give this our very best effort."

"I will remember," Iris said, with just a touch of a smile—the first since they'd arrived at her suite. "I think I am fortunate I meet you at the gallery. Also, what you said about trusting in your God…" She broke off shyly. "My parents taught me to believe." Her smile drifted down. "It is easy to forget, to look away." She dropped her eyes but quickly added, "Maybe you have helped me to remember."

Celia's return with a tray halted the conversation. "These were the only pastries they had," she said, balancing a tray with one hand and replacing her hotel key card in the pocket of her tan skirt. "Just these berry muffins." Her quick, glittery eyes roamed from one to the other, perhaps trying to decipher what had transpired in her absence.

"This will be just fine, thank you," Meredith said, reaching to help Celia with the refreshments.

"Is everything all right?" Celia asked, still scanning the three faces around the little table.

Was Celia merely being attentive to Iris? Did she have her charge's best interests at heart? Julia recalled how Celia had been listening at the door when Iris was in her office.

As they headed back to the agency, Julia pondered possible connections at the art school Helena had briefly attended. "Iris doesn't have any information about friends or acquaintances at her granddaughter's school," she said with a sigh.

"So, let's head there in the morning," Meredith said decisively. "Let's try to find someone who knows something to ease that poor woman's burden. The place is just north of Charlotte, but we need to start early to get back to Savannah at a decent hour. Real early. How about five thirty?"

"That isn't what I would call decent," Julia responded with a groan. She wasn't an early riser like Meredith, who saw frequent sunrises. "But you're right." She sighed. "I'll drive. I'll pick you up promptly at five thirty."

"Good girl!" Meredith said. "We've got to find out once and for all whether Helena is Desdemona or not."

"Whoever she is, we've got to silence Melpomene and pray she finds a muse who whispers triumph instead of tragedy."

Chapter Fifteen

THE SMALL PRIVATE ARTS COLLEGE was nestled in a picturesque valley in a town of roughly fifty thousand people. The partners had made good time despite early fog and the rain that came in fits and starts.

"I'm glad this place isn't terribly far from Savannah," Julia said. "We can have a firsthand look rather than depend on internet surfing and virtual fact gathering."

"Uh-oh," Meredith said as they drew closer. "Where are all the cars?"

A handful of automobiles were scattered in the two lots on either side of the main building. A few cars appeared in a side area reserved for short-term parking. Startled, Julia consulted her activity tracker. "It's a weekday. Where is everyone?"

"Students should be arriving." Meredith groaned.

"Is this some kind of holiday without scheduled classes?" Julia asked.

Julia drew up in the closest lot and parked. "I should have checked before driving all the way here." After a moment she had a realization. "Students might not be much help anyway since Helena left more than two years ago. Dare we hope that the teachers are in and that someone might recall Helena?" She twined a strand of hair around her ear as she plotted their next move. "Well, we're here now. Might as well make the best of it."

"After nearly three and half hours on the road!" Meredith said. "But it may be difficult to get any information from the Administrative Office."

"Yes," Julia said. "FERPA and all that." The Family Education Rights and Privacy Act and laws like it were meant to protect students' privacy.

Meredith grimaced. "We'll just have to be interested tourists exploring the sights and hope to uncover something." She snugged her purse over her shoulder and pushed open the car door.

Julia popped her blue-striped umbrella open. "Let's check in and hope for a warm welcome."

The private college was nothing like Georgia Southern U, where Julia had earned her undergraduate degree, but it had that distinctive aura of academia right down to the smell. Its walls were replete with the usual complement of historic photographs, trophies, and sundry signage, but it was oddly quiet without the rush of students coming and going.

"Why does one always want to whisper in places like this?" Meredith asked. "It's like the walls are hiding secrets they've kept for centuries."

"I know," Julia whispered back. "But sometimes they give up a secret or two."

A door opened down the hall, and a thirtyish woman approached with a stack of manila folders. At first glance she appeared to be a student in jeans and sweatshirt, pale hair in a ponytail. Maybe a day without students allowed teachers a chance to dress down. She gave them a cursory glance and went on, passing an older man in khaki pants and open-necked polo. Peering at them over his half glasses, he came toward Julia and Meredith.

He had a slight paunch and thinning hair and was dressed more for a golf course than a college campus. But the unmistakable veneer of academia lay on his pleasant features. "May I help you, ladies?"

"We're looking for the administrative office," Julia said.

"First right," he said, pointing. "You're almost there."

"Students all playing hooky today?" Julia remarked as they began to walk away.

"And loving every minute of it," he said with a wink. "And so are we."

The admin office door opened into a medium-sized reception area, flanked on both ends with cubicles that were mostly empty. A woman approached the front desk. Sturdy and probably in her midsixties, she had salt-and-pepper hair in a smooth short style. She removed her glasses and let them drop from the chain around her neck. She wore a tailored knee-length skirt and matching brown blouse above serviceable shoes.

Meredith introduced herself and asked, "Would it be convenient to have a look around the campus?"

"We have a friend whose granddaughter was a student here a few years back," Julia said. "She's become quite a successful artist. No doubt what she learned here had a lot to do with that."

"I see," said the woman, whose name tag read GLORIA HALEY. "That's always very good to hear." She clasped small, ringless hands together and rested them on the dark oak counter. "We've been helping students develop their potential for over a hundred years."

She paused, glancing toward a mounted rack holding pamphlets likely outlining the school's merits.

Meredith took a colorful brochure from the rack. "Thank you so much."

"I am sorry, though, that you've come on a day when the students are not in class," Ms. Haley said. "This is a TD day. We have one or two a quarter." She smiled politely. "Teacher Development," she explained. "It's important for our staff—gives them time to catch up on the curriculum and develop their teaching plans."

She explained that there would be some training classes in the auditorium that afternoon, but that the campus would be open. "The Fine Arts building is to your left. I believe you mentioned your friend's relative took visual arts studies."

"Yes," Meredith said. "Definitely."

"I'll just ask you to sign the guest register and put on these badges."

Julia signed the book, tugged her purse closer across her denim blazer and prepared to leave. She smiled at Gloria Haley. Then as though expressing an afterthought, she said, "I wonder if you might perhaps remember our friend's granddaughter."

Ms. Haley only tilted her head, waiting, perhaps vaguely wary. After all, she would be trained to guard the privacy of their students.

"Her name is Helena Meyer, and she was enrolled in your Fine Arts program. Twenties, dark hair, dark blue eyes. You should hear her grandmother rave about her."

Ms. Haley's eyes registered recollection. "I do remember her. Quite a talented young woman, as I recall."

Julia gave a rueful sigh. "Actually, the sad thing is that our friend has lost contact with Helena. You—uh—wouldn't know what she might be doing now? I mean, did she say what she was planning to do when she left here?"

Gloria Haley's face showed no emotion. "I'm sorry," she said, all business now. "Our students' records are confidential. Even if I knew anything about your friend's granddaughter, I am not at liberty to share private information."

"Of course," Julia said, offering her brightest smile. "Thank you for everything."

"Please remember to return to this office and sign out," she said, turning away as a phone rang behind her.

"Well, that was interesting," Meredith said. "But it doesn't help us find Helena."

"No," Julia said, pushing a strand of hair behind her ear as they walked away from the administration office.

It was doubly quiet in the well-maintained Fine Arts Building. Several of the doors were closed, some offering a peek through a window, some rigidly holding their secrets. Open doors revealed a variety of classroom styles, some devoted to sculpture, some to interactive digital media or animation.

They walked down the halls, perusing tastefully posted photographs and drawings. Posters described classes offered for ensuing semesters as well as local art exhibits to supplement the regimen of classes.

They were still whispering, though for the most part the building was deserted. The accoutrements of art were everywhere. Easels, flat worktables, paint jars and brushes, projects in process. Canvas drapes covered tables in rooms reserved for the messier crafts like sculpting and ceramics.

"We need to talk to someone here who might know Helena," Julia said, pausing at yet another collage of artwork, none bearing Helena's name. Or style, from what Julia could discern. She searched her mind for ideas but discarded them. They needed an opening. Something to make this day more than the dismal failure it was shaping up to be.

"Looks like there's someone down at the end of the hall," Meredith said.

"Do you hear humming?" Or was it whistling? Julia exchanged a glance with Meredith, and they quickened their steps in the direction of the unexpected sound.

A man's jovial half hum, half whistle grew louder as they approached the room at the end of the hall. The door was thrown wide, and bright light flowed from it. Julia stopped at the threshold and stared at a stocky, seventyish man sweeping a brush across a canvas.

Sparse gray hair tufted at his ears and at the collar of his short-sleeved cotton shirt that extended over his trousers. He wore bulky sandals over dark socks, his feet balanced flat and even in front of a large easel containing a partly finished landscape painting.

Rugged mountains in blended blues and purples spread boldly from end to end on the canvas. Behind them white clouds bloomed in a busy turquoise sky. With a large brush the painter daubed at the foreground. Trees in various sizes and shapes magically appeared. With each blunt stab of the brush against the canvas, he accented the beat of the wordless song he was humming.

Julia stood, captivated by the magic of the developing landscape and the music that seemed to flow effortlessly, joyously from its creator.

Suddenly the painter turned, brush suspended in air. Warm gray eyes in a round flushed face. More tufts of hair interspersed on a balding pate, curly white sideburns. "Oh! I didn't hear anyone." He pronounced "one" with a *v*, as someone of Germanic ethnicity might.

"We're sorry to disturb you," Julia said, finding her voice. "But we were so fascinated by your painting." She stared into his wide eyes and the deep laugh lines at their corners. His mouth made a round *O* beneath his bushy mustache. "We came to see the Fine Arts Department. We were just looking around...." She tapped her visitor's badge, not sure how to proceed.

She was looking at this rotund, happy little man and thinking of William Alexander with his "mighty brush" painting "happy little clouds" on television and YouTube videos. He had died in 1997 after forty years of teaching his technique. Was this man a relation, and how did he relate to today's modern students?

"I see. I see," he chirped, setting his palette and brush down on a cluttered table. "You are *velcome*. Come in, come in." He gestured to some chairs at the front of the classroom.

"We don't want to interrupt," Meredith said, seeming as charmed as Julia.

"No, no. I was just enjoying a little painting time. A little practice for my students. It's a teacher development day, they call it. So, I have been developing! Do you like it so far?" His round cheeks grew rosier. "I am Hamel Velker, by the way, but my students refer to me as Mr. Ham." He laughed, making his jowls shake.

It was refreshing to think of an artist really enjoying art. No depressing angst. No streaks of pain or unutterable emotion. "I like it very much, Mr. Velker," Julia said.

"The colors are so deep and beautiful," Meredith added.

"Have you been teaching here long?" Julia asked, leaning forward and swiveling a little in her chair as Hamel Velker sat down adjacent his easel.

He pulled a handkerchief from his pocket and wiped his broad forehead. "Ah, I have become a fixture around here. Ten years. No! Eleven. Bless my soul!" He went on to tell them how he had settled in the area to be near the mountains and waterfalls that South Carolina afforded. The same vistas along the Cherokee Foothills National Scenic Highway that she and Beau had often traveled.

"Eleven years," Julia exclaimed, feeling suddenly more hopeful. "You've taught a lot of students in that time."

"More than I can count, and I should say it has been a pleasure. *Vell,* most of the time. Bless my soul!" He stuffed the handkerchief back in his shirt pocket.

"Mr. Velker, we're here because we're working on a case," Julia said. "We're private investigators. Magnolia Investigations in Savannah."

Velker took the business card she handed him and squinted to read it. He brushed a hand across his chin and searched their faces.

"You see, our client's granddaughter was a student here," Julia said quickly. "Her family has been estranged for some time, and now she's anxious to reunite with her granddaughter. She has traveled from Athens, Greece, to Savannah, believing she will find her in this area."

Velker seemed to be considering his response. A tinge of sadness crept into his gaze. "*Ach*, the young and the old. Sometimes they do not know *vat* to say to each other. They stand at opposite sides of the bridge *vhile* the mist is falling. It grows thicker until they can no longer see each other." An uncomfortable silence followed the man's poetic response, and Julia wondered what personal sorrows the artist might camouflage with his happy painting.

"Her name is Helena," Meredith said, assuming her practiced business persona. "Helena Meyer. She started here three years ago and left last year. Her grandmother is a well-known sculptor from the Athens area—a place called Marousi."

The moment of nostalgia ended, and Velker folded his thick hands over his ample stomach. He sighed, making a soft, sad sound. "Helena." He said her name gently. "*Ja*, I remember a young woman named Helena. Bless my soul, she was one of the most gifted of my students. But not like them. So quiet, always looking inside. Sad blue eyes, and yet when she painted, there was a glow like a lamp turned on inside." He shook his head, making the tufts of white hair at his ears shiver.

Julia tried to do the math in her head. Helena had spent two years at this college. She'd left about a year ago—with someone probably.

"Did you ever have occasion to talk together? You know, about her life, why she didn't continue her studies here?"

He shook his head again. "She spoke only with her paintings. I was disappointed when I learned she had dropped out before finishing her education."

"Did she have any friends that you knew of?" Julia asked quietly. "Anyone she talked to or seemed close to? A roommate perhaps? Or a boyfriend? Did she ever mention someone named 'Dilly'?" When he only shook his head slowly to Julia's string of questions, she added, "I know that privacy rules are important, and we wouldn't be asking if it wasn't important. Her grandmother believes she's very troubled and needs help."

He leaned forward in his chair, said softly, "If I could help you, I would. The truth is that I do not know. Wherever she is, I think she must be painting; she should succeed. Very gifted. Ja, she should do well in the art world." He swept a hand over his chin.

"The paintings on display," Julia began, "are any painted by Helena?"

"There was one, but when she left, she asked to have it back. Took it with her, frame and all, and we never saw her again." Velker seemed genuinely grieved. "I hope you find her. And I am sad for the grandmother who has lost her." He shook his head again. "And so, I send you back without helping." He glanced down at the business card again for confirmation. "To Savannah, you say?"

Julia nodded, but before she could speak, he brightened. "Savannah. Do you know my friend, DeLuca?"

Julia flinched. DeLuca? Did he know Marco DeLuca?

"Eduardo," Velker supplied. "He owned a gallery there in Savannah. We met when he came here to lecture. A fine man. The college invites artists and collectors to visit. Critics too. They come to share their knowledge of the art world. Many come and go." He frowned, pursing his lips. "I heard about Eduardo's stroke.

I hoped he would recover and come back to speak to our students."

Julia swallowed. "I'm afraid he's not doing well. His nephew is running the gallery now."

The frown deepened, shadowing his eyes beneath the bushy brows. His mouth turned down, forming a grim line beneath the shaggy mustache. The paintbrush held aloft in his fingers seemed immobile. "Ja," he said slowly. "He lectured here too."

"Marco DeLuca lectured here at the college?" Julia's pulse picked up.

"A couple of years ago," Velker said with a sigh and looked across at his easel, as though yearning to get back to his happy mountains. After an awkward pause and a slow shake of his head, he added, "He is not Eduardo."

"Did he come to lecture often?" Julia asked when she found her voice.

"A few times. But funds are tight in our department. When a school must cut back, it is the arts that are sacrificed. We schedule very few outside instructors now." He drew his feet back, preparing to stand. "I am sorry," he said softly. "About Eduardo. And about Helena. I am sorry I cannot help."

Julia swallowed. "Mr. Velker, did Eduardo's nephew know Helena? I mean, did he ever discuss her paintings or have occasion to—to talk with her?"

The gentle, rotund man drew a deep breath and sighed. "He was—popular with the students. It is likely he talked with your young friend." He shrugged as though suddenly weary. "It is a different age, ja? I know nothing more to help you." He spread his hands. "I must get back to my work."

"Thank you for taking time to talk with us," Julia said, rising. "If you think of anything else that might help us find Helena Meyer, will you call?" She nodded to the business card on the edge of his easel.

He bowed slightly in assent and turned back to his palette and brush, no longer humming.

Chapter Sixteen

JULIA HEADED TO HER MOTHER's house after taking Meredith home. She was weary from the trip to North Carolina and troubled by what might have transpired between Helena and Marco DeLuca. He had lectured at the college to the relatively small group of Fine Arts students during the time Helena had been there. He had to have encountered her. Perhaps he had done more than simply encounter her. Could he be the reason she had left abruptly? Was he the man Helena had spoken of in her letter to Iris? *He is strong where I am weak—and he likes my painting.*

Julia recalled the quick frown from the sweet-tempered Velker at the mention of the younger DeLuca and knew he had not liked the man. He had clearly drawn a negative comparison. *He is not Eduardo.* More than ever, she was certain that Marco was the key to finding Helena, whether she was Desdemona or not. Could she confront him again? Would he simply reiterate his denials? They had to find something to either prove his connection or admit it did not exist. But for now, before she could go anywhere else, it was important to check in on Mom. Cassie was worried, and Julia feared her sister had good reason to be.

The neighborhood slumbered in the hazy afternoon gloom as Julia climbed the porch steps of her childhood home. From inside there were no sounds—no voices, real or mechanical. The television usually blared in Mom's house. Not that she watched it, but she turned it on for company. Sometimes the radio or CD player would fill the emptiness. But not now. Julia lifted her hand to knock but was surprised to find the outer door partially open. She gave the screen door a gentle push and stepped inside the quiet hallway.

"Mom? Cassie?" she called. Not too loudly lest her mother was taking a nap. She often rested for an hour or so, sometimes in her chair in the living room, less frequently in her room. She seldom owned up to napping in the middle of the day, however, viewing it as a weakness or a sign of old age.

The stillness was unsettling. She glanced around the living room and found it tidy in a way it hadn't been on Friday. The carpet appeared to have been vacuumed recently, the tables polished, throw pillows artfully arranged on the soft beige sofa. In recent weeks, Mom had taken little interest in housekeeping. Another signal that all was not right with her. But maybe she had decided to spruce things up.

Julia hurried into the kitchen. Maybe Mom and Cassie were having coffee. Tea at night, coffee in the afternoon—usually Amaretto, an aromatic blend that drifted into other parts of the house. But the air gave no hint of almond, and the kitchen was void of human habitation. No dishes in the sink this time. If Cassie had worked this miracle it would really be something, she thought. But the smile teasing her lips quickly faded.

Where was everyone? Had Cassie succumbed to the charms of Calvin, who said he and Cassie didn't need a piece of paper to seal their commitment to each other? Some commitment! He was committed to her bringing home the bacon and him eating it. Had Cassie left Mom on her own? Surely not. Not without at least calling her sister.

Mom! Hurriedly she climbed the stairs to her mom's bedroom. The door was slightly ajar and opened wide to her touch.

"There you are!" Julia exclaimed, relief flooding in. Mom was sitting in the wing chair near the window. Dressed in dark slacks and white cable-knit top, she appeared to be looking out meditatively on the street. No book, no crochet project. Just sitting, her short hair curled around her right ear like a silver wave circling a shell. Aloof. Vulnerable.

"And here you are," she said, looking up, a hint of a smile on her lips.

The quick-witted response was reassuring, but Julia thought her mother looked pale. She hurried across the room and bent to kiss her cheek. It was cool to the touch. "Are you all right?"

"I'm fine," she said, resetting her left arm in the hospital-issue sling. She sat up straighter, giving her daughter an indulgent smile. "What brings you here in the middle of the day? No mysteries to solve?"

Of course she would be here—whenever and as often as possible, especially after her mother's fall. "Just checking on you because you're my favorite mom." Julia dropped down on the end of the bed close to her mother's chair so she could look her full in the face. "What are you doing?"

"Well, I don't suppose I'm doing anything right at the moment." It was a typical Mom response, but her stone-washed blue eyes were dreamy. She peered out the window once more. "Looks like a front is moving in with all those gray clouds looming."

Julia noted the proximity of the photo of her father and mother taken at their twenty-fifth wedding anniversary. It rested on the round table under the window, only inches away from her chair. A handsome, hazel-eyed Dad posed for the camera in a black tux and bow tie beneath his chiseled chin. Next to him was her mom with something of a Mona Lisa smile. Just above the curve of her sleek black gown was the dazzling diamond necklace, the treasured heirloom that Julia had found on the floor by the closet the night Mom had fallen. Julia suddenly remembered. Today was her father's birthday. She'd been aware of it and knew her mother often became pensive when this time of year rolled around. But in the press of work and the day's activities, she'd temporarily forgotten.

She knew better than to refer to her mother's state of mind, so she touched her hand gently where it lay in her lap. "Can I get you anything?"

Mom snapped her gaze away from the window—or was it the photo? She shrugged. "I have had a bit of good news today, though," she said. She nodded to a small stack of magazines on the end of her bed close to her chair. "The Arts Committee newsletter came today. Only comes out twice a year."

Julia picked up a thin glossy leaflet. "This it?"

Mom drew a satisfied breath. "It's on the second page—bottom of the second column. Eduardo is out of rehab and recovering at home." Her eyes took on a rare gleam. Whatever she had been brooding about was for the moment superseded.

"That's really great news." Julia scanned the brief report offered by his wife and felt a rising optimism. If Eduardo could receive a visit—perhaps on behalf of his old friend Bonnie Jean Waverly—could he provide any information about the runaway artist exhibit?

"Your sister has been cleaning up a storm today," Mom said, breaking into Julia's quickly developing plan to pay Eduardo a visit. "The oven, the cupboards, the closets, and I don't know what else. I heard the vacuum buzzing all morning. Honestly, I don't think I ever saw that girl work so hard. Not that the house needs all that cosseting. I'll get to it once I get rid of this infernal harness."

Domestic occupation wasn't like Cassie, Julia thought as she listened to the feverish pitch of her mother's voice. *We're both wondering what she's up to,* Julia thought. "But where is she?"

Mom shrugged, then winced at the pain the action had caused. "I sent her to the attic with some boxes from the hall closet. I've been meaning to take them up myself and order the chaos up there. But as long as she's here…" She raised her eyebrows. "Besides, it gives me some peace for a while."

"Ah," Julia said. An excuse for Mom to take a nap, though what she had been doing was staring out the window and thinking. Thinking what? Something had been bothering her for weeks, distracting her usual pursuits. It was more than the approach of Malcom's birthday, more than worry over her youngest daughter. "Well, good for Cassie," she said, thinking it was high time her sister had taken some responsibility for her family.

"If you're going up to see your sister, take that stack of old blankets with you." She tilted her head toward a chair near her closet.

"Get some rest," Julia said, kissing her mother's cheek again as she left the room.

She ascended the shallow steps to the attic, her arms laden with blankets. *No way should Mom be climbing these stairs*, she thought as she painstakingly navigated the narrow space. She hadn't heard any shuffling or clunking during her brief visit with Mom downstairs, and she heard nothing now as she gave the partially open door a shove with her hip.

A startled Cassie looked up from her perch on a low box on the cluttered attic floor. Her face was obscured by the lid of a nearby trunk. "Oh! It's you," she said, craning her neck and dropping the shoebox she had been exploring into her lap.

Julia peered into the gloom. Inside the trunk were various and sundry items from decades of living. Scarred shelving units and old curtain rods were scattered around it, along with an American Flyer sled and other objects no longer in use.

"Mom said you were up here," Julia said, taken aback by the vacant look on her sister's face. Her cheeks were pale as alabaster in contrast to the bright hair that frizzed around her shoulders like a red halo.

"I was trying to clean up some of this stuff for Ma and…" She sat back a little and stretched out one leg. "I came across this old trunk and got to remembering things." She tried a smile that teased the dimple in her left cheek and quickly disappeared.

Julia dropped the pile of blankets onto the top of a nearby plastic tote. "I know," she said. "Cleaning the attic always takes longer than you think because the memories are so loud."

"I had no idea this stuff was still here." Cassie tilted her head to the trunk. "Your cap and gown are in there, you know. And the 4-H purple ribbon you won for design. You made everything for a bedroom, from curtains and spread to wastebasket to window reading nook. Remember?" She held the ribbon in her palm for Julia to take.

"Barely," Julia said, feeling something like awe. She passed the "Best in Show" ribbon back to her sister. "Five decades is a long time to keep anything."

Cassie held the ribbon in her hand for a long moment. Then she looked up. "You know, I've always been proud of you. Even when I acted like I hated you." She gave a little half sigh. "You succeeded in everything you did."

Julia drew in her breath. Would Cassie draw the line between them again? Point out her own failures in comparison? She looked at her sister, expecting the "You go your way; I go mine" flippancy she often had exhibited.

"I can understand," Cassie continued. "I understand why Dad was so proud of you and why Ma loves you so much."

"Cassie," Julia interrupted. "They were proud of both of us. And Mom loves you. Surely you know that." How often had she caught Mom staring at the photograph of Cassie that hung prominently over the fireplace with the wrench of aching love visible in every line of her face? How often had worry drained the color from her face when Wyatt brought disheartening news of her youngest daughter? She'd never been one to say a lot of sentimental words, but both Mom and Dad had demonstrated their love in many ways to the insecure and headstrong Cassie.

Cassie took the lid off the shoebox that lay in her lap. She set it aside on the floor. "I never believed Ma loved me the way she loved you. But I've been sitting up here looking at stuff she saved, stuff I thought she would have thrown out years ago." She lifted out a piece of notebook paper, its blue lines intersected with crayoned stick drawings. "I made this for her in second grade. It's a valentine." She traced her finger over the flimsy paper, a nostalgic smile trembling on her lips.

"You see, don't you, Cassie?" Julia asked softly. "You were always loved. I used to be jealous of the way Daddy could never say no to you."

A tremor passed Cassie's lips, and Julia knew she was thinking about her own failures and of the worry she had caused her mother over the years. "Mom said you were cleaning like a whirlwind today. The house looks good. Really good. In fact, I haven't seen it so clean in a long time."

Cassie's face brightened like an internal lamp had been lit. "Well, it needed to be done, and I thought, why not? You certainly don't have time to be cleaning with all you have on your plate." A frown drew her pale eyebrows together. "I wish she would hire someone to help with the heavier work."

"Yes, well," Julia said with a sigh. "You know how independent Mom is and how she likes things just so."

"There was someone for a while—a long time ago," Cassie said, tipping her head in thought. "Wyatt told me about a very efficient young woman who used to help with housework and such when he was young. I think he liked her a lot because he was really sorry when she left." Sadness swept over Cassie's face. "I know it wouldn't have been necessary to have household help if I had been here—if I hadn't..." Her voice trailed off. She rubbed her fingers aimlessly over the ancient drawing that still lay in her lap.

"Well, it means a lot that you're here now," Julia said softly. "You've done a really good job helping to nurse Mom back to health."

Cassie lifted her gaze to Julia, the sadness still there, but something else—something grateful and almost proud. "Well, it was the least I could do. You've been here all this time. I don't know how you managed with your heavy schedule."

Julia sighed. "It's true that there's a lot on my plate right now." She hadn't intended to talk about it, but she found herself telling Cassie about Iris Floros, about the granddaughter who might be painting beautiful works of art under the name "Desdemona," but nobody knew who or where she was. "Mrs. Floros is an artist too, a sculptor. She traveled all the way from Athens, Greece, because she believes her granddaughter is in trouble."

Cassie listened intently, her eyes round and blue as a summer sky. "Wow, that's really sad—and beautiful that she would come so far to find her."

"Iris has a letter that hints something is wrong. She thinks that Helena is desperately unhappy, and that something bad may have happened to her. She has hired us to find her granddaughter, but every lead so far has failed. We can't seem to find her."

Cassie's brow knit tightly. "People come to see her and buy her paintings, but they don't get to see her or to know anything about her?" She looked down at her childish drawing again. "She must be proud of her art, must want to show it to the world. It would be awful if something or someone kept her from doing what she loves to do."

"Yes," Julia said softly. "No one should have that kind of power over another person." Only after she'd said those words did Julia realize that Cassie was probably in the same position. Different, perhaps, but maybe not so different. Cassie stayed with Calvin because he loved her and needed her. Fear of being unloved could have powerful consequences.

"I hope you can find your client's granddaughter." Cassie looked up at Julia, her blue eyes hopeful. "I'd put my money on you—if I had any." She laughed softly. "Bad joke, but what I mean is you always succeed, and I think you will now."

Julia shook her head. "No one *always* succeeds. What's important is that we keep on trying and learn from those times when things don't go the way we expect." She paused, hoping she didn't sound like Pastor Markham on Sunday morning. "You know, I used to pray that God would help me win in whatever I was doing; now I know that it's more important that I do my best and trust the outcome to Him. His ways aren't always clear, but they are best."

"Well said, Sister," Cassie said, pressing the lid of a memory box closed and replacing it in the trunk.

Julia glanced at her sharply, expecting to see mockery in her sister's eyes. Instead, she saw genuine warmth.

Cassie angled her head to one side and let out a puff of air. "I'm really glad you came up here. Glad we could talk." She pressed her lips tight.

"Me too," Julia said.

"We didn't really get to know each other when we were young, did we?" Cassie went on, fiddling now with her fingers. "The age difference between us seemed like such a lot. And now..." She left the sentence unfinished, but her eyes seemed to hold an ocean of regret or perhaps hope.

Julia smiled, feeling an uncommon tenderness for her sister, a sense that something important had passed between them. "And now, we'd better go downstairs. I bet Mom is through napping and ready for coffee."

Julia followed Cassie down the narrow stairs, her heart whispering a prayer of thanks for whatever God might be doing in all their lives.

Chapter Seventeen

"DESDEMONA CAN'T BE HELENA!" CARMEN stood poised in the doorway of Julia's office, a hand on one hip, abundant hair tumbling to the shoulders of her coral pink blazer. "She can't be Mrs. Floros's granddaughter!"

"What?" Julia peered into the brown eyes lit with excitement.

"I read what Mrs. Watson wrote. You know, the journal entry you left for me."

So Carmen had read the pages from Delyse's journal. Julia waved her in. She had come to the office early to get a head start on paperwork. It had been a busy morning, and now at eleven, Meredith had gone to pick up Iris Floros at the Andaz. The plan was to take her to a quiet restaurant and over lunch compare notes with their client again. Away from Celia and with only one investigator probing her memory, Iris might remember more that would help in the search for her missing granddaughter.

Meredith had decided on the excellent restaurant housed in the Mansion Hotel directly across the park and not far from Magnolia Investigations. Meredith had hosted many events there with the historical society and could be assured of a quiet corner in the posh restaurant. Also, Iris would enjoy the owner's impressive art collection on display throughout the property.

"I'll join you for dessert," Julia had told Meredith and arranged for her to call when they were ready.

Now, Julia waited for Carmen to settle herself into the chair across from her desk. "What exactly was it about Mrs. Watson's journal entry that makes you think the runaway artist isn't Helena Meyer?"

Carmen crossed one leg over the other and smoothed her aqua A-line skirt. She cleared her throat and jutted her chin forward. "Because I think she's the Dove. It was the ring. I had forgotten about it. But when I read what Mrs. Watson wrote, I remembered." She tapped a pink-nailed forefinger to her temple. "The Dove always wore it on a long chain because it was too big for her finger. I remember how it sparkled when it bounced on her chest."

Ah, the ring Delyse had described. The one she saw when the girl dropped her pencil and stooped to pick it up. Julia recalled the brief mention but had thought nothing of it.

"I told her she was crazy to wear it," Carmen said, shaking her hair back over one shoulder. "I told her somebody was bound to knock her over the head someday and steal it."

Julia raised an eyebrow. "A lot of young girls wear rings and lockets. They might look valuable, but usually they're just costume jewelry—discount bling." Once in junior high, she had bought a mood ring and hung it around her neck pretending Joey Blaze had given it to her as a sort of pledge. She smiled remembering her long-ago, short-lived crush on the handsome math whiz.

"It's not just that," Carmen protested. "The girl she wrote about sounded like Ophelia or Virginia or whatever she called herself on any given day—"

Julia tilted her head to the side and regarded Carmen. "Do you know anything about this graffiti artist, really? Her background or family? You said you didn't know if she had a home to go to, and you don't even know her real name." She softened her challenge with a smile. Carmen was smart and savvy, but she had a flair for the dramatic along with a very vivid imagination.

"No. No, but—" Carmen puffed out a breath, frustrated. She uncrossed and recrossed her legs, fiddled with a button on her bright blazer. "It wasn't just that. It was the way Mrs. Watson described her. You know, how she would get quiet, not answer, and draw pictures when she was supposed to be writing. The Dove was like that." She tapped her temple again. "It was odd, you know. When I read it, I was transported back to that time on the streets. I was there again." She broke off with a wistful sigh.

"The girl in Mrs. Watson's memoir was only ten or eleven. The one you remember was what? Fifteen? Sixteen?" Julia smiled gently. "A lot of years went by, and that girl was living in Atlanta at the time."

"Me too," Carmen said. She was quiet a long moment, seemed to be considering her position. Then she looked up sheepishly. "Do you think she could be Desdemona?"

"It's possible," Julia said. "Anything's possible."

Carmen stood. "Well, we can be pretty sure she's not Helena Meyer since the writing on the signature didn't match the letter Mrs. Floros showed you." She tucked a pencil behind her ear that immediately disappeared into the rich profusion of her dark hair. "Did you find out anything at that college?"

Now it was Julia's turn to sigh. "An art teacher—Hamel Velker—remembered her, said Helena was talented. He was sure she would make it in the art world." She made a tent with her fingers. "He knew Helena, though, and I believe he cared about her. I think he cared about all his students really. It was quite refreshing." Julia heard herself sigh again. "He didn't know where she went when she left, and the receptionist in Administration wasn't about to release any information. But we do know that Marco DeLuca lectured there. Apparently, he was popular with the Fine Arts students. But Mr. Velker knew nothing about her showing at the Winston—or the name 'Desdemona.'"

Carmen turned, gave a quick wave of her fingers. "Okay," she said. "*Lo que sea.*"

The Spanish phrase for "whatever" made Julia smile.

"But I'll keep surfing. You never know what might turn up. Desdemona can't hide forever."

Or be hidden, Julia thought, wondering if Iris Floros's fears were a result of an active imagination akin to Carmen's.

"Oh, here's Maggie Lu!" Carmen said before popping back in behind Maggie Lu.

The elegant woman stepped into Julia's office, wearing her usual understated but tasteful attire. A loose dark jacket over a beige dress with small buttons down the front. Only today she had tied a jaunty powder blue and purple scarf at her neck, giving her a festive look.

"Charlene and I are off to take Clarissa to lunch," Maggie Lu announced, dark eyes twinkling. "It's her birthday, and we're gonna celebrate. Like my Granny Luv used to say, 'Don't just sit on a log when the dancin' starts.'" She smiled proudly. "I'm taking them to Elizabeth's on 37th Street. Charlene is about to have a fit, says I shouldn't spend my money like that. But this is special. I told her, 'What good is money if I can't spend it for love?'" Maggie Lu pulled something from her tapestry handbag. "Charlene's waiting in the car, but I found another entry about that child artist. At least I think it's the same one." She handed Julia a folder and snapped her bag shut again. "It's just a page, but I think it's worth taking a look."

Julia said goodbye and wished Maggie Lu a great day. Carmen had probably heard the interchange. Julia might have to fight her assistant for a first read. Could they be on the wrong track thinking Desdemona was Helena? Could she be Carmen's graffiti artist of long ago? Or was Desdemona someone else entirely?

When the door was closed, Julia took the folder to the comfy loveseat she'd installed near the window. No dates were inscribed at the top of the page—not even a "circa." The writing was a little less steady than the first excerpt. Still, within seconds Julia was hearing the gravelly patois voice of Delyse Watson. In her mind's eye she could see the whiskered tabby curled in her lap.

I tell you, Sydney, teaching high school these days can bleach your poor old bones, and yet some things just don't change— even from those one-room school days. My teaching days are coming to an end, but when they need a substitute they call on this old woman.

Things ride a more even wave now, depending on how you look at it. But trouble is trouble, no matter how you dress it up, and I never saw a time limit on hate. The whole world is chaka-chaka (disorganized and messy) like that girl I saw slapping paint on Old Callaway's warehouse.

She turned white as a ghost when the lights from the squad car started flashing. Lit up the whole alley. The cops chased her, and she ran hard, a towheaded little boy in unlaced tennis shoes stumbling after her. Before I could get out of the way she slammed smack-dab into me. And Coo-yah! (Look here!) *I knew that child, though she'd gone and grown up considerable.*

"Simmer down, or I'll put the cuffs on ya," the biggest cop said as his partner went running after the little boy.

The child I first met in grade school lurched as though to go after the boy too. Her eyes were wild, frightened, but she simmered down like the cop said and just stood there like someone had drained her from the inside out.

"You responsible for that?" The policeman pointed to the warehouse brick where gorgeous alien flowers bloomed and spread like they were growing while we watched. Even in the dark I could see a look of grudging admiration in his eyes.

She had a can of yellow spray paint in her hand and just stood there looking into space. A scarf that had been tied over her wild hair came loose in the wind and flew away like a frightened red bird. She said nothing, even when I came around to look her full in the face and demand, "Girl, what are you up to?"

"You know her?" the big cop asked. I nodded, told him who I was, and he said he'd be taking her to the police station and bringing her parents in too. "You know her folks?"

I said I didn't, but I convinced him to let me go along to the station because I could see she was scared. Just stood there in her sandals shivering.

I knew someone had been spray-painting in the neigh-borhood; it was a perfect place—old abandoned buildings and such everywhere and no one caring much. I should have moved out when the blight got bad, but I never lived any-where else. Home is home, aye, Sydney? Besides, when I leave the home fires, I just naturally take more caution than a wood rat with the owl out.

Lots of kids roamed the streets day and night marking up stuff. But I never suspected that shy, skinny child who never got up to mischief in class.

"Where you suppose she stole that?" the policeman asked sarcastically. "That" was the ring I had seen in my classroom. Once more it had slipped from beneath her shirt and gleamed in the flashing lights of the parked patrol car.

She scrambled to retrieve it. "No. It's mine!" she said, her voice small and frightened. She scooped it up and pressed it inside her dark jacket. And I remembered the day she had bent to pick up her pencil. She was grown up some, but she was still a small, hurting thing.

I tell you, Sydney, it was a long night. After a while they released her to her parents. The boy too. He couldn't have been more than six or seven. The father looked haggard and unshaven, said he worked nights on the dock and didn't know what "that foolish girl" got up to. The mama came looking mad and almighty put upon. She kept hold of the boy's shoul-der, pulling him against her belly and staring daggers at her husband and the policemen. Hardly gave the girl a glance, just left her standing there alone in that scary place!

In the end, it was yours truly, Sydney, who convinced Hutch Calloway not to press charges. That old warehouse was no prize, and besides, this wily old woman knows some things about the owner he doesn't want to become common knowledge. But as I sit here remembering, my heart lies in me like a hot brick about to burst into flame. I keep wondering what will happen to those kids. Who's gonna protect them in this chaka-chaka *world they never asked to be part of?*

What? That was it? Julia turned the page over, hoping to find more. But there was nothing more. Delyse had ended the account abruptly, giving no names, no hint who those children were or what happened to them afterward. Julia's mind went to Carmen's tale the first night they visited the Winston. Was the towheaded little boy in untied tennis shoes the child who would later fall to his death from some scaffolding?

Well, Carmen, here's more fuel for your fire. Looks to me like Delyse may just have crossed paths with your long-ago street buddy. Julia's thoughts raced, and as they played themselves out, she felt disillusionment like a physical weight in her stomach. Delyse's jottings from days gone by were interesting but did nothing to shine a light on their case. Whoever the graffiti artist was or wasn't, they were nowhere closer to finding Helena Meyer.

Julia jumped when her cell phone erupted inside her purse lying on her desk. "On my way, Mere. See you in five." She clicked off and left to join Meredith and Iris at the Mansion Hotel's restaurant.

Julia followed the young waiter to a table set off in a small alcove of the restaurant. Meredith was consulting a menu. Across from her,

Iris held both hands around a cup and appeared to be staring into it. She wore a dark dress with a fringed paisley shawl. A circular beaded comb secured her snowy chignon at the nape of her neck, but tendrils of white hair had escaped and wisped about her face.

"It's good to see you, Mrs. Floros," Julia said, nodding to Meredith and simultaneously slipping into an adjacent chair. She noted their client's wan complexion, the worry lines in her forehead as she looked up with polite acknowledgment. "I hope you had a good lunch and saved a little room," Julia said, taking in both Iris and Meredith. "That the dessert menu?"

Meredith passed it to her. "I'm going all out for the mini Dulce de Leche Lava Cake. It's the specialty here. I recommended it to all my tourists when I conducted tours." She gave Julia a wink. "Even the mini order is enough for two. Want to share?"

"Works for me," Julia said. "And how about you, Mrs. Floros?"

"Has it not been long enough we know each other so you call me Iris?" She proffered a weak smile. And looked very tired.

"Of course. Iris," Julia said obediently. The elegant Greek woman seemed to command respect as for an elder. But there couldn't be more than a decade between them.

"I think I'll just have some more of that coffee. It's good and strong, and I..." She broke off with something of a sigh. "I'm still a little tired. Morning is usually my best time, but lately, I wake up tired." She held up her cup as a waiter approached, a silver pot in hand. "Maybe I should stop taking the pill to sleep."

Julia exchanged glances with Meredith. Lots of women took sleeping aids, and of course, Iris was a heart patient who would need adequate sleep. But it was no longer morning, and shouldn't she be more awake at one in the afternoon? "Do you always need help to sleep?" she asked casually.

"Sometimes, but Celia says the doctor wants me to get good rest while I travel. So, I take it, and I sleep." She set her cup down and smiled wearily. "I will stop so I am more awake in the day. Maybe I can remember more to help find my Helena."

When Meredith left to take Iris back to the hotel, Julia walked slowly through the lobby of the Mansion Hotel, vaguely disconcerted over Iris's pallor and her confession of feeling tired during the day. Maybe they could convince her to see a doctor here in Savannah, one who could no doubt consult by phone with a doctor at her Athenian clinic.

She allowed herself a slow walk through the hotel, taking in the art that adorned its walls. There were lavish displays everywhere as she meandered past conference rooms and toward the spas and more secluded areas of the grand hotel.

She headed back to the lobby, only slightly disoriented. One could use a GPS walking through this place! She had just passed a boutique marked CLOSED when she spotted two women standing together in a small alcove. Stunned, she realized that one was Celia.

Julia stepped back to keep hidden and peeked around again to make sure. No mistaking that rigid figure in a gray pantsuit the woman had worn before. Hatless now, dirty blond hair—or was it brown—pulled back over her ears. The face severe and attractive at the same time trained on her companion.

Surprise number two! Julia knew the woman in the crimson dress, dyed blond hair draping one side of her face. It fell to her shoulder while the other side was drawn dramatically back. Julia had seen her only once, but she knew her instantly. Deirdre Something who had poured a pink lady over Marco DeLuca at the Olde Pink House restaurant the night of Julia's double date with Meredith.

Julia pressed back against the wall, drawing in her breath. What was Celia doing here? And with the blond woman in the red dress whom DeLuca had introduced? She peered around the corner again. She was too far away to know what they were discussing, but she could hear hushed tones occasionally rising and falling. Julia peeked around the corner again. This time she saw Deirdre push back the billow of hair on her right side, revealing the distinct half-moon scar on her cheek. No mistake. It was her.

Suddenly the two women moved toward the corner where Julia huddled. But they made a right turn past her hiding place, not noticing her. Julia watched them walk away, Deirdre in wobbly high heels, Celia in Cuban heeled comfort shoes. They walked side by side, their matching steps oddly similar. They would be about the same height without shoes. They stopped talking, and at the end of the long, unpeopled hall, Celia turned left. Deirdre veered right. Neither looked back.

What were the chances that a nurse living in Greece would know Deirdre?

Chapter Eighteen

JULIA PROPELLED MEREDITH INTO HER office like a ship at full speed into harbor. She directed her to the couch by the window and told her what she'd seen while perusing the halls of the Mansion Hotel. Meredith's eyes widened. "It's very odd that Celia, who lives in Athens, would know Deirdre."

"And Deirdre knows Marco DeLuca. He may be the common denominator," Julia said. She could see the wheels turning in her partner's methodical mind. It was Meredith's way to take her time corralling her thoughts, but Julia had to force herself to sit still. They had to do something. Clearly the two women she had seen engaged in secret conversation knew each other. Julia could feel her pulse racing, ready for action. But what action?

Meredith pursed her lips briefly and gave voice to her thoughts. "It's possible that the two women might have a connection that has nothing to do with DeLuca. We know that Celia worked in Baltimore before going to Athens to take care of her mother-in-law." She frowned, an indication that she might not have convinced herself.

"I suppose we could simply confront Celia. Ask her straight out about Deirdre," Julia said.

"Yes, but we'd want to be careful not to convey suspicion if…"

"If there *is* a connection to DeLuca," Julia finished for her.

And if so, what did it mean? Julia felt a shiver pass through her. "Well, the first thing we need to do is have Carmen work her magic and see what she can bring up about both ladies. We probably should have done it before now." Meredith picked up the phone.

"Glad you're back." Carmen appeared in the doorway of Julia's office as though she'd been summoned. "There were a few calls while you were out." She glanced from one to the other, brown eyes alert and inquisitive.

Wily girl, Julia thought, marveling again at Carmen's perspicacity. It was Meredith's word for her and meant, quite appropriately "the quality of having ready insight."

Meredith waved Carmen in, quickly getting to the point. "We need you to find everything you can on Celia Angelos, Iris Floros's companion and nurse." She paused, scribbling details on a pad. "She says she was raised in Baltimore, Maryland, but moved to Athens to take care of her husband's ailing mother. Then she entered the home health care system in that city, or maybe in one of the suburbs like Marousi, where Iris and her husband had their studio."

"Yes," Julia added, excitement rising. She recalled that Celia had claimed to have studied art herself—"dabbled in pastels." "Maybe Celia heard about Iris's plan to come to the States through some local artist's guild."

"Sí, *entiendo*," Carmen said, signaling that she understood. Her eyes widened. "You think she's not what she says she is?" An intriguing glint shone in her brown eyes.

"We just need to check her story," Meredith said.

"And there's one more name we want you to plug in," Julia said as Meredith scribbled notes for Carmen. She had been searching her brain for Deirdre's last name. Jones? James? She knew it was one syllable and began with J. A common name, unlike "Deirdre." Finding her might be difficult without a confirmed last name, but Julia was confident that Carmen could locate her.

"And I will see what other information I can dredge up," Julia added, straightening her shoulders. After all, she was no slouch navigating the information superhighway.

When Carmen was gone, Julia stood up, her nerves popping. "Coffee. I'll get it," she said without preamble and headed to the door. She turned back before going through it. "There's something else troubling me right now."

Meredith waited, setting her pen on the low table by the couch.

"That business about sleeping pills. Iris said they were Celia's idea, that her doctor ordered rest while she traveled abroad. You don't suppose—?"

Meredith picked up the pen again, tapped it on the table. "You're thinking Celia might be deliberately keeping her sedated?"

Julia shrugged. The thought had crossed her mind, and yet Celia didn't strike her as someone who would deliberately endanger another person.

"Iris went off half-cocked when she left the hotel on her own to go to the gallery," Meredith said. "Later, she disappeared again and confronted DeLuca directly. With her heart condition, some restraint might have been necessary."

Julia drew a long breath. That was a reasonable explanation. "All the same, we need to keep our eyes open."

"And make sure Iris is all right. I am going to have a talk with her," Meredith said, eyes narrowing. "She needs to be checked by a physician here. One who will consult with her doctor in Athens." She paused, tapping the desk again.

"How about your cardiologist?" Julia suggested.

Meredith tilted her head. "Of course, Dr. Parker is exactly who Iris should see. He's excellent in his field—and besides, he's very attentive and caring." She frowned. "But also very busy. Still, when I called on him in a pinch when one of our tourists got sick, he stepped in to help." She leaned forward, brightening. "I'll call him right now. With any luck he'll be able to fit Iris in, maybe even this afternoon."

"Great," Julia said. She glanced at the clock on the wall. "While you do that, I'm going to pay Mr. Eduardo DeLuca a visit. My mother arranged for me to go on her behalf. When she read that he was well enough to go home, it really made her day."

"And if he has any information on the current art exhibit his nephew is hosting, it will make our day!" Meredith added with a hopeful grin.

Julia headed away from the agency, taking along the get-well card her mother had asked her to deliver. Her instincts told her that Marco DeLuca was involved somehow with the fabled "Desdemona," and she was determined to get to the bottom of it. Maybe with a little help from Eduardo and Oneta DeLuca.

The aesthetically pleasing home was tucked back from the street and heavily shaded by beautiful maples that had probably stood there for many decades. The front door of light oak boasted a decorative oval inset of frosted glass. All in all, the aspect was one of good taste and old money, the kind of surroundings one might expect of an art collector and gallery owner for thirty years or more.

After a few minutes, the door opened to reveal a petite woman with short gray hair drawn back from a lean face. Expressive gray eyes widened warily and quickly warmed.

"I'm Julia Foley—Bonnie Jean Waverly's daughter...."

"Yes, of course," she said, a smile softening her anxious face. "We've been expecting you." She kept her cultured voice low, presumably because of the proximity of her convalescing husband. "Please, come in."

"My mother asked me to bring this." Julia handed her the pale blue envelope bearing her mother's careful script. "She is very happy that Mr. DeLuca is doing so much better."

"Oh, how kind," she said, glancing down at the card. "Bonnie Jean was always so thoughtful." She looked back up at Julia, concern etched in her genteel face. "And how is your mother? It's been such a long time since I've seen her."

"She's fine, Mrs. DeLuca. She had a slight fall recently but she's mending well."

"Call me Oneta, dear—and please, come in." She gestured as she moved into a large living room, the walls of which were tastefully adorned with beautifully framed art. Julia recognized the styles of impressionism and rococo—classic works she supposed had enjoyed prominent places in the Winston under earlier management.

She followed her host into an alcove off the main parlor where Eduardo sat in a wheelchair, a plaid blanket across his knees. He wore a long-sleeved polo shirt of dark blue that contrasted sharply with the thick white hair that waved back from a high furrowed brow. Curious blue eyes with an unusual dreamy aspect regarded her.

"Eduardo, this is Julia Foley. Bonnie Jean's daughter." She touched a hand to the man's shoulder. "She brought this card from her." She showed him the envelope containing his name and placed it on a small table near his chair. "We can read it together later, but Julia wants to speak with you."

Eduardo bent slightly forward as though in a formal bow. His eyes registered welcome, but his lips barely moved.

"I'm very happy to meet you," Julia said. She held his gaze as she sat down on the love seat across from him. "Mother speaks highly of you as well as the Winston. She so enjoyed serving on the arts committee you chaired."

"You wanted to see Eduardo about something related to the gallery." Oneta's voice lifted in inquiry while simultaneously her eyes conveyed a warning to be brief.

"Yes," Julia said. "You see, I'm trying to locate a young artist who might have a connection to an exhibit at the gallery."

Quick interest sparked in Eduardo's watery blue gaze. "The gallery," Eduardo repeated haltingly. Only the left side of his mouth formed the words.

"The reopening was wonderful," Julia hurried on. "It was really an excellent event. Our client who was present believes she knows the artist who was featured."

Eduardo nodded, but it was Oneta who spoke. "Julia is a private investigator."

A wary look sprang to Eduardo's face, but he made another little bow to register that he understood.

People were often put off guard at the mention of the word *investigator,* but Julia couldn't help wondering if there was more to his reaction.

"A missing person case," Julia said casually, to put him at ease. "We inquired about the artist—a young woman—but your nephew was unable to provide any information." She heard a quick intake of breath from Oneta. The formerly soft eyes had narrowed in her pleasant face, but she said nothing.

"Marco showcases many artists," Eduardo said slowly, taking visible care with his pronunciation.

How difficult, Julia thought. *The mind moves quickly but its expressions are laborious and awkward.* And she felt deep sympathy for the cultured man so limited by the effects of his stroke.

Eduardo spoke slowly, eyes trained on Julia's face. "Marco's contacts are broad—like his father's."

Oneta broke in with a hint of irony. "In between his various travels he seems to have taken fresh interest in his uncle's gallery." She gave a dismissive shrug of her shoulders. "For years he barely had time for a holiday visit. Now..." She pressed her lips together as though to withhold something she had wanted to say. After a moment she released a weary breath. "Eduardo feels obliged to look after the boy's interests now that his brother Paulo is gone."

The tension was palpable. Oneta DeLuca didn't approve of Marco. Julia appealed to them both. "I was wondering—perhaps from your long association with artists and agents—if you might know the name 'Desdemona.' Perhaps your nephew might have said something about her?"

Eduardo's brow furrowed more deeply, and his blue eyes clouded. "I am sorry," he said, the affected side of his mouth rigid. Then he closed his eyes and leaned back in his wheelchair. The plaid blanket began to slide off his knees.

Oneta quickly stood to right it with a meaningful glance in Julia's direction. "My husband needs to rest." She released the brake on his chair. "I'll be back in a few minutes if you care to wait."

"Sorry," Eduardo said again but did not raise his head.

As Julia waited for Oneta to return, she studied the lovely alcove and the living area beyond with its luxurious paintings and furniture. A shelf near the window contained books about art as well as figurines and mementos no doubt meaningful to the DeLucas. A bronze sculpture of a dancing nymph, an art deco figure of a child. Julia wondered if Iris had created such objects in her Marousi studio.

Julia glanced at the small table near the spot where Eduardo had been sitting. Cards, books, and envelopes were scattered there and, adding to it, the blue envelope from her mother. No doubt Eduardo would sit in this spot to enjoy the sunshine during his convalescence. Oneta reappeared, pushing back a lock of hair that strayed over her forehead. She seemed weary—and no wonder. Caregiving was hard work. Yet she stepped lithely into the alcove and sat, drawing her skirt over her knees with a sweeping gesture like a dancer.

"There now, Julia, can I offer you coffee or a cold drink?"

"Please don't bother," Julia said. "I appreciate the opportunity to talk to you and Eduardo."

"Even though we have little to offer you in the information department," she acknowledged with a sigh as she began to order the tumble of cards and letters on the table. "My husband is often too generous, especially where Paulo's family is concerned." She pushed her lips out briefly in a contemplative gesture. "After Paulo died, Eduardo felt he had to watch out for those left behind."

"Like Marco," Julia said. "But he seems to be quite self-sufficient."

"Self-sufficient, perhaps, but never satisfied. His father provided an adequate inheritance, but Marco has expensive tastes." Her eyes narrowed again. "He's become Mr. Attentive now after many remote years. Sends gifts and cards, trinkets from his travels. Postcards…like this one." She tossed a colorful card casually across the table to Julia.

It was a rendering of the Acropolis at sunset, golden light splaying over the ancient structure. She felt her pulse jump but made herself turn the card over slowly, as though only mildly interested and read a scrawled message: "There's nothing like the Acropolis this time of year. Wishing you well and hope Uncle Eddie is recovering by leaps and bounds. Yours always, Marco." The signature was a scribbled oversized *M*. Julia cast her eyes up to the postmark and was immediately jolted. Marco DeLuca had mailed it from Athens less than three weeks ago!

"Eddie," Oneta said with undisguised scorn. "Eduardo hates being called that." She stopped fiddling with the objects on the table and leaned back against the chair with another sigh. "Well, I'm sorry we can't aid you in helping your client, but I do hope she finds her granddaughter—wherever she is."

Julia realized she hadn't paid attention to what Oneta had said but recognized that the visit was nearing its close. "Well," she said brightly, "it was really wonderful to meet you. My mother has spoken of you, and now I have met you. Thank you." She paused, turning the postcard over nonchalantly. "As it happens, my client is fond of the city of Athens. Would you mind if I borrowed this to show her?"

Oneta seemed not to think the request strange. She made a sweep of her hand again. "Take it. And keep it. No need to return it."

Julia tucked it into her purse and pushed forward in the upholstered chair. "Thank you again for taking time to see me. I will be praying for your husband's continued progress, Oneta—and for you. The role of the caregiver is not an easy one."

"For Eduardo, I would give a hundred years if it was needed." She gave her head a little dignified toss, but her deep gray eyes misted.

Julia shook her hand and left the DeLuca home, the postcard burning through the fabric of her purse. That Marco had been in Athens at the same time Iris was planning an imminent trip to the States wasn't conclusive of anything. But she did have a handwriting sample—from which an investigator worth her salt could learn a lot.

As she drove away from the DeLucas' home, she switched on the device connected to the radio and checked her messages. The first was from Cassie, asking Julia to call her. She pushed the button and waited for her sister to pick up.

"Cassie?"

"There you are," Cassie said, sounding weary or worried or harassed.

Julia sat up. "Is everything all right?"

"Well, I'm not sure."

"I'm sorry I missed your call earlier. I was out on an errand and I... Never mind. What do you mean you're not sure?" Julia felt sudden irritation—she was in no mood for guessing.

"It's Ma. She won't eat. Won't eat anything I fixed for her today. I know I'm not a great cook like you, but I thought we were doing okay."

Julia groaned.

"I mean, she ate half a piece of toast at breakfast and went up to her room. I brought her lunch up on a tray when she didn't come down."

"Did something happen. Is she sick? Did you call her doctor?"

"She just sits there staring out the window. Or at the photo of her and Dad." Cassie's voice rose in worry or frustration. "I ask her does she feel all right, and she says she's fine. Half an hour later I look, and she's still sitting there doing nothing."

Julia waited as her mind absorbed what Cassie was telling her. She sighed. "It's that time, you know," she said finally. "Dad's birthday. Mom gets that way." She heard the resignation in her own voice.

"I'm sorry...," Cassie began.

"You've nothing to be sorry about. I'm just glad you're there. You're doing a good job, Cassie." She paused. "Mom's happy you're there too, I know. It's hard for her right now." She said goodbye and hung up. She was itching to get back to the office and show the postcard to Meredith. But she would have to check on her mother first.

She speed-dialed Meredith. "You'll never guess what I found out today while visiting Eduardo and Oneta DeLuca."

"Tell me it's good news," Meredith said.

"It's better than good. I have a handwritten postcard from Marco to his aunt and uncle—dated three weeks ago from Athens."

Silence. Julia could almost hear the wheels spinning in her partner's analytical mind. Three weeks!

Finally, Meredith said, "Proves only that he traveled to Greece—possibly in connection with his export business." She paused. "But it wouldn't hurt to have Curt Constantine take a look."

Chapter Nineteen

Julia climbed the familiar steps to her childhood home, wondering what she would find. Would Mom still be moping in her room, staring out the window? It was already past four o'clock. Surely she had snapped out of it. It wasn't like her mother to pine away, even in illness. Except perhaps on Dad's birthday. But something had been eating at her. Julia would wager, if she were a betting woman, that it was something more than nostalgia for the man she had loved. She lifted a prayer for her mother and for Cassie and for their small struggling family.

She tapped lightly at the front door, leaving the spare key above the lintel. Mom insisted on leaving it there, despite warnings that the old-fashioned practice just didn't work in these days of new-fashioned crime. Old habits were hard to break, and her mother's stubborn will even harder to manage.

Cassie appeared, a tea towel over one shoulder. Wisps of russet hair clung damply around her face, which appeared flushed, her blue eyes red-rimmed. She looked as though she might have been crying, but she flashed a brave smile when she saw her sister at the door. "Come on in. I was just cleaning up a spill on the kitchen floor. My fault. I wasn't looking where I was going and dumped a whole pot of coffee. At least it didn't break." She scurried back to her task.

Julia followed, amused to see Cassie in her new domestic role. It was strange to see her once well-enameled nails blunt and ragged. She grabbed a handful of paper towels and bent to help her sister with the cleanup. After wiping up the remainder of the spill, she dropped the paper towels into the trash. "How's Mom now?"

Cassie wiped up the last dregs and dropped down in a kitchen chair. "When she came down for breakfast this morning she hardly said two words to me. And she only ate half a piece of toast. Then she picked up that African violet you brought and went upstairs. She's been there all day."

Julia frowned, scanned the windowsill where Mom had told her to deposit the plant. She stared at the bare spot. Mom never put plants in her room.

Cassie shrugged and spread her hands. "She's been very strange the last few days. Sometimes she seems glad I've come home, and then other times it's like I'm not even here." She looked down at her reddened hands.

Julia's heart melted. It hadn't been easy for Cassie, but she seemed to be trying hard to make up for past failures. "Are you all right?" she asked softly.

Cassie pushed her wild hair back from her forehead. "Sure, I'm fine. You know me. Roll with the punches Casandra Sue." But the cocky tone had lost its resiliency. She tossed one blue-jeaned leg over the other and began to fiddle with her fingers.

Casandra Sue. Julia had rarely heard Cassie's full name. Dad used to tell her that her name had its origins in Greek myth, though they'd chosen to spell Cassie's name differently. Cassandra was a Trojan princess, the daughter of Priam and Hecuba. She was given the gift of prophecy by Apollo, but when she spurned his advances he cursed her so nobody would believe her prophecies. Julia wondered if Cassie remembered this and thought ironically of Iris Floros and what recent developments could mean for finding her granddaughter.

But one problem at a time.

"I'm not going back to him." Cassie's flat statement fell on the air in a tone so soft Julia wondered if she'd heard right. *Back to whom? Calvin?*

"Not this time," Cassie continued, fixing her glance somewhere over the top of Julia's head.

"Oh, Cassie," Julia whispered.

"Don't say you're sorry. I know you always thought he was wrong for me. Of course, he was, but I thought I loved him. I thought he loved me. I'm beginning to understand that I don't know the first thing about love. Somehow being here…" She let her words fall away, and for some minutes neither sister spoke.

"He emptied our joint account," Cassie said, her voice flat. "Says he'll replace my half as soon as he gets on his feet. 'Trust me,' he says." Fresh tears sprang into her eyes. "I never really trusted him. Just loved him—or thought I did." The last words were barely a whisper.

Julia didn't know what to say. In the quietness she simply prayed for her hurting sister and for the balm that would heal them all.

Abruptly, Cassie stood. "Right," she said, as though the past few seconds hadn't happened. "Let's go see how Ma's doing." Julia followed Cassie out of the kitchen. "She came down this morning in her best baby blue sweater set and poured herself a cup of coffee. Said yes when I asked her if she slept well. End of conversation. Half a piece of toast and off upstairs, carrying that plant with her good arm."

Julia stepped into her mother's room after tapping lightly on the partially open door. All was quiet, orderly, the bed neatly made with the hospital sling lying on her patchwork quilt. Mom sat in her chintz-covered chair with her hands folded in her lap. Silver-white hair coiled around her ear and fell gently to her shoulder. She wore a cashmere cardigan of pale blue. Her eyes of the same color were fixed on the late afternoon landscape beyond the window. Maggie Lu's violet rested on the small round table. Next to it were the faux hurricane lamp with hand-painted roses and the photograph of Dad and Mom in her diamond necklace.

Julia embraced it all in a single glance, thinking that the picture would be engrained in her mind for all time to come.

Mom's head made the smallest turn toward her daughters. "Well, since you're both here, you might as well come on in," she said without taking her eyes from the window. Her voice seemed tired and weak, despite the usual ironic twist to her invitation. "You might as well know what a dismal failure your mother is."

The words had the effect of a slap, and Julia stopped in her tracks. She caught Cassie's eye, saw her own shock registered there.

"Mom?" Julia began, ignoring the elephant in the room. "I just stopped by to see how you are." She stepped around the chair to sit down on the end of the bed and face her mother. Cassie sat down beside her. To anyone watching, it might appear that they were poised to listen to a favorite story before being trundled off to their beds.

Mom turned to look at the two of them. Her eyes, usually bright and calculating, were dull and clouded. She said nothing, looking from Julia to Cassie and shaking her head slowly.

"Mom, what are you talking about?" Julia asked, leaning forward, and engaging her mother's attention. "You aren't and have never been a…" *What was it she had called herself? A dismal failure?*

"Ma? You all right?" Cassie asked in a frightened voice.

"I am what I said I am," Mom said. "I failed you and your father. Others too." She clasped her good arm over the sprained one, wincing as though it hurt, or as though a blast of cold air had chilled her. "All these years I hid the truth. Your father died without knowing."

Julia's breath caught. *Knowing what? What truth could she be talking about?*

"The young woman I hurt… She didn't deserve it," Mom said, a shudder passing over her fragile form. She stared out through the window and spoke in a ghostly whisper. "You girls never knew."

No one said anything—the stillness in the room lay heavy and too deep to penetrate. Julia looked at Cassie—saw her own confusion reflected in her sister's blue eyes.

A nostalgic sorrow crept into Mom's voice. "She was a good worker—a really good worker. I never had to worry when I was away working late on some committee or other. She'd have dinner ready and never complain. She'd take on the heavy work I couldn't do— always said it wasn't hard, that she loved making our lives easier."

Julia swallowed against a lump in her throat. What could a decades-old connection have to do with her mother's strange confession? "Mom?" Julia heard her own voice as though it came from far away.

Her mother lifted the photograph from the table and held it in front of her, clouded eyes full of sadness. "It was hard on Malcolm," she said, sniffling back tears. "Your father liked her—said hiring her was the best thing we'd done. The truth was she became like part of the family. You girls were living your own lives...."

Julia longed to reach out to her mother, whose pain seemed palpable, but she dug her fingers into her palms and waited.

Mom traced her fingers over the necklace in the photograph and said nothing for a long moment. Then she took a breath, released it, and resumed. "For a long time, I haven't been able to look at that necklace, let alone wear it." In a softer voice, she added, "I loved it, you know—not just because it was beautiful, but because it belonged to the aunt who was so special to me since I was a child."

Julia knew Aunt Faith had been Mom's favorite, but she hadn't realized the depth of their relationship.

A tear fell on her mother's blue sweater. She made no attempt to wipe it away.

Julia heard Cassie's breath catch. She touched her sister's hand to signal that they should wait. Mom had more to say.

"When my necklace disappeared, I was absolutely distraught. Your father and I looked everywhere. And then I thought I knew." She drew another deep breath. "I remembered seeing *her*. She was in my bedroom. She often picked up after me when I was especially busy. But that day I remembered how she had coiled my necklace around her neck and admired it in the mirror before putting it away in its box.

"Oh, Ma," Cassie whispered.

"She denied taking it. But the more time passed, the more bitter I became. I was sure she was the one who had taken it. There had been no break-in, and nothing else was missing. I accused her unmercifully, and I made your father let her go." She shook her head. "I can still see that terrible wounded look in her eyes.

"We didn't make an official complaint, and she left. I didn't know where she went or what became of her in the years that followed. Then one day, I discovered..." Her voice dropped to an even lower whisper. "I...I found the necklace wedged into a crack in the floorboard behind my dresser."

Julia's heart ached for her mother—and for the young woman her father had sent away. "Oh, Mom, I'm sorry."

She rushed on, her eyes flashing now. "I convinced myself that she was fine—she'd go on with her life. But I could never forget, especially when your father's birthday comes around. I have lived it over and over. He fired her on the day she'd made his birthday cake that I was going to decorate in a golfing motif."

Mom's sad eyes sought Julia's. "She did make something of her life—despite my terrible wrong. And then Magnolia suddenly became part of your life and I learned that Charlene was her daughter...."

"Charlene?" Julia whispered.

"Yes, it was Magnolia's daughter, Charlene, who I blamed for my lost necklace. I couldn't face them, couldn't face myself and admit what I had done all those years ago."

Julia felt her own eyes fill. No wonder her mother had been troubled. The guilt must have been awful. She who always tried to do the right thing, to help people and to fight for justice hadn't been able to face this very personal truth. Julia reached to clasp her mother's hands. "But you're admitting it now, Mom. And God will forgive you, as we do. And as Charlene will."

Cassie got up to put an arm around her mother's shoulder. "God knows I've made bigger mistakes than you in my life, Ma. Admitting them is the first step—for both of us."

"I'm glad you told us, Mom," Julia said softly.

"My girls," Mom said with a deeper tenderness than Julia had ever heard from her mother's lips. The tears slid quietly down her face.

Maggie Lu had known a long time ago that Julia was Bonnie Jean Waverly's daughter. Julia was sure of it. And she thought she knew the moment Charlene had made the connection. It was that day in the restaurant when she'd gone all silent and wide-eyed at the mention of the name "Bonnie Jean Waverly." All this time, neither of them had mentioned it; mother and daughter had merely reflected the grace that lived in their hearts. It was a grace that would extend to Mom when they received her apology all these many years later. Julia knew that apology would come very soon. Once her mind was made up, Mom would waste no time. What a blessing that would be.

Julia left her mother and sister with a light heart. The source of Mom's angst had been revealed. Her mother would make things right with two people she had hurt by her long-ago deception. And her own recovery would be expedited. Not to mention that Cassie too was on her way to her own healing. What more could a girl ask?

"Wisdom for what to do about Iris Floros and Helena Meyer!" Julia whispered. Marco DeLuca, Deirdre, and Celia Angelos had to be linked by a common bond—one that most certainly included the granddaughter of Iris Floros. It had become even more likely since discovering that Marco had been in Athens as lately as three weeks ago.

Chapter Twenty

It had been too late to return to the agency, but Julia had checked in with Meredith by phone once she and Beau had dined on a late supper of ravioli and sunflower salad. She had learned that Dr. Adam Parker confirmed the diagnosis of chronic stable angina but that Iris was doing pretty well considering all she'd been through.

At the office the next morning, Meredith picked up the thread of Iris's visit to the cardiologist. "She takes a medicine called 'Glycerine trinitrate.' Dr. Parker says he concurs with the treatment prescribed by her doctor in Greece. It's what he would have recommended—along with rest and avoiding stress."

Julia frowned, realizing how much stress Iris was experiencing now. "What did Iris have to say about all that?" Julia asked.

"That she's just fine, thank you very much!" Meredith laughed. "By the way, Celia checks out with the Home Health Services in Athens. She's been with them for five years, plus a few months. Her record's clear."

Curious, Julia thought. It was a relief to know that Celia was who she said she was. But how did she know Deirdre? And how did Marco DeLuca fit in the picture? He'd been in Athens three weeks before—while Iris and Celia were planning a trip. Was it all a huge coincidence?

"Maggie Lu found something very interesting," Meredith said, breaking Julia's reverie. "Something Carmen will particularly be anxious to see."

"*¿Qué?*" The familiar voice of their receptionist emanated from the doorway. "What will Carmen be anxious to see?"

Did the girl have a pipeline to their thoughts? Or a high-tech military-grade hearing device?

"And good morning to you," Julia said drily, waving her in. "Have you turned up anything interesting on nurse Celia?"

"*¡Aye!* Not about nurse Celia, but I found something on the other lady."

"Deirdre?" Julia leaned toward Carmen.

"Deirdre Jaynes." Carmen narrowed her eyes and read something from a paper in her hand. "PR specialist. University of Georgia, 1998. Business Manager for M.L. DeLuca Enterprises, Savannah, Georgia, since 2016."

Ah, Julia thought. *So, Deirdre is indeed a colleague of Marco's. Interesting.*

Meredith absorbed the information silently, running a hand through her short blond curls. Then she reached into the bottom drawer of her desk and withdrew a leather binder. "Maggie Lu found an interesting news clipping in a box belonging to Delyse. I've made copies for each of us." She handed them to Julia and Carmen.

Julia exchanged a glance with Carmen and saw the young woman's eyes widen in anticipation. She was convinced that the girl Delyse wrote about in her journal once roamed the streets of Atlanta with her.

Holding the original clipping, Meredith cleared her throat. "It's dated August 13, 2009. No picture and just these spare lines: 'Atlanta police discovered the body of an eight-year-old male in the warehouse district. His death has been attributed to an accidental fall from an alley scaffolding where he had allegedly been playing with other children who fled the scene. The boy has been identified as Desmond Satterlee of 3411 Peachtree Court.'"

Utter silence reigned as Julia absorbed the significance of the name. Not the unfamiliar surname "Satterlee," but "Desmond." Could he be the little boy who purportedly followed "the Dove" around as she painted warehouse walls? Could it have significance for the name appropriated by the runaway artist Desdemona?

"Des…," Carmen whispered. "I remember now. The Dove used to call him Des!" Her brown eyes, saucerlike, flew from Meredith to Julia and back to the copy of the newspaper clipping. "She loved that little boy. She—"

"Was he her brother?" Julia's thoughts tumbled over one another in rapid-fire succession. But the art connection! And the secretive behavior of Marco DeLuca, Deirdre Jaynes, and Iris's nurse companion. Was Desdemona Iris's granddaughter or Carmen's old street acquaintance? Iris said she had no knowledge of another child in the family, but was it possible that Donald "Duke" Meyer had remarried after Iris's daughter died, and that there had been a child? But what of the name "Satterlee"?

"It doesn't follow conclusively that our disappearing artist called herself 'Desdemona' after Desmond," Meredith said, vigorously tapping her fingers on the conference table. "The similarity gives one pause, but it could be a coincidence." Her brows knit together in a golden line.

When Carmen left the table to respond to someone in the outer office, Meredith got up and closed the door. "There's been nothing clear-cut about this case from the very beginning," she said, pacing from door to desk and back. "We've been focusing on the DeLuca connection, and I still think he's involved." She held Julia's gaze. "I asked Carter to do some checking into DeLuca's import/export dealings, particularly involving international finance."

Julia felt her pulse rise. "Anything?" she urged.

"Well, DeLuca has no convictions attached to his name, but there's at least one ongoing investigation into the fraudulent sale of some expensive paintings. And five years ago, he was a suspect in an insider trading scam. It was settled out of court, but our gallery owner's art dealings leave a lot to be desired. And judging by his hostile reactions to our inquiries, I'd say he has some secret he doesn't want the world to know."

Julia shivered, recalling her confrontation with DeLuca.

"The man could be dangerous," Meredith said. "But at least for a couple of days he's out of town. I had Carter check."

The conference phone buzzed. "It's Mr. Constantine for you," Carmen said when Julia picked up.

They had asked Curt to analyze the handwriting on the postcard Oneta DeLuca had given Julia. He was to compare it with Desdemona's signature from the painting Iris had bought for $1,200. Julia switched the phone to speaker and, sitting down, exchanged a hopeful look with Meredith.

You had to listen carefully due to Curt Constantine's husky voice combined with his Scottish brogue. Julia imagined him now, his thick head of white hair that had once been ginger, the little goatee that bobbed against his bow tie when he spoke.

"I've had a wee look at those signatures. I can't be sure how a court would deal with it if it came to that, mind ye," he said. "But I can tell ye that the two signatures were penned by the same individual."

Julia stared as Meredith thanked Curt and ended the call. Nothing about this entire case made sense. She felt an overwhelming weariness. It wasn't so much a physical fatigue but an emotional one. So much had happened with Mom and Cassie.

"This is terrible," Meredith said, fingers tapping wildly on her desk. "If DeLuca signed Desdemona's name to those paintings, why would Helena allow it?"

"Maybe she doesn't know," Julia said, her mind buzzing. *Or doesn't understand that she's being manipulated?* Maybe there was no Desdemona. And if that was the case, Julia wondered, had Iris Floros been completely deluded about her granddaughter? If such a young artist did exist, perhaps she was the young woman of Carmen's memory. Or someone no one knew at all.

Julia became aware of scuffling sounds in the outer office. Raised voices, Carmen's placating tones. Then a quick rapping on the office door. Before she or Meredith could rise to open it, Carmen came in, face flushed.

"I'm sorry. I told her you were busy, but she wouldn't wait."

Iris Floros burst into the conference room, green shawl flapping over her black dress. Strands of white hair that had escaped their confining combs trembled around her face. Eyes like hot coals blazed.

"Mrs. Floros! Iris!" Julia exclaimed, rising.

The fiery Greek sculptor drew herself up to her full height, struggling to maintain decorum as she came toward them.

"Please, sit down," Meredith said, indicating a chair by the desk.

Iris remained on her feet. "I'm sorry to intrude, but I have decided." She clutched her purse against her chest. "I do not wish to retain you detectives further." Iris shook her head so vehemently that more wisps of hair came loose from her chignon. Bright spots appeared on her pale cheeks as she fumbled with the clasp of her purse. "I am prepared to pay what I owe for your time."

Julia searched their client's ashen face. Had Iris hired a taxi? Walked to the agency? What had come over her? "Iris, where is Celia?"

"She is outside, waiting in the car. I come to pay what I owe." She shook her leather bag with trembling fingers.

"Mrs. Floros, we can see you're upset," Meredith said calmly. "Please sit down. Tell us how we can help."

She sat heavily and attempted visibly to collect herself. Sniffing, she thrust her head up. "I thank you for your efforts, but it is clear you cannot find my granddaughter, and she does not wish to be found. I have decided. I will return to Marousi. Celia has arranged tickets for tomorrow."

"But, Iris," Julia broke in, astounded. "We are so close. We are finding things out. Surely it won't take much longer before we are able to…"

"No! My mind is made up." She clamped her jaw tight, and Julia could see the rippling veins at her temples. Then she opened her mouth again. "I have much business back home. I must go back. You have only to tell me what I owe." A look of sudden desperation flared from her nearly black pupils.

"What is wrong, Iris?" Julia asked, her heart racing. "You were so intent on finding Helena. What has happened?"

"What has happened is that you do not find her!" Her voice turned brittle, accusatory, as on the night she had confronted Marco DeLuca at the gallery. "So I put a stop to this now. You do not need to look further. I will write a check to pay!"

What had frightened Iris away from the mission that had brought her across the ocean? Something had gotten to her—or someone.

Julia narrowed her eyes to pierce the dark ones across from her. "What are you afraid of, Iris?"

"I fear nothing!" she said, rising from the chair and fumbling in her purse. She thrust a business card onto the table. When Julia and Meredith only looked at it, she blew out her breath. "Very well, when the bill is ready, you send to me. I will pay." She fled to the door.

"Iris, please." Julia watched the relentless march of sturdy black shoes across the floor.

What could they do, aside from physically restraining her? Rush to the waiting car and confront Celia? Demand to know her connection to Marco DeLuca and Deirdre Jaynes? There was the noisy rush of the front doors closing, then the whirr of an engine racing away.

Carmen appeared in the doorway of the office. "What in the world has gotten into her?"

"That's what we'd like to know." Julia, furiously twisting her hair around her right ear, stopped in mid twirl. "Carmen, check all outgoing flights to Athens for tomorrow."

"Got it," Carmen said, turning to carry out the instruction. Then, pausing to stroke the door frame, she said, "Do you still want to know where to find Deirdre Jaynes?"

Julia stared at their resourceful assistant. "You found her?"

"Got the coordinates to her place outside Savannah. And believe me, without them you'd never locate that house."

Julia turned to Meredith. "Iris has dismissed us, but are you thinking what I'm thinking?"

"What are we waiting for?" Meredith asked, reaching for the suit jacket. "I'm not buying our grandmother's story."

"There's something else," Carmen said, her eyes dark with mystery. "Deirdre Jaynes was Deirdre Hamilton before she married Enoch Jaynes, but I traced her back to her maiden name. It was Meyer."

Julia's heart beat double time. Could Deirdre be related to Donald "Duke" Meyer? What did it all mean?

With instructions for Carmen to text flight information and any other developments, they piled quickly into Julia's car.

The coordinates Carmen had mapped out took them to the far end of Skidaway Island, near the Wassaw National Wildlife Refuge. A dozen turns led them deeper into a remote area. Houses grew fewer and farther apart until the road turned into something akin to a cow path. Dense trees and heavy foliage made visibility difficult. Added to the problem was the heavy rain that had morphed into a full-blown thunderstorm.

"Can this be right?" Meredith asked, poring over Carmen's directions.

"I guess we'll know when we get there," Julia said, peering through the rain-slashed windshield. "If someone wanted to hide out, this would be a perfect place." How had Helena and Deirdre gotten involved with Marco DeLuca? At least DeLuca was out of town; maybe they could scour the truth from Deirdre Jaynes, née Meyer.

After several more turns, a house came into view. A sturdy stone and brick structure likely built in the '90s stood on a broad stretch of land dense with pines and hickory. A low fence surrounded the house. A late-model Kia was parked at the end of a winding driveway.

Rain pelted Julia's car, and a clap of thunder broke the afternoon air. Meredith stopped near a grove of loblolly pines and reached for her umbrella. Julia pulled up the hood of her anorak.

They climbed out of the car and scurried toward the house, grateful that DeLuca was away. Hopefully, miles away from Savannah! Julia prayed that no one in the house was watching, perhaps scrambling to lock them out. Light shone from a window on the lower level. Serene. Domestic. Ordinary. Maybe…

They reached the door as lightning flashed and a rumble of thunder shook the ground. They had decided to walk right up to the door and confront whoever was inside. But they were still stunned when Deirdre herself opened the door.

Gone was the glamorous figure in a crimson dress. Deirdre might be any fortysomething homemaker in faded jeans and oversized shirt. A bandana held back her platinum hair. Gray-green eyes peered at them with an unreadable expression. The crescent moon scar at her right cheek was clearly visible.

Deirdre dropped her arms to her sides, inclined her head slightly, and stepped back from the door with a sigh. Tired sage-colored eyes focused on Julia. Her voice when she spoke was heavy with resignation. "I wondered how long it would take you to find me."

"Deirdre Jaynes?" Julia asked, though she had no doubt about the woman's identity.

"Of course," she said simply.

"You expected us?" Julia asked with quiet incredulity. She broke her gaze from Deirdre to scan the home's interior. A large living room with vaulted ceiling. Light oak furniture, tasteful accents. A curving staircase. Who else was here?

"Dilly?"

A young woman appeared near the bottom of the stairs. Slender, fairylike, with a maze of dark hair spilling over a flowered smock, she observed them with probing eyes the color of sapphire. One delicate hand rested on the bannister, the other held a paintbrush poised as though about to stroke an unseen canvas.

At the young woman's voice, Deirdre turned. "I believe these ladies are looking for you," she said in a world-weary way. She returned her gaze to Julia. "And this," she said with a sweeping gesture, "is my niece, Helena Meyer."

Julia stared at what seemed an apparition. They had wondered if she was really flesh and blood and not a ghost that lived in a frightened grandmother's imagination.

Helena descended the final two steps, blue eyes wide with apparent confusion.

Julia sidestepped Deirdre to face Helena. "Do you know that your grandmother is looking for you? That she traveled all the way from Athens to find you?"

Helena's left hand flew to her chest, grasped something beneath her clothes. "Grandmama? My grandmama is here? But when? How?" The blue eyes flashed to Deirdre. "Dilly?"

"I wanted to tell you," Deirdre told her in a small voice that gradually gained strength. "I tried to find a way. I tried to get him to stop all this—this..." Both hands flew to her temples, then dropped away.

"You've been keeping her hidden away here!" Julia said, the anger and frustration of recent days spilling over.

"You might as well come in," Deirdre said, taking another step back. To Helena, she said, "Give me that brush before you get paint on everything."

"Helena?" Meredith repeated, steel in her voice. "Or Desdemona?"

Helena gasped. "You know my work? Mr. DeLuca says it's very good, that people like it." Her dark brows drew together. "But Grandmama! Tell me about my grandmama. She never answered my letters, but now you say she is looking for me?" Astonishment rose in her voice.

"Your grandmother wrote that she was coming," Julia said, "but you never answered her letters—the last one she got from you was over a year ago."

"But..." Helena turned a flustered face to her aunt. Deirdre—the mysterious "Dilly."

Deirdre's head dropped to her chest, her silence confirming what Julia had already guessed. Like everything else in the young artist's life, Helena's mail had been censored. "Your grandmother bought one of your paintings for $1,200."

Helena's mouth dropped open. Was she not aware of the prices DeLuca charged for the runaway artist's paintings?

"He never said…" Helena looked from Julia to Deirdre in consternation. "You never told me…"

"I'm afraid there are a lot of things your aunt and Mr. DeLuca didn't tell you," Julia said. "Including that your grandmother confronted DeLuca about your whereabouts, and he denied knowing you or Desdemona."

Helena didn't look up for a long moment, then she spoke in a stunned hush. "Mr. DeLuca said I needed something to interest people in my work. I must trust him to sell my paintings, so I became this runaway artist, Desdemona—after Desmond."

"Your brother?" Julia asked.

"No." She lowered her head. After a moment, she added, "But he was like a brother to me. After my mother died, my father…" Her eyes darted wildly from one to another. "Des came with the lady my father brought to our house." She seemed unable to go on.

"Was her name 'Satterlee'?" Julia held her gaze.

She nodded. In a whisper she said, "Des was kind to me where his mother was…" She cut herself off once more and took a deep breath. "I used the name 'Desdemona' because it made him seem closer. Des, I mean."

Tears made her eyes glitter in the dim interior lit only by a flowered faux hurricane lamp. "It was just until I got established. Mr. DeLuca said he would put the name on the paintings himself so no one could trace my signature and ruin the secret." She shook her head, as though trying to understand. "He said some day when people pay more than $100 for a painting I could reveal my identity and put my real name to my work."

Julia recalled Carmen's description of the girl she'd known from the streets of Atlanta. *She was* ingenuo, *naive,* she had said. *You could tell her anything and she'd believe you.*

Meredith pressed toward Deirdre, closing the space between them. "Have you told Helena about the enormous success of her shows, that people pay thousands of dollars for her paintings?"

Helena stared, openmouthed, her fingers trembling as she clutched the neck of her smock. Was she grasping the ring Carmen had recognized? The one Delyse had described in her journal?

"But he said…" Helena stared at Deirdre.

"Don't you know he's been lying to you?" Deirdre shouted at Helena, her eyes green fire. "He's been lying to you for months, and I…" She lowered her head. "And I've been lying too."

Meredith's explosive charge and the confusion that followed gave Julia a quick moment for a text message. She touched Carmen's name on her phone and quickly typed, H is here. Bring Iris. Carmen knew where they were. Iris needed to know her granddaughter had been found. Carmen would find a way to get her here.

"I'm so sorry!" Deirdre's eyes spilled over with sudden tears. "I wanted to stop it," she continued to rant. "I wanted to, but I—couldn't!"

Suddenly the door flew open, bringing in a wild rush of wind and rain. And Marco DeLuca.

Chapter Twenty-One

JULIA FROZE. SO MUCH FOR DeLuca being out of town. And now, they might just be running out of options. Everyone stared in shocked silence.

A rain-drenched Marco DeLuca stood in the doorway, gray suit soaked, silver hair slicked against his head. His dark eyes flashed with eerie amber light, and beneath the gray mustache his mouth was a grim line. After a few seconds, his stunned expression morphed into a kind of condescending amusement.

"Well, isn't this an interesting little tea party!"

No one spoke. Meredith stared. Deirdre's explosive sobs had subsided, and she looked like a deer caught in the headlights.

"It's the ladies from the Magnolia Agency, isn't it?" DeLuca said, closing the door against the storm and brushing rain from his damaged suit jacket. "Out calling, are we?"

"Well, you seem to know Desdemona well enough to just walk into her home without knocking," Julia said, heart quaking against her ribs, ire roused to a fever pitch.

"Correction," he said, moving to the mantel a few feet from Helena, on whom he smiled indulgently. "It's my house, which I am leasing to her and her aunt out of concern for the career of a developing young artist."

"An investment earning you a rather sizeable personal return," Meredith said with dripping sarcasm. "When were you going to share the profits you've been pocketing during this subterfuge of yours?"

DeLuca nodded his head slowly from side to side as though he were dealing with simpletons and was running out of patience. "You two are determined to destroy this young woman's career, which depends, for the moment, on the mystique that is drawing the interest of the public to her art."

"Mystique?" Julia parroted indignantly. "You mean lies! You are lying to the public and to Helena, and to the woman who appealed to you to find her granddaughter!"

"That would have come in time. Surely, even an overly dramatic Greek sculptor would not want to ruin her granddaughter's chances of becoming truly famous. She would have understood that I'm guiding our Desdemona toward the greatness she deserves."

He turned a limpid gaze on Helena. "She'll tell you how important this is to her, won't you, my dear?"

Helena rushed toward him. Her eyes had deepened to a stormy ocean blue. "You didn't tell me Grandmama was here. You didn't tell me that she wanted to see me!"

"Now, *chérie*, you of all people must understand the need to remain away from the public eye. Haven't I given you everything you need, and many lovely gifts besides? Didn't I just bring you your favorite perfume from that boutique you like so much? Surely you understand that your career depends on…"

"He means," Meredith put in, "that your talent can't stand on its own, that you must rely on falsehood. And above everything else, he is using you to make money!"

"Is it true you sold a painting to my grandmama for $1,200?" Helena demanded, planting her feet just inches from DeLuca.

"Isn't it wonderful that our customers are realizing how gifted you are?" DeLuca asked, unperturbed.

"Did you tell her you didn't know me?" Helena demanded, her voice rising to near hysterics.

"Calm yourself, *chérie*," DeLuca said with sarcastic bravado. "Your grandmother will understand. By now she's safely on her way back to her own studio."

Julia stared in disbelief. He knew Iris was going back to Marousi. What had he said to convince her to stop looking for Helena? Julia could hardly believe the man's arrogance, the French endearment, the way he manipulated an impressionable young woman to trust him.

Suddenly, Helena whirled around. "And you, Dilly. All those letters I gave you to post to my grandmama! You never mailed them, did you?"

"It was for your own good!" Deirdre said. "Marco said nothing must distract you from painting." Her face became wan and desperate. "But I—I made sure you had everything you needed—got you the art training...."

A memory suddenly flashed in Julia's mind. It was Iris who had paid for art school! She had been grieved that Helena hadn't acknowledged her gift. *She never said thank you.*

"Really?" Julia said, breaking into Deirdre's list of proud accomplishments for Helena's good. "I think you mean Iris paid. You only confiscated the check and said the money came from you."

"I had to!" Deirdre glanced at DeLuca.

DeLuca flashed Deirdre a deadly look. "Watch yourself," he spat under his breath.

Deirdre bit her lip but turned again to Helena. "I made you comfortable in a big beautiful room where you could paint. I brought you supplies. I made your meals and took care of you." Her words trailed off, and she began to wither under Helena's stricken gaze. "I did it—for you."

Helena stood still, shaking her head, enormous blue eyes filled with shock and sadness. Julia longed to go to her, to comfort her.

Deirdre claimed she had done DeLuca's bidding for her niece's benefit, but Julia wasn't buying it. The man was holding something over Deirdre, something that perhaps was wearing the woman down. Had she tried to intervene for her niece the night she threw a pink lady in his face? What had DeLuca said that made Iris halt the investigation?

"Who is Celia?" Julia demanded in the tense gap that followed.

DeLuca and Deirdre both snapped their heads in her direction but remained mute.

"I saw you together at the hotel." Julia pierced Deirdre's averted eyes, and in another flash of knowing realized what it was about Celia and Deirdre that had bothered her. It was the similarity in the two women's features. "She's your sister, isn't she? You arranged for her to answer Iris's ad for help."

"I'm really getting bored with all these histrionics," DeLuca said, folding his arms across his rain-spotted chest. "And I don't intend to put up with any more of it." He took a firm step toward Julia and Meredith. "This is my house and I am asking you Magnolia ladies to leave. I have things to discuss with my protégé."

Julia also folded her arms across her chest, willing her pulse to slow down. "You may own this house, but it's leased to Deirdre here. It's her home—and Helena's. You've no right to speak for them."

"Quite right," DeLuca said with undisguised venom. "Deirdre, isn't there something you would like to say to these ladies?"

Deirdre drew a long breath. She swiped her face with her hands and stared directly at DeLuca. Several seconds passed before her lips parted. "There *is* something I wish to say." She cast a glance at Helena, who had backed up to the stairs and sat on the third step with her head bent down over her scrunched-up knees.

Gripping the back of the couch, Deirdre drew herself up to her full height and took a steadying breath. "Since it's my name that appears on the lease for this house, and it is still in effect, I'm asking *you* to leave instead."

"Have you forgotten, Deidre dear, that your name also appears on another document, one I'm sure the authorities will be interested in?"

"I haven't forgotten, but I won't allow what you are doing to Helena to continue." She drew another sustaining breath. "Besides, I could share some things with those authorities you're threatening me with. Things that you won't like at all."

Julia watched, amazed. Was Deirdre a victim too? Perhaps Celia as well?

"What I am doing to Helena?" DeLuca repeated, incensed. He sounded wounded to the core. "What I am doing is engineering an amazing career for this young woman! Without me she'd still be painting graffiti on alley walls."

Helena's thin body shook with new sobs, but she remained with her head bowed over her knees.

"Just go away and leave us alone!" Deirdre shouted. Her gaze suddenly flew to the window.

A car had driven up to the house. Julia heard the engine halt as Deirdre said, "It appears I have guests to attend to."

DeLuca appeared momentarily stunned but quickly recovered. "As you wish," he said with undisguised contempt. "I'll show myself out, but we'll discuss this later—when you come to your senses." He turned on his heel and, with a brief glance in Helena's direction, exited, leaving the door standing open to the wind and rain.

As one, Julia and Meredith rushed to the door. A moment later Carmen appeared, holding a dripping umbrella over Iris Floros's head. Behind them, Celia Angelos pressed close.

"Are you guys all right?" Carmen stepped inside, ushering in a fretful Iris in a lime-green raincoat. Tendrils of white hair dripped around her flushed face. Her dark eyes flashed immediately to the figure hunched on the curving staircase. But she made no move toward her.

Helena looked up with an incredulous face blotched with tears. She stood unsteadily and grasped the railing with both hands. "Is that you, Grandmama?" A small, tremulous voice. Eyes sapphire clear sparked in wonder.

"Are you all right, Helena?" Iris pushed aside Celia's arm and took two faltering steps toward her granddaughter. "He said he would ruin you as an artist if I didn't go away. I came because I need to see you. Because…"

But she seemed unable to go on. She and Helena stared at each other unmoving for what seemed a long time. Julia stood back with Meredith and Carmen, not sure what to do. Then a smile broke out on the young artist's face, and she cleared the space between her and her grandmother in quick running steps.

"I hoped you would come! I thought you didn't want to see me anymore!" She flung her arms around Iris, and the two held on to each other as a string of unintelligible Greek comfort words surrounded grandmother and granddaughter.

Deirdre, who had stepped back when the rush of bodies entered, seemed to awaken. "Won't you all sit down?" She touched Iris's shoulder and smiled at the tearful Helena as she urged them both toward the flowered couch.

Celia, standing close to Deirdre, watched Iris with worried eyes. "I guess we all have a lot to talk about," she said. "Carmen told us that Helena was here and that we should come." She made a hands-up gesture of confusion, looked at her sister helplessly, and threw apologetic glances at Meredith and Julia.

Julia could imagine that it hadn't been easy for Carmen to convince the two women to accompany her to this remote place. That would be a story for later, complete with dramatic flair. She glanced gratefully at their resourceful assistant. Winging a hopeful prayer heavenward, she signaled for everyone's attention.

"Celia's right," she began firmly. "We do have a lot to discuss. But first we can be grateful that Helena is all right. It's true that Marco DeLuca has been hiding her from public view, convincing both Helena and her aunt Deirdre that no one should know her real identity. And sadly, he has been profiting handsomely and keeping that a secret too."

"I am so sorry," Deirdre said, her eyes filling once again with tears. "I should have known better. I should have *done* better. I knew

Helena has been unhappy." She turned toward Iris. "I hated keeping your letters from her—and hers from you." She took a shaky breath.

"She thought she had to do what he told her," Celia said, coming to her sister's defense and tucking an arm through Deirdre's. Her eyes narrowed in quick disgust. "She believed he would ruin Helena's chance of success, but he was blackmailing Deirdre too. He said he will turn her in if I don't get Iris to leave."

"Did it have something to do with the sale of a painting a few years ago?" Meredith asked. "I had my son research that fraudulent Kusama that's being investigated."

"My name appears on the contract," Deirdre said, shaking her head. "I believed it was legitimate, and I agreed to sign it for him. I am so ashamed." Her tears fell once more as in the stillness Julia tried to absorb the rather twisted tale that had brought them all together.

Celia pulled a handkerchief from her bag, handed it to Deirdre. But her words were for Iris. "When you wrote a letter to Helena telling her you were coming, he intercepted the letter. Deirdre and I worked it out to get you to hire me so we could keep an eye on you and keep you away from Helena."

No doubt she was absorbing what was being said, but Iris seemed unable to keep her eyes off the fragile young artist. "It has been such a long time," she said, still intent on her granddaughter. "I have failed you. And your mother." She put a hand to her chest.

"Grandmama!" Helena said, leaning toward her.

"No, it is all right," she said. "I am all right." She shook her head, returned her hand to her lap, close to Helena's. "I wish it had been different, that I could have been here for you and for Rhea." She took a shuddering breath.

"Grandmama," Helena said, suddenly clutching the small bulge at her neck. She pulled out a slender chain that held a ring glittering in the lamplight. She held it out to Iris. "Mother said I must keep this for you. She said it is yours and that I should take care of it always until I could return it for her." She dropped her head. "I didn't give it to you when you came for my birthday all those years ago because it reminded me of Mother, and I didn't want to give it up."

Iris clamped her jaw tight against the emotion that seemed to engulf her. Julia realized that this was the expensive ring Rhea had taken the night she'd left her parents' home in Greece to come to America.

Carmen, who to this point had been silent, only watching through huge bewildered eyes, gasped. When Helena looked up at her, Carmen said, "When I saw your paintings, I thought it was the Dove who painted them. We were just kids, but I always knew you would be a great artist someday."

Helena cocked her head, peered closely at Carmen. "Oh," she breathed, her blue eyes lighting up. "It is you." She shook her head back and forth as though she couldn't believe it.

Iris looked from one to the other, obviously not quite under-standing, but nothing could dim her joy. She turned to Deirdre. "You have been not all right, but you have been protecting my Helena from that man, yes?"

"Yes," Deirdre whispered. "I'm sorry that I—"

"Whatever that man made you do, I thank you. I thank you for taking care of my Helena after Rhea and Duke are gone."

Deirdre's face glowed as she absorbed these words of apprecia-tion, gratitude where certainly none was due. Forgiveness where no pardon was deserved.

And now what? Julia wondered. One thing she was quite sure of: It would mean a drastic change in their lives. Somehow the young painter with her hand clasped tightly in her grandmother's would become Helena Meyer instead of Desdemona, the runaway artist. With her grandmother's support she would no longer run from her true self. Love could triumph over the failures of the past—even as it had for Mom and Cassie. Their lives too would change. But in this moment, anything seemed possible.

Julia was already thinking of ways she could help Deirdre get out of the mess DeLuca had gotten her into. She wasn't an experienced lawyer and judge for nothing. And Meredith's amazing Quin could help too.

"What should I do with these plane tickets?" Celia asked suddenly, breaking Julia's reverie.

"You won't go back to Marousi now, will you, Grandmama?" Helena implored. "Surely you can stay a while."

"Please do!" Deirdre broke in. "This is a big house. I still hold the lease. You could stay here with Helena and me for a while." She hesitated, her expression unsure, no doubt wondering if they would trust her after the trouble she had caused.

"Grandmama, please stay," Helena said. "There is so much I want to know, so much I want to tell you."

"Of course we will stay," came the reply from the bombastic Iris Julia had met that first night in the gallery. Julia heard her laugh for the first time. Despite the knotty problems that might need solving, there was no hiding now. Together they could work it out. Ties with DeLuca could be severed, even if they had to take out a restraining order to keep him away. She might just suggest that. And Julia had a notion that

Helena's career would continue to flourish with the love and support of her family.

"I'm going to make some coffee!" Deirdre said with a gleaming smile. "And I have almond coffee cake. Celia and I will have it ready in two shakes."

Julia looked at Meredith and saw reflected in her eyes the satisfaction she herself was feeling. It had been a difficult case with many twists and turns, but Helena had been found. They had held on to hope, believing for a miracle.

"This God of yours," Iris began, smoothing her hair back from her face with one hand. The other still held Helena's. "I looked away from Him for a very long time. I thought He did not care for this foolish woman who made so many mistakes."

Julia thought Iris Floros had never looked so beautiful.

"But I believe it is like you say in your prayers. I mean, when you asked Him to help us, I think He listened. I think He is the One I shall give the biggest thanks."

"Absolutely, Iris." Julia could hardly wait to go home and tell Beau, and to plan a get-together with Mom and Cassie, Wyatt's family, and of course Maggie Lu and Charlene. They'd need to put two more leaves in the dining room table. Especially if Iris and Deirdre agreed to come too, along with Celia and Carmen.

Julia's heart leaped. They had witnessed hope and renewed faith, but the love that held them each in a tender embrace was the greatest of all.

Dear Reader,

It is a signal honor to be part of the exciting Savannah Secrets series established by Guideposts and fostered by its remarkable staff. Having written the first book in the series, I consider it a privilege now to supply the tenth, featuring the talented sleuths of Magnolia Investigations.

Our ladies are embroiled in a mystery surrounding a "disappearing artist" and the determined grandmother who crosses an ocean to find her. Family ties and the enduring power of love are paramount in this story, in which Julia has her own personal struggle with an estranged sister. With dogged determination and enabling faith, they learn that love is no artifice but the greatest thing in the world.

Signed,
Marlene Chase

About the Author

MARLENE CHASE IS A LIEUTENANT colonel in the Salvation Army, having served in various communities in the Midwest for forty-three years. She retired as Editor in Chief and Literary Secretary for the Army's National Publications headquartered in Alexandria, Virginia. She continues to serve the ministry endeavors of the organization and to write from her home in Rockford, Illinois. She is the author of twenty-one books and numerous articles, poems, and stories. She has two daughters, four grandchildren, and two great-granddaughters. She holds a Bachelor of Arts degree from MidAmerica Nazarene University in Kansas and is an ordained minister in the Salvation Army.

The Truth Behind the Fiction

THE FICTIONAL ART GALLERY FEATURED in this book is named "the Winston" in honor of Sir Winston Churchill, the prime minister of the United Kingdom who led his country to victory in the Second World War. He reviewed US troops at Fort Jackson, South Carolina, in June 1942. "Impressive and convincing," Churchill wrote of the soldiers there. Though our troops were at the time inexperienced in ground combat, Churchill wrote in his memoirs, "The troops in Carolina bore themselves like veterans."

Another facet of this remarkable man was his interest in art. He began painting early (1895–1899), his landscape drawings inspired by places he saw all over the world. He became more enthusiastic about painting after resigning from the government in 1955. Churchill had a true craftsman's dedication to art. He consulted teachers admired for their professionalism and learned from their knowledge and experience. We are told that Churchill sought and found tranquility in his art. He is quoted as saying: "When I get to heaven I mean to spend a considerable portion of my first million years in painting, and so get to the bottom of the subject..."

The owner of this story's "Winston Gallery" favored and collected Churchill's art and opened a gallery in Savannah's City Market, one of the city's most frequently visited places. The Market is a mixed-use project in the historic district which began in 1985. Developers established an art center with working artists occupying about 19,000 square feet of space. Other tenants operate the District's most popular restaurants and businesses, to which tourists and Savannahians alike flock to enjoy its attractions and the ongoing cultural heritage of the South.

Walk the shaded streets of Savannah, where magnolias bloom and carriages take you to the heart of City Market. Explore the bistros and galleries and be serenaded by local musicians. Enrich your mind and soul with inspiring art such as "the Winston Gallery" affords and enjoy the varied characters you meet inside.

SOMETHING DELICIOUS FROM A
Downhome Southern Kitchen

SCORED FLOUNDER WITH APRICOT SHALLOT SAUCE

Ingredients:

Vegetable oil	Pepper to taste
1 whole flounder	3 tablespoons melted butter
½ cup milk	2 tablespoons brandy
½ cup flour	2 peeled and chopped apricots
Salt to taste	½ cup shallots

Directions:

Preheat a cast-iron pot half-filled with vegetable oil to 375 °F. With a sharp knife, score the skin of the flounder, making a crosshatch pattern. Place the scored fish in a shallow casserole dish, cover with milk and season with salt and pepper.

In a separate casserole dish add the flour and season with salt and pepper. Dredge the flounder in the flour, then immediately dip the fish into the fryer and let cook for 5 to 6 minutes.

Melt butter in a small saucepot over medium-high heat. Add the brandy, apricots, and shallots. Simmer for 3 minutes or until thickened. Remove flounder from oil and place onto a platter. Serve with the sweet apricot and shallot sauce.

This quick and easy taste of the South will serve 4. Prep and cook time 10 to 12 minutes.

*Read on for a sneak peek of another exciting book
in the Savannah Secrets series!*

Patterns of Deception

BY RUTH LOGAN HERNE

"WHOA." WYATT WAVERLY DIDN'T JUST look surprised by Meredith Bellefontaine's request the first week of March. He looked dumbfounded. He got up, shut his office door with a solid *click*, and retook his seat before he said another word. "Payroll Inc. has hired you two to do what? Look for some kind of money leak that professional auditors couldn't find?"

"I know it sounds unlikely," Julia Foley said. Wyatt's aunt Julia had partnered with her old friend Meredith to reopen Meredith's late husband's detective agency. She motioned to Meredith. "Meredith and the CEO are old friends."

Meredith cut in quickly. "Not like *real* friends," she told Wyatt, but that only made the furrow between his brows go deeper. She took a breath and sat forward in the chair. "Ron and I knew Carolanne and her husband, Rusty, from the early days. Decades ago," she added in explanation.

"Russell Van Valken was called Rusty?" That seemed to surprise Wyatt even more.

"Back then, yes, but as the payroll corporation grew everyone called him Russ or Russell," she went on. "Anyway, we were all young together. Ron had left the police department to open the detective agency and Rusty saw that companies were outsourcing all kinds of things via technology, so he thought, Why not payroll? Why not us? Why not now?"

"He created a mega start-up before start-ups were a common buzzword," noted Wyatt.

Meredith nodded eagerly. "Yes, and that's just the kind of people they were. He and Carolanne both had degrees in accounting and business, but Rusty had coupled his with technology skills. He programmed his own software, so when he launched the company, it climbed the ladders of success solidly until it became the multibillion-dollar corporation you see now." She made a face, acknowledging Wyatt's expression of disbelief. "Look, I know it's weird that they came to us."

"Not weird," he said flatly. "Frankly unbelievable. And that's not an insult to you or my wonderful aunt," he assured them with a look of affection toward Julia. "Payroll Inc. can have the best of the best of anything. Why would they come to a newly formed agency that only has a year of experience? And that doesn't have a skillset for investigating computer or financial crime, if that's what's occurred?"

"Because Carolanne and I both lost our husbands within weeks of each other, and we bonded," Meredith said. "Not like best friends bonding but bonded by loss. And by the changes in our lives. We even"—she sighed softly and gripped the handle of her spring-floral quilted purse more tightly—"went to the same grief counselor for a while. When she approached me earlier today, I asked the same questions you just did." Meredith met Wyatt's gaze firmly. "She told me they've had big auditing companies come in and snoop around, and they saw nothing wrong, but she has a couple of inside people who believe there could be a leak. They just can't find it. If it exists, she has to do everything in her power to track it down. She's afraid if she doesn't, she'll have the board micromanaging her every move."

"So if the professional auditors can't find it, how does she figure we might stand a chance?" asked Julia. "I have to agree with Wyatt, that doesn't make a lot of sense."

Wyatt raised a hand. "I'm not saying it doesn't make sense," he said, and when Julia looked surprised, he continued. "It seems odd, but the reason forensic auditing differs from traditional auditing is that we go further. We begin with the suspicion that something is wrong. In a general audit, if the company's numbers fall within one percent of the total worth, it's considered clean."

"Which means that a two billion-dollar company can hide twenty million and be listed as clean?" Meredith's voice fairly squeaked on the question. "Seriously?"

"Theoretically, yes. It's more complicated than that," Wyatt explained, "but that's how the numbers roll. The more layers a company has, like major university hospitals and medical insurance billing and corporations running a full stable of other corporations under one massive umbrella, the more opportunities for criminal activity. About the only way you find a needle in that very big financial haystack is if you have a whistleblower."

"I had no idea." Julia stared at him, then Meredith. "But that brings us right back to the question of why would Carolanne bring us in?"

"Because people talk to us," said Meredith.

Julia looked skeptical, but Wyatt lifted a brow of interest.

"We don't go at things the way other places do," Meredith went on. "Carolanne thinks that if we listen to what people are saying and ask the right questions, we might figure things out before the next major quarterly meeting."

"When is that scheduled?" asked Wyatt.

"The first week of April in Miami. It's always off-site so they can talk more freely. But here's why we need you, if you have some time and don't mind helping us." She smiled at him. "Carolanne is correct. Julia and I have the people skills. At our age we've learned the art of listening. We read people well. But if we say yes to this, I want a numbers person on board. A person who's willing to look beyond the obvious—because I honestly don't know what that would be in a financial corporate setting. Give me a small-time swindler or someone stepping out on their spouse, and I can follow the rabbit trail. But I don't think your aunt and I can say yes to this without expert backup. And that means you."

He frowned.

Then he folded his hands together and stayed quiet for what seemed like a long time. After slow beats of the clock and Meredith's heart, he leaned forward. "I'm overseeing two cases right now, but fortunately they're in the discovery phase and that leaves me a little time. Not a lot," he told them, "but I have to say I'm intrigued by the idea of someone skimming off a major corporation like this, a corporation that makes money by simply channeling funds where they're supposed to go. If we find it, I want to be able to use it as one of our firm's credits. Is that agreeable to both of you?"

Julia didn't waste a moment. "Absolutely. Give credit where credit is due."

Meredith nodded. "Of course. But I'd like to keep your involvement quiet initially. I think Carolanne is right, that people might slip and say something in front of us that they wouldn't say if they know you're on the job."

"Agreed," he replied. "And while you two make friends with the folks inside the walls, I'll do some quiet digging on Payroll Inc. A company is only as strong as its weakest link, and if that weak link has access to financial controls, then it should show up somewhere. But not always," he reminded them. "It's a huge operation after all."

"So you're in?" Julia stood up.

"I'm in."

She hugged him fiercely. Then she took a step back. "And you're sure we're not imposing?"

"If you were, I'd have said so, Aunt J. Promise."

Their look of sweet affection tugged at Meredith's heart. Julia had helped her parents raise Wyatt, and he bore more resemblance to his aunt than his absentee mother, Cassie. It was there in his looks but also his devotion to giving a job 100 percent. His two girls called Julia Nana, and she treated them like her own.

"Thank you, Wyatt." Meredith extended her hand. "I'm grateful."

He took it, but he didn't just shake it. He folded her hand between both of his and smiled down at her. "Walk in there and be yourselves. Pretend to chat while you're listening. Act more than your age. Or stand in a corner looking utterly bored. Any one of those ruses will keep people talking around you if not at you or to you, because you'll be invisible. Like faded wallpaper. With ears."

Meredith wasn't sure she loved being compared to old wallcoverings, but it was sound advice. She nodded as he loosed her hand. "I like how you think. We'll keep you posted, all right?"

"I can't wait to hear what y'all glean. But Aunt J?"

Julia paused at the door. So did Meredith. They both turned back.

"Don't forget that you're dealing with a multibillion-dollar corporation. Even a tiny percentage of that is more money than most of us see in a lifetime. And plenty enough to kill someone over."

Julia's mouth dropped open.

So did Meredith's. She swallowed hard. "I hadn't really thought about it that way."

He met her eye to eye with a firm expression. "You can't think about it any other way," he said. "Gather what you can but don't put yourselves in harm's way. It's only money, and it's never worth endangering yourself over. Understood?"

Julia dipped her chin. "Understood. And Wyatt, thank you for the help and the reminder. It's easy to see the people side of things but tough to realize what some folks will do for money."

"Tale as old as time," he said. "Love you."

"I love you too."

They walked outside and climbed into Meredith's car. Then Julia let out a breath. "We're really doing this? Looking into a major corporation like this? And what kind of fee do we charge a monster-sized company, Mere?"

Meredith told her the amount she'd proposed to Carolanne.

Julia's eyes went wide. "That's a year's salary on the bench." Julia had served as a judge in the juvenile courts for over a decade.

"Then clearly our judges are underpaid," Meredith retorted. "We're working hourly, but I said that was the base rate and Carolanne didn't blink. Not once."

"I'm not accustomed to working with ultrarich people," Julia said as she snugged her seat belt into place. "We saw some in juvenile court, but it wasn't the norm by any means. Beau and I have been blessed abundantly, but when we start talking millions and billions, my money-meter goes on high alert."

Meredith's phone interrupted their conversation. She hit the Bluetooth connection and answered smoothly as she pulled out of the parking lot outside Wyatt's building. "Hi, this is Meredith."

"Meredith." Carolanne's voice came through the car speakers in just above a whisper. "Come quick. Someone has hacked into our computer system, and they may have taken over everything. And I mean everything!" It was impossible to miss the panic in Carolanne's voice. "Hurry. Please. I honestly don't know what to do right now, but I know I need help. Serious, serious help."

The phone went dead.

Meredith looked at Julia.

Julia pointed straight ahead. "Take that next left. It will get us around the traffic, and we can be there in a few minutes. If we can park nearby."

Meredith darted across two lanes of traffic and took the left before the light had time to fully change. "Are you thinking what I'm thinking?"

"That Wyatt is right and people will do anything for money?"

"Well that and—" Meredith accelerated to merge then slipped into the exit-only lane about two thousand feet up the expressway. "This might be the most exciting job we've gotten yet. I'm totally psyched. I'm not sure what that says about me." She signaled the exit and took the curve. "But I know exactly what it says about Magnolia Investigations, my friend. We've arrived. Literally." She signaled right, made the turn, and then made another hard right into Payroll Inc.'s corporate parking lot. "And figuratively. Now let's go inside and see what in the world is going on."